I0629867

IN PURSUIT OF STARLIGHT

ROB PECK

Copyright © 2025 by Rob Peck

All rights reserved. No part of this publication may be reproduced, distributed, or transmitted in any form or by any means, including photocopying, recording, or other electronic or mechanical methods, without the prior written permission of the publisher, except in the case of brief quotations embodied in critical reviews and certain other noncommercial uses permitted by copyright law.

This is a work of fiction. Names, characters, places, and incidents are either the product of the author's imagination or are used fictitiously. Any resemblance to actual persons, living or dead, events, or locales is purely coincidental.
For information, contact: rmp0628@gmail.com

ISBN: 979-8-218-77082-2

Cover Illustrations and Title Design by Brittany Evans
(@bybrittanyevans)
Printed in the United States of America

For those we walk beside, and the promises that carry us forward

August 7th
Before Junior Year
(Logan)

Logan sprawled his hands on the shower wall and closed his eyes to the rhythm of the water drops beating on his back. His dad was out at work, and he remembered his mom telling him something about groceries in the morning.

By myself on a summer day, he thought. *By myself on any day really.*

He sat down on the floor of the tub, drifting asleep. The bathroom filled with steam, and the water began to cool. He shook his head and jumped out to dry himself off. He changed into only shorts and hung over the side of his bed, picking up two dumbbells in the process.

"Hate this shit. But you gotta do it, Logan. You gotta do it," he muttered to himself.

The regular workout had served him well for the last two years. He'd been a varsity pitcher for Springvale High's baseball team. He hung backwards over the side and began crunching. Up, down, repeat. He dropped the dumbbells on the floor and sat back up. He glanced back at his phone. 1:34 in big white numbers stared back. He got off his bed to flex in the mirror. Suddenly, the doorbell rang.

"Yeah, give me a minute!" he yelled, not caring whether the person at the door could hear him.

A furious knock came soon after, followed by a few more rings of the doorbell.

"I'm coming! Christ," he said throwing a shirt over himself.

He ran down the stairs and opened the door to see a familiar face standing on his front step.

"You know, for a kid who stays home all day you're awfully hard to get a hold of," the boy, about six feet tall, said back with a smile.

"I'm not that hard to find if you'd come to my house every now and then," Logan answered back.

Brayden Lewis was Logan's best friend, teammate, and signal caller behind the plate. Brayden, originally a transfer student from the city, was a senior to be and was widely regarded by local and national media as one of the best baseball prospects in the country.

"That's not fair. You know why I don't come around here. I always get these looks from your mom," Brayden said imitating her darting eyes.

Logan laughed to mask the truth. Logan's mom hadn't been a fan of Brayden's, but she'd never taken the chance to get to know him. Many of the students at Springvale had once felt the same way. He was physically imposing, never said much, and didn't go out of his way to make friends. Underneath his appearance was an unmatched heart, kindness and mind. Logan usually had to be the one to bring Brayden into the spotlight.

"Trust me. It's nothing, Bray. Don't worry about it. So, what did you have in mind? You came here to find me after all, right?"

"I don't really know. I just didn't want to be home I guess," Brayden answered. "Want to see what Amber's up to and take the kids to the park?"

"Oh yay, babysitting." Logan rolled his eyes.

"Come on. It's better than sitting around here all day and doing nothing."

Logan groaned. "Alright. Fine. Let's go."

They walked down the street towards Brayden's house to pick up his little brother, Julian, and sister, Angela. Once inside, it didn't take long for the little girl to fly down the hall and jump into Logan's arms.

"Logan's here!" Angela shouted down the hall.

Julian came out of the kids' room and ran over to hug Logan as if he were his older brother too.

Logan smiled. "How ya doing, buddy?"

"Good!" Julian answered.

Having little children run over and treat him as a big brother always warmed his heart.

"Logan!" Brayden's mother walked in from down the hall.

"How are you, Mrs. Lewis?" Logan hugged her.

"Tired! Taking care of these three is an all-day job. Sometimes I wish I could switch places with my husband." She laughed. "How are things at home, darling?

Logan looked over at Brayden. "Things are fine. My mom is having a bit of a hard time with my dad I think, but she'll be okay."

Logan's parents had been hitting a rough patch since the summer started. Logan's dad, a contractor, was spending less time at home and more time on the road, which had caused his mother to grow wary of his actions.

"Nature of the job." Logan's dad had always opened with that line whenever Logan or his mother would ask why he didn't come home on certain nights.

"I'm sorry to hear that, Logan. But, if you need anything, our door is always open to you," Brayden's mother said to him.

Logan had always felt a sense of belonging to Brayden and his family.

"You guys wanna come to the park with me and Logan? Amber and her brother will be there!" Brayden said to his brother and sister.

"Can we play catch when we get there?" Julian, an almost miniature version of Brayden, asked with a pinch of excitement in his voice.

Brayden laughed. "Yeah sure, buddy, let me get my stuff out of my room. I think I have a glove that can fit you."

Logan took the kids outside and waited for Brayden to come out.

"Be home later!" Brayden shouted towards his mother as he walked out the door.

With the children in tow, Logan and Brayden continued into town and towards the municipal building where the park was. Brayden had his brother up on his shoulders and held his sister's hand. Logan trailed behind. Angela separated from Brayden to walk alongside Logan as they approached the park.

"Brayden! Let's play catch!" Julian yelled from atop Brayden's massive shoulders.

"Okay, okay, hang on. Let me get my stuff out of my bag." He laughed. "You trying to play catch with us, Logan?"

"I'll sit this one out. You guys have fun. I'll hang out over here with your sister and the other two."

Logan walked over towards the swing-set with Angela and saw Amber pushing her younger brother, Michael, on the swing. Amber Donovan and Logan had grown up together since grade school. They were always at the top of the class, a perfect complement for one another. Amber's father pulled her out of Springvale Elementary in favor of a nicer private school in the next town over. It was hard to reconcile losing his best friend because of something out of his control. Logan hadn't seen her for almost five years until the end of this past winter; she had re-entered public school following the death of her father.

After catching a glimpse of Logan, Amber whispered something to her brother and walked over to Logan. She hugged him and her black hair brushed against his face.

7

"Hey," she said looking up at him with her ice-blue eyes.

"Hey yourself," he answered with a slight smile. "Did you dye it again?"

"The brown was starting to come back in, so my mom helped me out a little." She laughed. "Thanks for noticing. Let's go have some fun!" She took Angela's hand from Logan and ran towards the swing.

Logan glanced back at Brayden, who shot a look over at Amber, then back at Logan and he smiled a little. Angela sat down on the swing and Logan began to push.

"Higher, Logan! Go higher! He's beating me!" Angela yelled as she looked at Amber's brother.

"Yeah, Logan, put some effort into it. You don't want to embarrass yourself by letting me be stronger than you, right?" Amber giggled from the side.

"Oh, I didn't know it was a contest. You're on! Don't worry. I'll make sure you're touching the sky by the time I'm done!" Logan replied.

Logan felt like a kid again, as if he didn't have a care in the world. He watched the two children go higher into the sky and it made him think of when his mom would push him on the very same swings when he was little. His arms grew weary.

"Angela? Think you can pump yourself for a bit?"

The girl nodded.

"Michael?" Amber asked.

"I'm fine!" Michael replied.

"Come on! Let's go sit down on the grass!" Amber grabbed Logan by the arm and pulled him to the ground.

Amber sprawled down onto the grass and looked up to the summer sky. She closed her eyes, took a deep breath and reopened them. Her eyes appeared to brighten. She sat back up and brushed the grass off the baby blue t-shirt that complimented her eyes so well. She unfurled her hair from a ponytail.

She seems so at peace.

Logan had envied her for that. For everything Amber had endured during her life, she seemed so happy with herself. She swung her legs back underneath her, swept remaining blades of grass off her dress and tossed them up for the wind to carry away.

"Hey, Logan?" She paused. "Do you remember coming here when we were little? I remember you'd always have a small baseball glove and bat. You rambled about how you would be the greatest baseball player ever."

"You remember that?" Logan laughed.

"I remember a lot of things about you," she answered.

Logan reflected on back then. He would come to the field with his dad when he was no older than Julian was now. He and his father had practiced until the lights came on, working on hitting, pitching and fielding.

"Atta boy," his father would say after every strong throw and every solid hit. Thinking of his dad in the moment put a weight on his chest he couldn't quite shake.

"Was I any good then?" he asked.

"You were getting there." She smiled. "I think you decided then that you wanted to play baseball forever!"

Logan watched Brayden and Julian tossing the ball back and forth. He looked back to make sure Angela and Michael were still on the swing. Logan watched the two laughing and swinging back and forth. Brayden fell to the ground as if his brother's throws were forceful enough to knock him to his back.

Julian ran over into the waiting arms of his bigger brother who pulled him towards his chest and used his power to lift him to the sky from his back. Logan smiled a bit.

"Life was easier back then I guess," Logan replied.

"It was. But! Things will get better, Logan. You just have to believe everything happens for a reason. You'll be okay. I know it."

"How can you be so sure?"

"I just know you." She lowered her eyes and fumbled with her hands. "I've always known you. You were always the first one to speak up in class. You always chose to be the leader or captain of all the games. You've always been a source of light for everyone you surround yourself with. You're strong. Not just outside, but inside too. I just know, okay?" she said as she kept her eyes down.

"Well, at least I have your confidence," Logan answered rolling his tongue into his bottom lip.

Logan looked away from her. It didn't seem like it would happen. That's when he felt a faint touch on his leg. He looked down and saw Amber's fingers tapping on his calf. He looked up to meet the unrivaled luster in her eyes.

"You always know, don't you?"

"Know what?" She giggled.

9

"When someone is upset or when someone isn't quite feeling themselves. You always have a way of knowing that. I don't know how you do it."

"It's just body language, Logan. It's nothing special!"

She was the girl that'd just give someone a hug to show that the world wasn't ending. Logan smiled as he grasped her hand in his before he heard a voice behind him.

"Are you and my sister in love, Logan?" Michael asked. Logan never noticed the two stopped swinging.

"What?" Amber pulled her hand away. "No. No. We're best friends. We care about each other very much, Michael. Love is something totally different! You'll understand when you're older!" Her usual pale skin flamed red as she tried to laugh it off.

"It looks like love!" he answered. "Mommy and daddy held hands all the time, and they were in love."

"Your sister and I…we aren't in love, Mikey. We weren't holding hands, we were uh…high fiving each other!" Logan stuttered trying to cover himself. "See? Look. Give me a high five buddy!"

Logan exchanged high fives with Michael and then with Amber to show that Logan and Amber were just best friends. This wasn't the first time someone had accused Logan and Amber of liking each other. Back in the third grade, a boy in their class had written an innocent story about two fish named Amber and Logan that were in love. The two of them had become good friends in school and even then, the little children could pick up the faintest signals of human interaction. As the child who wrote it read the story aloud, kids in the class had given Logan and Amber looks.

"Logan and Amber are in love!"

"Logan and Amber sitting in a tree…"

One boy even had stood up and yelled, "They're gonna get married!"

They laughed. They played along. They were two friends that just happened to be opposite genders. They never saw the big deal, at least Logan didn't. Michael's question had brought him back to that third-grade classroom. That's how he had remembered Amber before he ran into her last March. He looked at her and once again saw the petite, conservative, brown-haired girl with a melodic laugh and intelligence that surpassed his own.

What if? he wondered to himself.

10

He didn't want to think about Amber in that way. He couldn't afford to. He never had before. Why start now? Amber was his best friend. That was it. The last thing Logan wanted was to hurt Amber out of a stupid passion.

He stood to help Amber up off the ground as he saw Brayden and his brother coming back from their catch.

"How is the superstar in the making?" Logan chuckled.

"I'm fine, but the kid definitely has potential!" Brayden replied. "How was grazing in the grass?"

"Shut up Brayden! Aren't you a city boy? What do you know about grazing in the grass anyways? Don't make me hurt you in front of your little brother and sister!" Amber snapped, jabbing Brayden in the arm. "I'll wait for my mom to come get me. It was fun! We need to do this more often."

Logan and Brayden nodded, and they took Brayden's siblings and started to walk home. Logan looked back at Amber waving and smiled. Logan had felt like being around his two best friends made everything okay. Brayden protected Logan from anything outside that could harm him and Amber often protected Logan from himself.

"So, what's going on with you two?" Brayden asked.

"Who two?"

"You and my brother…no you and Amber, ya goof. Who did you think I meant?" Brayden prodded.

"What? Me and Amber? Nothing. Why?"

"Mhm. Nothing." Brayden laughed.

"She's my best friend. I've known her for years! There's nothing there. Trust me."

"You're afraid because you think she might actually be something special."

Logan walked ahead of Brayden. "Yeah, thanks for the diagnosis. Next time you want to offer your opinion on my love life? Make sure I ask you first." Logan walked faster.

Something WAS there though. He thought about her smile and demeanor that could turn any bad day into an okay one. That's what he liked most about her. He felt his nerves coming back to him. They arrived back at Brayden's.

"Look, I'll talk to you later man. She was right. We definitely have to do this again," Brayden said as he and Logan slapped fives.

"For sure," Logan answered. "Bye guys!" He hugged Julian and Angela and walked up the road back towards his house.

When he walked in, he heard his mother banging about in the kitchen.

"Mom! I'm home!" he yelled in her direction.

"Logan! Can you give me hand setting the table please?"

"Dad gonna be home?"

"I think so sweetie."

Logan pulled plates and cups out of the cabinet above the oven and set the table. He could smell seasoned chicken in the oven. He walked over to his father's place and put down the plate and glass.

"So, how was the park?"

"Fine."

"Just fine?"

"Yup." He kept his eyes away from her and on his plate.

"How's Amber doing?"

"She's okay."

Logan looked around the house and felt like a few things were missing but couldn't quite put his finger on what they were. Before he could answer, he heard the garage door opening outside. His father was home.

His father walked in with a dirt-covered navy-blue T-shirt, dusty jeans and the same pair of work boots that he'd owned for years. His face was sunburned from being outside for a full day and then some. Logan looked over at him warily. He unloaded his tools in the garage, then returned to the house and looked down at the table.

"Just in time for dinner?" He chuckled.

"I'm surprised you actually made it home for this one," Logan snapped back at him.

"How could I miss out on such a good meal? This is your mother's finest work!"

"Why don't you sit down, Mark? I'll get everything set." Logan's mom interjected.

His dad walked away to wash up.

"I'm…" Logan paused. "I'm gonna go ahead and eat up in my room, if that's alright."

"Are you okay Logan?"

"Yeah, I'm fine. I just wanna watch the game and stuff. Don't worry. I won't forget to bring my dishes down."

Logan went back upstairs for the rest of the night to catch the Yankee game on TV. He flopped down on his bed and focused on the screen. He muted his TV for a moment, snuck towards his door and opened it. He stuck his head in the hallway to hear the clashing voices of his parents arguing over where his father had been.

"I spoke to the foreman today. He told me you left work at 2:00. It doesn't take you nearly three hours to get home, Mark!" Logan's mother screamed.

"I moved to another job site on the way back to oversee some things. You're overreacting," he snapped. "Besides, what are you doing calling him anyway?"

"Overreacting? I know you were there seeing her. If you want her so much, go live with her! Stop coming home and pretending everything is okay!"

"Everything IS okay! Or at least it would be if you…"

Logan slammed the door in his bedroom as he stormed back in. He didn't want to hear any more of his parents' arguing. His parents had got along all his life. They were married for twenty years. How could two people, who appeared to be so in love at times, be so ferocious towards each other? Logan rolled over and gazed up at his ceiling. With the muffled sounds of his parents arguing mixing with the commentary of the game, voices swirled around inside Logan's head. Suddenly, he heard a loud crash coming from downstairs. He raced back down into the kitchen.

"Mom? Dad? Are you alright?" Logan exclaimed.

He looked around and saw shattered dishes lying on the tile floor, and he watched as his mom limped to gather a dustpan and broom.

"What happened?"

"Nothing, son, your mother missed the counter by this much," Logan's dad answered pinching his fingers together. "Nothing to worry about."

Logan squinted at his father and walked over to help his mom with the shattered pieces of dishware.

"It's fine, Logan. I'm fine. Thank you. Go back upstairs, honey."

Logan helped his mother stand back up and walked back towards the stairwell. He looked back down by the kitchen and glared back at his father.

"I'm just glad you're okay, mom."

He never saw his parents argue like this. He flopped back down on his bed and opened one of his schoolbooks from the previous semester. He threw the book to the side because he knew he was just looking for something, anything to provide a distraction. He regretted not hearing the rest of his parents' argument.

"What did you do, dad?"

He kept his door open to see if he could hear any more of their conversation.

"He's lazy. He doesn't push himself hard enough. When are you going to make him give a damn about his life?" Logan heard his father say.

"He's doing just fine! Mind you, he does it despite your constant shouting at him and everyone in his life."

"I am pushing him to be better. I am pushing him to be better than me, than either of us!"

"The only place you're PUSHING him, Mark, is away from you."

"Don't tell me how to raise him. I've done just fine for 16 years."

"You? Just you? I didn't have anything to do with raising our son? Who stayed home with him all these years while you worked? Or whatever it is you do?"

Logan shut the door again, loud, so they could know he was listening. He looked over at his trophies, certificates and accolades from both his athletic and academic careers and knew that despite what his father said, he cared about his life.

I don't give a damn?

Logan picked the book back up and continued to flip through them before his arms grew weary from holding the book above his head and his eyes grew tired. The book crawled down onto his chest, his arms fell to his side, and he drifted asleep with images of broken dishes and his parents fighting. He heard his phone buzz but didn't answer it.

"I'll show you who I can be, whether or not you want to be here to see it."

2

17 Months Ago
March 2nd
(Brayden)

After a freshman year that saw him move to a new state, a new school, and make few friends in a new town, sophomore year was going to be easier. That's what he told himself. For the most part, it was. His grades were fine and while he may not have made a ton of friends, the kids on the baseball team seemed to tolerate him a little more by the end of last season.

This season's gotta be better, he thought.

He walked over to where the coach posted the roster list for the upcoming season, just to see if there were any new names. There weren't many. The turnover for the Springvale baseball team wasn't great. Once you made it, you were there until you graduated. If you were a freshman, you had better try your luck next year. Brayden was the first freshman in almost seven years to make the team. The funny thing about it was, he didn't even try out. He arrived at Springvale long after tryouts and the roster was seemingly set.

During the baseball module in gym class, Coach Stevenson had caught Brayden tossing a ball from center field to home plate like a cruise missile. An injury had put one of his players on the shelf and from that day forward, Brayden was a member of Springvale's baseball team. He ended his freshman year leading the district in almost every measurable statistic. Seeing his name on the roster wasn't a surprise. He flashed a confident smile and walked away.

A yell ripped through the hallway. "YES!" the voice screamed.

Brayden turned to see an auburn-haired boy, maybe about five and a half feet tall staring at the list with his fist clinched. Brayden chuckled to himself and walked over to the kid.

"You must be a freshman. Don't worry. I think everybody gets like that when they make it the first time," Brayden said.

The boy wheeled around, and his eyes widened as he looked up at Brayden. "You're um…uh…I'm sorry, I don't remember your name."

"Brayden. Brayden Lewis. You?"

"Logan…Anderson, and yeah I'm a freshman."

Brayden tilted his head up trying to remember.

The pitcher, right. The one with the strong arm. "Oh yeah! You're that pitcher, right? Pretty good stuff from what I saw this week, a little wild, but good. Looks like I'll be catching you all year."

Logan had stood out the most from the incoming crop of potential new players. Brayden knew he didn't recognize Logan right away, but he had no idea he was a freshman. Brayden nodded awkwardly since Logan didn't say anything back.

"Anyway, see you around, Logan," Brayden said and walked away towards his first class.

* * *

Practice was to start at three but most of the team convened well before then, especially on the first day of practice. Brayden greeted his teammates as he walked towards the same locker he had used last season. He sat down and started to change into his practice gear. With most of the team assembled, the door opened again, and Logan Anderson walked in. His eyes were wide, much as they were when he turned and saw Brayden earlier in the day.

Make a move, kid.

Brayden watched Logan walk over towards two of the senior pitchers on the team, Tommy Darvill and Darren Yates. Logan perked his head over in his direction. He was the center of their conversation. However, their conversation quickly turned into confrontation.

"What position do you play Logan?" Tommy asked.

"I'm a pitcher," Logan chimed with a confident looking smile.

"Oh really?" Tommy stood up and towered over Logan. "Well, Darren and I are the two best pitchers on the team. It's been that way for the last two years. You'll have to earn your spot like everyone else," he said putting his finger in Logan's chest. "Hey, Darren!" he called. "This new kid thinks he's taking our spot!"

Darren looked at Logan and then looked at Tommy. They both began to laugh. Logan balled up his fist.

Don't do it, Logan. They aren't worth it.

Logan rested his balled-up hand and smiled again. "Look, I don't want problems. I'm just going to work my ass off this year and if that means I take either of your spots, that's just the way it is." Logan smirked.

Brayden sighed. "Aw shit."

As Logan turned to walk away, Tommy grabbed him by the shoulders, turned him around, and thrusted him into the lockers drawing a gasp from the rest of the team. Nobody stepped in, though. Logan tried to throw a punch, but Darren stopped him.

"Oh! You got a bit of fight in you, don't you!" Darren patted Logan on the head as Tommy held him up against the lockers.

"Yeah, put me down and you'll see how much fight..." before he could finish, Tommy lowered one hand and socked Logan in the ribs.

"Jesus." Brayden glared at the rest of the kids in the locker room and got up.

He marched over towards the fight, though mugging would be more appropriate, grabbed Tommy by the shoulders and yanked him off Logan. Brayden positioned himself between Logan and the two seniors. He squared his shoulders, ready to make a move if either one of them would be dumb enough to test him.

"What the Hell, Brayden?" Darren shouted. "We weren't going to hurt him. We just wanted to show him the ropes."

Brayden scoffed. "I notice you guys weren't showing me any ropes last year. He's smaller than you are. He's an easy target. So, what are you gonna do now?" He leered at them.

"Forget this. Didn't know you were mister high and mighty," Tommy said.

"I'm not, and won't pretend to be, but what doesn't make sense to me is why you'd bully a new teammate on his first day," Brayden answered.

Instead of responding, Tommy rolled his eyes and with Darren, walked back to his locker. Logan was still on the ground behind Brayden. He turned around and extended his hand.

"You gonna take my hand, or are you just gonna lay there like a punk?" Brayden joked.

Logan hesitated for a moment and looked around the room before he grabbed Brayden's hand. "Thanks."

"You gotta watch your mouth around here, man. Some of these kids...they don't care about you. They don't wanna be your friend. They'll be your friend if you're good enough and if you blow smoke up their ass." Brayden stopped to look back at all the other kids gazing at him.

"Yeah, I got it. Thanks, Brayden," Logan muttered.

Brayden laughed. "What? You mad at me for saving your ass from those two? That hotshot attitude isn't gonna fly here and I'm not always gonna be here to bail your ass out."

"Nobody asked you to help," Logan snapped back.

Brayden smiled. "You got fire. I'll give you that. Just be careful around this place. I haven't been here long, but I know how dudes like them can be. Most of the team though? They aren't like them. Do your talking on the field and be on your way. I'll make sure you look good out there," he replied with a wink and a playful punch to Logan's shoulder. "Just trust me."

Logan still didn't respond. Brayden walked away but Logan called out after Brayden turned his back, "Hey, Brayden?"

Brayden stopped and looked back at him.

"You know what? Never mind."

Brayden smiled and walked back to his locker to finish getting ready for practice. Brayden shot a look back in Logan's direction and grinned a bit. The team ran out onto the field for their warmups. The coaches split off all the pitchers with various fielders to show off their arms. Logan sought out to catch with Brayden.

"Pairing off with Lewis, Anderson? Not a bad way to make yourself look good," Coach Stevenson bellowed in between spewing sunflower seeds.

"I figure if I want to be good, I'll have to develop chemistry with our best player, coach."

"Damn right you will. Go easy on him, Lewis. Break him in a little."

"Yes, sir," Brayden said as he tossed the ball over to Logan.

The two began to develop a feel for Logan's game and for each other. Just like his personality, Logan pitched with ferocity. Every pitch came with bad intentions, and he didn't waste time. He threw hard and often. Brayden smiled after every throw. After about twenty pitches, they both stopped and looked around. The two boys from before were watching them. In fact, the whole team stopped warming up to watch them.

Some watched with mouths open. Some watched with arms crossed. This group was a team in name only. Everybody had already sectioned themselves off into various groups. None of those groups seemed to include either Logan or Brayden just yet.

Brayden walked closer to Logan. "Looks like it's just you and me, kid."

Logan looked around at the other guys. "Yup. Seems that way."

"Well? Let's give'em something to talk about then," Brayden said as he trotted back into his catching crouch. "Best player, huh?"

"Don't flatter yourself. I plan on being that guy sooner rather than later." Logan smiled.

Brayden just shook his head and ran back over to catch some more pitches.

"Brayden!" Logan shouted over.

Brayden stood up.

"Thanks for before." He paused. "I really mean that."

Brayden nodded. "Yeah, no problem, man. I got your back. Don't worry."

Brayden stretched his glove out and signaled for Logan to continue. Logan wound up and fired the hardest fastball he could muster up into Brayden's glove. The ball crashed into the glove with a sound like thunder. Logan smiled at Brayden, nodded, and then turned to the rest of the team.

"Get used to that sound, boys, and get used to these faces. We're not going anywhere."

The rest of the team stood almost entranced by what they had seen from their newest teammate. John Stevenson, the coach's son and a sophomore like Brayden, nodded at Brayden with a semblance of approval. Logan held nothing back and Brayden admired him in a way for it. When they ran laps, Logan sprinted to the front of the line. When they ran suicides from line to line, Logan was the first down and the first back. By the time practice had ended, Logan's face was red and was dripping with sweat. Brayden tossed him a towel and water as they reached the locker room.

"Take it easy before you have a heart attack," Brayden scolded. "It's only day one. At this rate, you're not gonna make it to the games."

"Just want to show that I'm not gonna be bullied out of my spot," Logan answered.

"I told you not to worry about it. Your time is gonna come and when it does? You're gonna show everyone why you made the team your freshman year. Just take it easy and enjoy it."

Logan stood up after he changed. "Yeah. You're right." He paused. "Hey, I don't take the busses home. I always like to walk. Wanna come with?"

Brayden raised his eyebrows. "Where do you live that you walk to and from school every day?"

"Church Street. It's almost two miles, I guess. I don't know. I started doing it to stay in shape, but I started to like it. It calms me down. It gets boring sometimes. Where do you live?"

19

"Oh, I live right down the street from there. Mason Ave," Brayden responded.

"No shit. Well, wanna come?"

Brayden nodded his head and he and Logan left the school to walk home. The walk back home hadn't been as bad as it sounded. The air was cool, and a light breeze hit Brayden's back and chilled his skin after a hard practice.

"Must be a nightmare in the winter," he said to Logan.

"Not as bad as you'd think. Wakes me up in the morning at least. Those idiots before told me that you transferred here last year, right?"

"Yeah, from the city. My parents thought it'd be better here for me, my brother, and my sister. You know, suburbs and stuff are supposed to be nice. It took a little getting used to at first, but I really like it here. It's quiet."

"I've grown up here my whole life. I don't know anything other than the quiet."

"You an only child?"

"Yep. I kind of always wanted a sibling though."

Brayden laughed. "Well, you ought to come over some time and meet mine. Maybe you can take one of them off our hands." Brayden stopped and looked at the front door of his house. "This is me. This was cool Logan. Thanks for having me tag along."

He put his arm up and Logan slapped fives with him. "Yeah, no problem! It was nice having someone to talk to instead of just looking at the cars going by and the trees swaying in the wind. Hey, here give me your phone."

Brayden slowly handed Logan his phone.

"I put my number in here in case anything pops up. I'll see ya around." Logan walked down Brayden's driveway but stopped. "Hey, Brayden?"

Brayden turned.

"I usually leave for school around six, six thirty. If you want, I could meet you and we can walk to school together from now on. You know, now that I know where you live and stuff."

"Yeah. Sure man, that'd be cool."

"Awesome. Okay! I'll see you tomorrow then."

Brayden waved Logan off, and he stepped foot inside. His mom had already begun to cook dinner, and his siblings were awaiting his return. Julian hopped off the couch to greet his big brother.

"Hey, little man. How was school?"

"Good! I got a good grade on my vocabulary test!"

"Oh yeah? What's a good grade?"

"85!"

Brayden chuckled. "Yeah. That's good. That's good. Let's get that up into the nineties next time alright?"

Julian nodded and Brayden patted him on the head.

"How was the first day of practice, sweetheart? Did the bus run late?" his mother asked from the kitchen.

"Practice went fine, mom. And no, I didn't take the bus home. I walked home with one of the kids on the team. He lives up on Church Street. His name's Logan."

"Oh, well, sounds like you made a new friend then."

"Yeah, I guess. I don't know. I pulled him out of a little scuffle with a couple of the older kids. He's a good kid though. I'm gonna leave for school with him in the morning, if that's alright."

"Brayden, you're sixteen years old. I think it's okay if you forego the bus to walk to school. Now, go wash up. Dinner will be ready in ten minutes, and your father will be home soon."

Brayden walked down the hall to his room to change. He flipped his phone onto his bed and went into the bathroom to wash up before dinner. He smiled as he looked into the mirror. His mom was right. He DID make a new friend in that locker room earlier in the day. He got back to his room, and his phone was lit up notifying him of a new message.

Look I know I said it a bunch already but thanks for having my back. It might seem small but seriously, I'm glad I didn't start my high school career with a black eye.

I told you it wasn't a problem. Don't worry!! Brayden replied.

So are we like, friends, now?

Whoa, whoa. Don't you think we're moving a little too fast? I mean, we just became teammates right? Brayden chuckled as he hit send.

Well, I am picking you up for school tomorrow :P

Yeah whatever. I'll see you in the morning.

Brayden tossed his phone aside and walked back down the hall to have dinner with his family. His father just walked in and greeted his son with a hug. Springvale had finally started to seem like a home he could grow to love.

21

3

5 Months Ago
March 22nd
(Amber)

Springvale High had allowed her to transfer her fall semester credits so she wouldn't miss any time or be held back by a semester or even a full year. Her mother had to pull some strings to get her in after the winter semester had started. Her father died in February, so it wasn't easy to get back in so soon, but she had made it back. She had been away from public school for over five years. It had taken her a little while to become acclimated to being around so many students again, but she missed it, even if none of the kids remembered her from grade school. Not seeing Logan hurt the most. She'd been back nearly two months and even in passing, he never so much as said hello to her.

We were best friends once you know.

The bell rang and she got up to go to her last class of the day. She went to Logan's last baseball game the day before. His team lost but he had played well, or so she thought. Lost in her thoughts, she collided with another student in the hallway. Her books fell from her hands, and she crashed down onto the floor. A few kids gasped, some went on their way and others just laughed.

"Oh, Jesus. I'm so sorry!" a boy said, presumably the person she crashed into.

She felt a little disoriented and rubbed her head. "It's fine!" she answered. She saw a hand extend down to her.

"Hey, are you o…." He stopped. She looked at him a little closer and stared into his hazel eyes.

"Logan?" she replied.

"Wait, do you know me? I mean, of course you do. Do I…?" He lifted her hair out of her face and looked right at her. "Amber? Amber Donovan?" he stammered as he helped her to her feet. "It's been years. I thought you were in Catholic school or whatever."

"My Dad passed away last month." She looked down. "I tried to get through the year at the school I was at, but my mom moved me back here. I've been back since February."

"What? Really? And you didn't say anything to me?" He sighed. "Wow. I'm sorry about your dad. Are you okay?"

"Yeah. I'm fine. Thanks. Watch where you're going next time!" She giggled. She ignored him about her going up to him since she'd come back.

She lived across town. She and Logan had gone to the same grade school, so they became better friends in the classroom. Before starting fifth grade, Amber's father had moved her to another school in a different town where her mom would take her to and from every day.

* * *

"It's my last day," Amber said.

"What do you mean?" a young Logan asked.

"Daddy says I can't be in this school anymore. I'm going somewhere else."

"Why?" Logan sounded like he was on the verge of tears.

"He said I can learn more if I wasn't with everyone here." Her eyes never met his.

"What about your friends? What about your teachers? What about your homework?"

She laughed. "Daddy said I'll make new friends at my new school, better friends."

Logan hugged her. "But you're MY best friend, Amber. I won't make new friends."

"Maybe you can come over and play if daddy will let you." She ironed out the bottom of her dress with her hands.

"I hope so." The embrace was still intact. "I'll miss you!"

"I'll miss you too Logan! You're my best friend too!"

* * *

"Shit," Logan said bringing her back to the moment. "Hey, Amber? I want you to meet someone."

Amber hesitated for a second before another boy, much taller than Logan approached the two of them.

"Amber this is Brayden. Brayden, Amber. Brayden's one of the kids on my team. He's also become something like a best friend over the past year."

"What do you mean something?" Brayden said punching Logan in the arm. "Nice to meet you, Amber." Brayden extended his hand.

"Best friend?" Those words stung, but she smiled. "Nice to meet you too, Brayden! Logan and I grew up together and then we grew apart. That's the short version."

"Yeah, and then we literally crashed back into each other." Logan laughed.

"Well, sounds like you two need to do some catching up! I gotta get to class anyway. I'll see you around, Amber. It was nice meeting you!"

23

"You too, Brayden!" He didn't seem like the typical jock type. He seemed like the total opposite of Logan, quiet, intuitive.

"So, where you headed to?" Logan asked.

"Before you knocked me over?" She giggled. "I was on my way to chemistry."

"Well, if your class is this way." He pointed behind her. "I could walk with you."

"Sure."

She caught Logan staring at her a few times. She wished she knew what was going on inside his head. Did he really forget about her all this time? Didn't he remember what their friendship meant?

"Logan? Are you alright?" Amber asked.

"Yeah. Yeah, I'm fine. Just glad to see you again. That's all," Logan stuttered. "You uh, you did something different with your hair from the last time I've seen you."

I'm sure you've seen me plenty. You just didn't know it was me. "Yeah, I dyed it a year or so ago, before my dad died. I didn't like it brown anymore."

"Well, it looks great. You look great," he said with frightening confidence.

"Thanks."

"So…this is your class?"

"Yup."

"Oh, well, I guess I'll see you around!"

"I'm sure we'll see each other again soon. Bye Logan!" She went to go for a hug, but he turned before she got the chance. He waved back at her as she took her seat. Before she knew it, he was gone again. She put her hand on her head and fretted. It wasn't the reunion she thought it'd be.

* * *

She pressed her head up against the bus window while looking out into the blur of colors on the way home from school. She thought of the boy she had collided with in the hallway earlier in the day, a boy she felt she might not see again for quite a while. Five years in Catholic school had separated her from her from her best friend. She had lost precious time with the one person she gravitated to as a child: the loud, brash, confident boy from across town, Logan Anderson.

* * *

Back then, her hair wasn't black but almost honey-like brown. Instead of jeans and sneakers, she wore long dresses. Their fourth-grade class was playing kickball. A

24

boisterous boy with auburn hair stood in the center of the field. Even though it was recess, Logan was serious. He had always taken sports seriously. His brows were low, and his eyes seemed to turn a dark brown from their normal hazel. She wasn't terribly good at sports, especially kickball, and here she stood staring down the best kid in class, well, staring at the ground while he stared at her. She kicked off her sandals and Logan stopped before rolling the ball.

"It's okay." He nodded to her. "I won't hurt you."

The other kids laughed, but he wasn't joking. She could tell.

"Easy out! Easy out!" the boy behind Logan teased.

Logan shot a glance in his direction and wound up as if he was going to roll the fiercest pitch he could muster. Instead, he slowed his arm down and rolled it softly, right to her. She swung her leg and didn't kick the ball very far, but just out of Logan's reach and she scored the winning run.

"You let her win!" one of Logan's friends yelled.

"No I didn't!" Logan yelled back. "You couldn't have done better!"

Just as the teachers called the kids in to go back to class, Logan pulled Amber aside.

"Nice kick," he said.

"Did you let me win?" she asked.

"No way!" He started to jog away but she grabbed his arm.

"Thanks." She hugged him.

"We weren't on the same team, but you're still my best friend!"

* * *

But Logan hadn't cared that they drifted apart for so long. Sure, he had laughed and joked, but he didn't give her the reaction she wanted. She wanted a long embrace, and she had wanted him to care about where she'd been for the last five years. Instead, he remarked about her being in Catholic school "or whatever," as he had put it to her. He walked away just as quickly as he arrived. Before she could see him when she looked back, he had scurried away to his next class. He just whisked away as if he had seen her as just another face in a school full of kids who knew Logan Anderson. He was a superstar. He was popular. He just forgot about her.

Her father had put her in what she would refer to as Hell on Earth.

"You don't need to learn with them other kids," his words echoed in her mind for years.

As she got older, she had started to break the illusion that whatever her dad did was for her own good. She realized her father could be just plain cruel to get her to live how HE had wanted her to live. That's why she had dyed her hair black, a tiny act of defiance, which she of course paid for.

25

* * *

"Amber Marie, you come over here right now!" her father called from the kitchen.

She hurried up the steps and heard footsteps behind her. She felt a hand grab her hair and a tug that yanked her down the stairs.

"This is going to toughen you up. It's for your own good."

He raised his hand, and she winced before the blow even landed. The slap knocked her down to the ground and she looked at the strands of black hair lying on the ground.

"Should have never gone behind my back and had your mom help dye that."

She sat on the floor and cried. She wasn't even a little girl anymore, and he still punished her that way.

"Are you going to apologize now?" he asked.

"No," she answered.

Another open hand, this time to the shoulder, just to knock her off balance.

"Are you sure?"

"I'm not apologizing. I'm not a little girl anymore. You can't treat me like this!" He knocked her into the step.

"Last chance."

"No."

He yanked her off her feet and threw her down with force.

"I wish you would just go away!" she screamed and ran up the stairs.

She ran into her room and dropped to her knees. "If you really exist, if you can really hear my prayers and if ANYTHING I've learned in that place is true, then you'll take my father away. I don't care how you do it."

* * *

Then, in the silence of a February evening, a little over a week before her sixteenth birthday, a massive heart attack had taken her father away. God had answered her prayers. She only cried the night the ambulance took him away. She didn't miss him. A bump in the road jolted her head against the bus window. The bus stopped and she rose up out of her seat to get off and head home. She waved goodbye to the driver and walked down the street to her home. Her mom was still working at the bank, and her younger brother Michael was still in school for another hour. She swung the front door open and breathed in silence. She sat cross-legged on the navy-blue couch near the window in her living room and glanced over at the picture on the end table closest to her. She saw herself in the photo at a younger age with her father, mother, and baby brother. She looked into the smiles of her parents, and into her own. Before she could become too absorbed in her thoughts, a knock on the front door surprised her.

Who stood on the other side surprised her more. She opened the door and saw a taller, auburn haired boy staring back her.

"Hey," he stuttered. "I hoped you still lived in this house."

"Logan?" she remarked. "What um, what are you doing here?"

"You're not happy to see me?" He laughed. "I just figured I would stop by, and, you know, catch up on the last couple of years."

"Uh, sure! Come in."

She picked her bag up off the couch and kicked various pairs of her shoes aside. Logan looked around a little bit before sitting down. She scanned his face as he looked over at the picture of her family.

"Do you miss him a lot?" he asked about her father.

"He was my dad, so, I mean..." she stuttered. "It's kind of complicated with me and my dad. Excuse me."

She glanced away from him and walked to the bathroom upstairs. She looked in the mirror and noticed herself tearing up and her face reddening. Logan knocked on the door.

"Are you alright?" he asked from the hallway.

She opened the door and smiled. "I'm fine, Logan! Go sit back down." She laughed.

"You got up and rushed away pretty quickly," he replied.

"I know. It's just...I haven't really talked about my dad with anyone since he passed, except for you know, the grief counselors at my old school, but that never went anywhere. It's just hard. Like I said, it's complicated. Don't worry about it!" She laughed again, this time, more as a defense so she wouldn't start to cry.

She wanted to tell him everything, but she couldn't bring herself to. She wanted to tell him about the things her father had done to her. When she was a little girl, she couldn't do anything about it. She couldn't even do anything about it now because her father was gone, so she just closed her heart to it. The scars remained. They stayed with her every hour of every day from when she woke up in the morning to when she laid her head to sleep at night.

How could Logan understand that? Logan lived with his perfect pair of parents, in his perfect house, with his perfect little life. He was smart, charming, good looking, and hyperathletic. Everyone in school admired and adored Logan now. People always told her how pretty her eyes were, but she used her hair to hide them most of the time. The only people who gave Amber any sort of attention at school were her teachers and a few kids here and there. She sat in front of all her classes and answered any question she could get her hands up fast enough for. Logan never ran into such problems. He had such a radiant personality that he blazed into any room he entered.

"You really don't want to talk about it, do you?" he asked looking up under her bowed head. She almost forgot they were still talking about her dad.

"I'm sorry, Logan. I just…I just can't right now. It's all so hard to bring up and talk about. I don't want…"

"Hey. Listen," he interrupted, putting his fingers under her chin to lift her head towards his eyes. "You don't have to explain anything. I'll always be around if you want to talk, okay?"

She smiled. "Okay."

The front door swung open and a brown-haired woman wearing a bright floral skirt rushed through the door and scurried into the house with a black leather purse slung across her shoulder.

"Oh! Sorry, sweetie!" she exclaimed. "I didn't realize you were going to have company over! Who is this handsome young man?"

Logan waved as he stood up. "You probably don't remember me, Mrs. Donovan, but I'm Logan…"

"Anderson! Logan Anderson? I haven't seen you in…

"Five years or so." He laughed.

"You look so much different! My goodness. You're all grown up!"

"Mom!" Amber interjected. "Do you mind?"

"Oh! Oh, I'm sorry again! I'll just pass on through. Great seeing you, Logan."

"You too, Mrs. D."

"Sorry about…you know, her." Amber smiled.

Logan just laughed off the whole situation. A bus rolled past the house and up the street. Michael was in third grade and had many of the characteristics of his father: dark green eyes, dusty brown hair, and chocolate-colored thin eyebrows. She looked at her parents' pictures from when they were kids hung over the entertainment center across from the couch and couldn't look at her brother without seeing her father in him. She knew he would probably grow up to be a spitting image of him, but at the same time, she knew that Michael would end up nothing like her father.

Michael blasted through the front door and hugged his big sister, almost ignoring the fact that a total stranger was standing next to her.

Amber had babysat him on days when their mother worked late at her second job. She cherished the time to spend with and to teach her little brother. Michael was one of the few blessings she could thank her dad for giving her. Michael tugged on Amber's shirt.

"Hey, Amber, is this your boyfriend?" the boy asked.

Amber blushed, and before she could reply, Logan answered, "Mikey, you were pretty much a baby the last time I saw you, but your sister and I have been best friends for a long time."

"How come I haven't seen you before then?" Michael fired back.

"Well, you know your sister went to a different school and I couldn't walk anywhere I wanted like I can now."

"Are you her boyfriend?" the boy pestered Logan.

"No," Logan laughed. "But my name is Logan and we're going to get to know each other a lot better, okay?"

Michael smiled, high-fived Logan, and ran upstairs to his bedroom.

"I wish I had a little brother or sister to see every day," Logan said.

"Really?"

"Yeah, I mean, don't get me wrong, I like being alone and being an only child, but there's something about caring about someone else that is really kind of, I don't know, special."

"I love my little nugget. I'd do anything for him," Amber responded.

"I can tell. I think that's an awesome trait to have. You've always cared about people Amber, and I've always admired you for it." He smiled as he stood to leave.

"I guess we'll have some more catching up to do, hm?" She giggled between smiles.

"Yeah, and I really look forward to it. I almost forgot how much I missed you all these years."

There it was. He did forget about her.

"Bye, Mrs. D!" he yelled into her kitchen. "Wait, um," he stuttered. "God, I don't know why this is so hard, but could I get your number?"

She laughed. "Give me your phone."

He handed it over and she typed her number in.

"Here," she handed it back. "Don't forget to save it!"

Before he turned to leave, he wrapped his arms around her and put her in a strong embrace. She wanted that squeeze ever since she ran into him in the hallway earlier in the day. His grip felt firm, strong, yet comforting to her as his arms wrapped around over her shoulders. She rested her head on his chest and closed her eyes for a moment that felt like an hour. She let go and looked up at him and for the first time, she felt a tiny spark. It wasn't overwhelming, but like something kicked her heart into an extra gear. She could recall the feeling as if it were always there, as if HE were always there. She remembered that jolt in grade school.

"You know," Logan muttered with his back turned to her. "Your hair really makes your eyes even more brilliant than when you had brown hair."

Before she could thank him or reply, he already made it down her driveway. Much like their encounter in the hallway, he disappeared. She felt much different than she felt earlier when he walked away in school. He cared this time. He meant everything he said, but she couldn't tell whether the quip about her eyes was just Logan being Logan Anderson, super charming, personable, flirtatious superstar, or whether he TRULY meant it.

"Thank you," she whispered to herself as she closed the door.

Her mother stood in the kitchen with a wide grin on her face.

"What?" Amber answered her mother's stare.

"Oh nothing! Just a mother's intuition at work. That boy has always been there for you, Amber, and you will always be there for him."

She nodded her head and smiled. Her mom was right. Logan was back and this time, she felt she wasn't going to lose his friendship again.

4

August 28th

Junior Year

(Logan)

Church Street was the same every single day. He could probably walk the streets with his eyes closed and make it through the neighborhood anyway. After every couple of steps, he looked up at the sky to see the fading moon and stars.

"Good morning, Mr. Brooks!" Logan waved to the old man tending to his front yard garden across the street.

"Morning, Mr. Anderson! Don't be late now." Mr. Brooks playfully chastised.

"Never!"

Logan walked down the street towards Mason Avenue to stop by Brayden's house. Before Brayden, the arduous nature of seeing the same trees, crossing the same streets, and seeing the same houses every day had annoyed him. However, after he and Brayden made a habit of walking together to and from school, he had grown to embrace it, even enjoy it. He approached Brayden's front door and knocked a handful of times. Checking his phone, he rang the doorbell a few times and heard footsteps on the other side of the door. Brayden opened the door with a less than enthused look on his face.

"You ready to start the last year of your high school life?" Logan asked.

"Man, I've been ready to get out of school for quite a while now," Brayden joked as he pushed Logan aside. "Putting up with you for the last year and a half."

"You've been working out? You look like you put on some weight." Logan grabbed Brayden's arms.

"Yeah," Brayden answered. "Except it's the good kind of weight, not like the pounds you put on over the summer."

"Screw you. I just like to relax in the offseason," Logan snapped back.

"Yeah, and judging by how you look? You've been doing an awful lot of relaxing," Brayden punched Logan in the gut. "Now, are you still in shape to walk to school?"

Logan nodded and they continued walking down the street to make their way to school. Logan looked up at the sky as it started to brighten.

Brayden was always quiet, but he seemed more reserved than usual. He kept his eyes forward and didn't say a word to Logan once they left his house. Usually, the mile and a half walk to school passed by quicker than this, because they spent it talking. Brayden's silence started to bug him as he ran out of houses to see, or cars to watch drive by.

Logan finally broke the silence. "How's it feel? You know, being a senior and all?" Logan asked.

"Doesn't feel much different yet," Brayden answered, tugging the straps on his book bag. "I'm sure that'll change in May and June, when the year starts to end."

Hearing that was the first time Logan had thought about the end of the school year. The end of the year meant Brayden moving on to college and leaving Logan behind.

"You want to know one of the best things I did?" Brayden asked as they approached the school. "Bailing your ass out of that fight."

"This again?" Logan sighed.

"No, I'm serious, Logan. Meeting you, playing with you, that's what turned everything around for me."

"You just had to see what kind of an impact you could be making if everyone knew you, instead of keeping to yourself all the time."

Brayden patted Logan on the shoulder. "As much as you thank me, I feel like I never return the favor. So, thanks, for everything."

They arrived at school a little early and hung around the front door until they heard the click of the front desk attendant unlocking the doors. They walked in and a rush of students quickly swallowed them as they came in for the first day of school. The quiet morning turned into a symphony of new students and old and "school-only" friends who greeted each other after not seeing one another for the entire summer.

"Do you think we'd be like that if we didn't hang out all summer?" Logan asked.

"Dunno. I think if we didn't see each other all summer, you'd know there was something wrong."

Logan fixed his attention on a particular kid in the hallway. His hair was all out of sorts, and he scurried around from side to side with a piece of paper in his hand. Every other second it seemed he was looking up at the room numbers in the hallway. He watched the boy fluttering about like a frantic butterfly trying to identify his proper classroom. Through the rush of all the students piling in, the young man stumbled over himself and almost fell. Logan laughed.

"What are you laughing at?" Brayden asked.

"That kid, you see him, right?" Logan snickered. "He has absolutely no idea where he's going. Come on, you know it's funny."

"It wasn't that long ago that was you." Brayden beamed. "I still remember a little baby deer stuck in the headlights of the baseball locker room on his first day."

"That was different, and you know it." Logan got defensive. "I was only like that because I was the only freshman there; this dude just has no idea where he's going."

"Oh, so you're the big man on campus now?" Brayden questioned. "You get to judge all the new kids all of a sudden? Don't start with that shit man, not on the first day."

"What do you mean?"

"That seniority entitlement bullshit. You're not even a senior. You can't just look down on these kids because they're new. Give them a chance. Let them get their feet wet. Shit, if I would've taken that approach with you, you would have started your high school career with a couple of black eyes."

Logan couldn't counter and Brayden laughed.

Logan fretted. "You're always right! I hate it, but you're always right."

"It's because I think about things before I say them. You still haven't learned that have you? You gotta relax, man. The weight of the world isn't always on you to prove yourself. Don't try so hard."

"It's just...I don't know. It's hard feeling like the sidekick sometimes."

Brayden stopped. "Sidekick? To me?"

"Yeah, to you! I feel like you casted this giant shadow over me and it's hard getting out from under it sometimes."

Brayden laughed. "Is that what's been eating you? Logan, I'm not casting a shadow anywhere. You're gonna be great. You can be everything I am now and even more. Trust me."

Logan didn't answer. The freshman boy found his classroom and disappeared out of view. They stopped at Logan's locker, and he began dumping his things into it. Out of his bag, he pulled a few headlines from the past baseball season, a reminder of what he needed to accomplish in the upcoming year.

SOPHOMORE SENSATION DAZZLES IN SEASON DEBUT

EAGLES WIN 14-0, ANDERSON RECORDS SHUT OUT
ANDERSON INJURY LEAVES SPRINGVALE SHORT-ARMED
FOR DISTRCTS

"I wish I kept all those newspaper clippings of the stuff I did the last three years," Brayden said, running his hands over the ink inside Logan's locker.

"Good thing you don't." Logan laughed. "You'd run out of room in your locker!"

"No, no that's not it. I just never really thought about looking back. I don't know. Never really saw a point to it. Not that I don't get why you do it. I just was never really motivated by that kind of stuff."

It was true. Brayden had proved to be a statistical marvel over the last three years. He didn't just lead the district in statistics like Logan, he had led the entire state in home runs, runs batted in, batting average, as well as posting no errors behind the plate every year he's played.

"Look man," Brayden opened up. "I gotta go to class. I'm not trying to be late on my first day. I'll catch you later. Lunch as always, right?"

"You can count on it," Logan replied.

Brayden walked away, but not before Logan noticed Amber across the hall.

"Hey, Amber!" Brayden yelled out from across the hall to the raven-haired girl.

"Oh, hey, Brayden!" Amber waved before embracing Brayden with a tight hug. "Ohhh, you smile nice today, Bray!"

"It's almost hard to see you down there little one. But me? That's that first day of school smell. Kinda like the new car smell, it's always best right at the start." Brayden laughed. "I gotta get to class though. We'll catch up later!"

Amber watched Brayden walk away. She turned her attention to Logan and snatched his class schedule out of his hand before he even had a chance to look at it. Her eyes scanned the paper as if she was studying for an exam. Suddenly, she thrust it back into his chest.

"Well, we don't have first period together, but we do have English second period and lunch together. So, it's not all so bad!"

"So, wait, you think spending more time together isn't a bad thing?" he joked.

She pushed him up against his locker. "You can be a real jerk sometimes." The way she flashed her eyes at him made him know that she knew he was kidding. "I'll see you next period, Logan."

He smiled and waved her off as he went in for his first class of the day.

* * *

Even though the first class of the day was over, Logan didn't feel any less tired. He always counted on the walk to school to wake him to counter getting up so early in the morning, but as he entered his second class, he spotted Amber, promptly took the seat in front of her and laid his head down on his desk.

He felt a nudge at the center of his back. "Are you kidding me?" Amber whispered.

"Just give me until the bell rings. I'll get up then." Logan shook her hand off and closed his eyes.

Logan heard his other classmates filter into the classroom. Suddenly the door slammed shut, which startled him. He propped one eye open to see the teacher walk into the classroom. He had never seen this guy before. He was a younger man with curly, light brown hair and his shirt cuffs were unbuttoned with the sleeves rolled to his elbows. The man strolled to the front of the classroom. He couldn't have been older than thirty, but the confidence with which he walked spoke volumes. He stood in front of the class, and his eyes grew wide.

"So, these are my esteemed juniors." He smiled. "Wonderful. Welcome to the first day of the most interesting class you'll take all year."

The class let out a collective half-laugh.

"I'm Mr. Anthony Pearsall. You can call me Mr. Pearsall, Mr. P, whatever suits your attitude. If you give respect, you'll get it in return. I promise you."

Logan slid up in his chair and picked his head off the desk. He opened his eyes a bit wider. He liked Mr. Pearsall almost right away. There was a quiet swagger in him that Logan admired.

"Oh! Ladies and gentlemen!" Mr. Pearsall exclaimed. "I was unaware that we had campus royalty among us! Why didn't anyone warn me? I would have dressed more appropriately," he said as he let his sleeves down and bowed before Logan.

"Oh no, no. No need for fanfare, Mr. P." Logan laughed. "I'm just here to enjoy that ride you promised me."

35

"And enjoy it you will," Mr. Pearsall reassured him. "I promised, didn't I? You're going for the ride for your life. So maybe next time, it won't wake you up when I walk into the classroom. It will merely increase your interest," he said with a wink.

"Most definitely, Mr. P. I'm all in." Logan replied. "Sorry about that. Long morning."

"Good, because all in is the only way you're going to have a good time in this class, Mr. Anderson."

The class laughed as Mr. Pearsall had begun to pass out his course syllabus for the upcoming year. Logan read over it and became dizzy looking at all the book titles and assignments that he was going to have to complete before the year was up.

He wasn't kidding about this.

Logan let out a big sigh and signed his name to the "contract" that was provided for him at the end of the syllabus. He stretched his arms out to Mr. Pearsall as the teacher whisked around the room to collect the sheets of paper from all the students. Logan paused for a moment before he handed in the paper.

"Here you go. I'm all in." Logan reached out with a smile.

"I see that. Now let's see if you boom or bust, my friend," Mr. Pearsall answered with a bigger smile. "Don't worry. I know the routine. None of you really want work to do on the first day. We are going to work, but we're going to focus on you as a group first before we focus on the work itself."

Mr. P handed out index cards. "On these cards, I want you to write down three unique facts about yourself. Where you're from, what your favorite color is AND why, anything that you feel is unique to you. It can be as fun or as deep as you want it to be, as long as it's UNIQUE. Then you're going to pass those cards forward and around the room to one another." He stopped. "I would prefer it if you DIDN'T use those two examples I just gave."

He drew a rough sketch of the classroom on the board and showed how they were to pass the cards around.

"Then in your notebooks, as you collect a card, write down the name of the student whose card you have and the most interesting thing he or she wrote about his or herself. That way, by the end of today's class, you'll all have a better sense of who your classmates are and what they're all about."

Logan glanced back at Amber. "Well, at least I know my first card will be easy."

Amber laughed. "You'd be surprised."

"Okay, take five minutes and then I'll give you the go ahead for when to pass your cards forward." Mr. Pearsall called out.

Logan sat looking at his card, blank and untouched.

What could I write that these kids don't already know? What's even interesting about me?

Logan was well known at Springvale due to his success on the field. He knew he'd have to dig pretty deep into his life at home to find something unique, a piece of his life he'd rather keep away from his school life. Inspired though by Mr. P and his upfront nature, he scribbled down on the card:

1. My middle name is Allen because of my grandfather on my dad's side.

2. Despite everything I do here, I have no desire to play baseball professionally.

He sat and thought about what to write for this third fact. Then, as if struck by something, he scribbled down:

3. My parents recently got divorced, and I don't care if I never hear from my dad again.

He had immediate second thoughts about that last bit, but before he got the chance to erase it or scribble it out, Mr. Pearsall had called them to pass their cards forward. Logan hesitated to pass his up, but he sighed and put the card in the hand of the kid in front of him. He reached behind him and smiled at Amber, plucking her card from her hand.

1. Black isn't my natural hair color, it's brown, but I dyed it black because my dad hated it.

2. I have one little brother, named Michael. That's got to be pretty unique.

3. My dad passed away in February before my 16th birthday, and I feel guilty because I prayed to God to take him away.

Logan put the card down on his desk.

He heard Amber whisper from behind him, "Not as easy as you thought?"

"I'm so sorry," he answered back without looking at her.

Almost at the same time those words left his lips, the kid he handed his card to wheeled around and just looked at him.

"Yeah, I probably didn't have to write something that heavy."

The cards went in rotation for several minutes before Logan finally had his back in his hand.

"Now that you're all done, get your cards to the front of the room so I can collect them and learn about you myself."

"Hey!" Logan interrupted. "How come you don't put anything up about yourself?"

"Patience, Mr. Anderson. I was getting to that. I'm going to write three things about myself now and you can take them down for your notes as well."

As Mr. Pearsall wrote his facts on the board, Logan looked back at Amber.

"Do you really feel like your dad dying was your fault?" he asked.

"I can't talk about this right now, Logan." Amber shut him down rather quickly.

Logan took down the three facts about his teacher as the bell rang and it was time for lunch.

* * *

Logan, Amber and Brayden met up for lunch. Logan and Amber sat closer to each other and Brayden sat on the opposite end of the small round table from them. He leaned back onto the two legs of his chair and kept quiet in the busy noise of the lunchroom. A teammate of Brayden and Logan approached them.

"Hey Logan! How's the shoulder?"

"Honestly? It sounds super cliché, but I've never felt better," Logan answered.

"Good to hear, bud," the boy said. "I hope that you stick around for the playoffs this year. We're going to need you."

"What's that supposed to mean? I'm not good enough anymore?" Brayden interjected.

"No, no. That's not it. It's just, pitching is light this year. Logan, we need you more than ever," the kid replied glancing at Brayden.

"I told you. I'm fine. Take all that pressure and put it on me. I'm ready," Logan answered.

The boy turned and walked away to his table.

"Man, you never shut that competitive switch off do you? Always focused, always serious when it comes to playing." Brayden said.

"Something else you want to be critical of?" Logan asked.

"Na man, not at all. I kind of admire it." Brayden dropped his chair down onto the ground. "Hey, can I talk to you guys for a second?"

"What's up?" Logan asked. Amber leaned in.

"I don't want to really get into this on the first day, but it's been bugging me since I got up." He paused.

"Well?" Amber prodded.

Logan leaned in and felt a pinch of concern

"You guys just take care of yourselves when I graduate, alright?" Brayden said out of nowhere.

Logan turned his head. "Where's this coming from?"

Brayden sighed. "A part of me that knows how shitty life can be, and it kind of just all hit me at once that this might be the last year we are around each other all the time and I just want you guys to be sure you're ready to go when I leave."

"You act like we can't just text you or call whenever we need you, Bray!" Amber interrupted. "Maybe one weekend, Logan and I can visit you when you're in school or come to one of your games! Don't worry about us!"

Brayden let out a breath. "Yeah, I guess you're right. Sorry, just a lot on my mind."

Amber reached across the table and put her hand over Brayden's. "It's okay. I get it. Graduating is scary and knowing that you're counting down the days, it's a lot to handle. I understand."

Brayden smiled. "You always do." Brayden grabbed the leg of Logan's chair and pulled Logan around to his side of the table close to him. He whispered, "Let her in, man. Just let her in."

"What is with you all of a sudden?"

"You two keeping secrets?" Amber asked.

Brayden pushed Logan away and laughed. "No, just some brotherly advice that he NEEDS to hear."

Logan looked over at Amber. Kids on the baseball team always asked him about her, though he never told her. Her long black hair and dazzling arctic blue eyes had often complimented her soft porcelain features, which added to her allure. She didn't belong with either of them from an outside perspective. She seemed wiser than most students were at their age. Logan would do anything in his power to protect her, and Brayden knew that too.

"You care about her so much, you'll protect her from you too," Brayden had once told him.

"What's that mean?"

"It means you don't want to hurt her by making things complicated."

They both guarded something from each other, to protect each other, and out of love. Brayden chuckled to himself.

"What are you laughing at?" Amber asked.

"Nothing, Amber. Nothing at all."

Logan kept his gaze on her and thought back to what she wrote on the card in class. He didn't know whether or not she was making a confession to the entire class, or just to Logan about the kind of anger she once had for her father.

5

September 22ⁿᵈ

(Brayden)

Upon coming home from school, Brayden and Logan noticed a strange but expensive looking car in Brayden's driveway. The car was a sleek navy-blue coupe with New York plates and a Syracuse University sticker mounted on the back windshield.

"Family from back home?" Logan asked.

"Na. Don't have any family that far up north," Brayden answered warily. "Let me get inside, I'll talk to you about it later."

Brayden walked inside and saw his mother sitting on the living room couch with a man. He was rather ordinary and just a little bit out of touch with the way he dressed. He wore a navy-blue overcoat and a bright orange tie. His grey hair was parted neatly to the side, and his moustache curled up on both sides of his face.

"Brayden Lewis?" the man said getting up off the couch. He extended his hand.

Brayden answered with a firm handshake and raised eyebrows.

"Brayden, honey," his mother said. "This man is a scout from Syracuse up north."

Brayden let out a breathless laugh. "Him?"

"A word Mr. Lewis?" the man asked as Brayden stood rather still. "Please, sit."

Brayden shook his head to bring himself back to reality. "Uh, sure, yeah," he said as he walked over to the couch and sat down.

"Brayden, I represent Syracuse University, and I love what I've seen out there over your past couple of seasons young man."

Brayden looked over at his mother. She did little more than nod her head and reassure him with her eyes. "Th…thank you sir. I don't know if you've seen any of our playoff games, but we can't seem to win those."

"A competitor! I love it!" the man shouted as he put his arm around Brayden.

Brayden narrowed his eyes.

"Look Brayden, I won't mince words with you. We want you to play for the Orange after you graduate high school next year. If you commit to us in the next few weeks, we're prepared to offer you a full athletic scholarship to attend Syracuse to be a part of our team, and our community after your senior year."

"A full ride? Like…I won't have to pay? I just go to college for playing baseball?"

"Well, yes, provided your grades are good enough."

Brayden sat completely still. He knew what he wanted to say, but he couldn't find the right words. This man had laid his future in front of him, right there in his living room, offering a chance for him to live out his dream.

"Man, sir, Mr…"

"Davies, Andrew Davies."

"Mr. Davies. This is a lot to get thrown my way. I wasn't exactly expecting all of this. I don't know." Brayden paused. "Why me? Why'd you pick me so soon?"

"You're a talented young man Brayden. We want you to come to Syracuse. You're a New York boy at heart. We want you to succeed on and off the field. We think we can give you the tools you need to succeed in life."

"But there's a bunch of other kids in this area of the country, but you found out about me." ·

"Well, you jumped off the screen at us when we were scouting talent in the region."

"Jumped out at you…" Brayden's hand clinched.

"Your numbers were amazing. In three seasons, you led the district every year in home runs, RBIs and have yet to commit a single error. You're a blue chipper Brayden, and we want to set you up for success. We know you're from the area and we figured we should try to bring you on home!"

Brayden sat, almost not blinking. Mr. Davies didn't know anything else about Brayden other than his height, his weight, and his baseball statistics. He had never seen Brayden before last year.

"Thank you, sir. I just can't make a commitment one way or the other right now. I hope you understand that. You won't be the last person I talk to. I don't think I'll be able to make good on committing any time soon."

"I understand. It's a big decision. Just keep in mind who came to you first, who talked to you first and who offered you the chance to talk to them first." Mr. Davies rose off the couch. "Thank you, Mrs. Lewis for letting me into your home. Thank you, Brayden, for giving me the time.

Please give my regards to Mr. Lewis as well." Mr. Davies pulled a card out of his coat pocket. "My number, give me a call sometime, not necessarily with a decision, but if you have any other questions about the university, the program, the academics, anything at all!"

Brayden extended his hand. "Will do. Thank you, sir."

"Thank you, son. Talk soon."

Brayden closed the door behind Mr. Davies and put his back to it. He was in such a shocked state that he almost let the card with the name and number fall right from his hands. Going to college at Syracuse would also keep Brayden closer to home. Brayden had grown to love Springvale over the past two and a half years. Nevertheless, he always longed to go back home to his home state and see his old friends again. He missed the city, the noise, the everyday hustle and bustle that New York provided him. He knew going to college in Syracuse wasn't the same as living in the city back home, but he felt a closeness with that area that Springvale could never replicate. The only things that kept him attached in Springvale were the obvious love for his parents and his friendship with Logan, which had blossomed into a fellowship between the two stars.

"So, what do you think?" Brayden asked.

"I think we should wait until your father gets home and talk about all this as a family."

"What's there to talk about? Why wouldn't I do this? They want to offer me a scholarship."

Brayden's mother sighed. "I know, baby, I know. It's still a big decision and I know you and your father don't always see eye to eye when it comes to your aspirations with playing professional ball but at least hear him out."

Brayden took off to his room and texted Logan all the details of the conversation between himself and the college scout.

My best friend is gonna be a D-1 superstar a text from Logan read.

This is cool and all, but he's just the first guy. He won't be the last. I need to be honest with myself. I gotta think about this, you know?

Think about what? Syracuse is a D-1 school. It's big. It's back in your home state. What's there to think about?

There's a lot to think about! This is my future man. I gotta talk to a lot of different people before I say yes or no to him. He knows that. That's why he just made all those promises.

Alright, but still, you gotta admit. It's pretty cool. ;)

Yeah, it is isn't it? Brayden heard his little brother and sister coming home from school. *Look, I'll talk to you later, kid.*

Rapid footsteps got louder and closer and Julian exploded into Brayden's room and hopped up on his bed.

"Whoa, drop the energy level there J. What's up?"

"Dad's home early!"

Wonderful.

Brayden walked out to see his mother and father standing in the dining room.

"Guessing you heard about the scout thing huh?" Brayden asked.

Brayden's father nodded. "I did. It's really wonderful son." His father grabbed him and hugged him.

His father didn't smile often. Brayden's father made good money commuting to the city working as a carpenter, but his job had laid him off a few months ago. His body had begun to fail him over the past few months. Nagging injuries seemed to last longer, bags had grown darker and heavier underneath his eyes from sleepless nights. His clean-shaven face had grown a greying, scruffy beard. Brayden saw his father aging day in and day out in front of his eyes. His parents had scrounged up money to send Brayden to a decent college, but nothing quite like Syracuse.

"I'll just say it right out pop," Brayden blurted out. "You guys won't have to worry about money for me anymore. You see that right?" Brayden smiled. "Take care of Julian and Angela. Take care of the house."

"It isn't that simple." His father's voice grew sterner. "This is a big decision and one you can't make lightly. Take some time to think about what you want to do in school, and I don't mean just playing ball."

It was funny. It sounded responsible when Brayden said it to Logan, but when his father said it to him, it sounded like a lecture.

"I know dad. I know."

"Do you? Do you even know what you want to go to school for?"

Brayden stayed silent.

"You still have to get through this last year. Don't let this man or the next man or any other man force you into a decision you aren't ready to make just because he's pitching the idea that the grass is greener back home, okay?"

"I got it dad. Thanks."

"Are you sure? Don't let any of your friends tell you that this is a golden ticket. Say you do take this scholarship, then what? You have to keep your grades up."

"You act like my grades are bad now!" Brayden shouted back.

"College is a different experience. You won't have your same friends to rely on. You won't have us to fall back on. You're going to be out there by yourself."

"Richard!" Brayden's mother interrupted.

"He needs to know what a big decision it is."

"I know what a big decision it is. What, you think I shook his hand and signed on the dotted line right then and there? I didn't. I thought about all the stuff you're saying. I told him I'd talk to him another time. I did everything the way you'd want me to."

"I just want you to really think about this, Brayden."

"I told you. I got it. Thanks for the talk."

Brayden stormed off back to his room and while he didn't slam the door, he closed it with enough force to make a point. Brayden looked at all his trophies around his room. He threw his notebook on his desk and opened it to a blank page. He began sketching. Drawing had always been an outlet for him. He drew a rough sketch of himself in the middle of a baseball stadium. He stood on the mound with lights pouring down on him. Blank faces filled the seats, and, in the dugout, he drew his family, Logan, and Amber.

He drew Logan behind him with a Springvale jersey on. He pulled out colored pencils from his desk drawer and started to fill in Logan's features. He did his best to replicate Logan's auburn hair and signature confident smile. Amber was next. He shaded her skin softer than the rough scratches he drew himself and Logan with at first. He used the faintest off white he could find to replicate her. He pulled two distinctly different colors, black and aqua blue, for her hair and eyes respectively. He had thought about putting her in the crowd, but she meant more to him than that.

He put her on the opposite side of himself, with her arm out of view behind him and close to Logan. He colored in her long black hair, which ran down near her waist. He tilted her head slightly to the side but made sure not to cover either of her eyes. Finally, he drew himself there. Instead of drawing himself with his face out like Logan and Amber, he drew himself with his back turned, with a big S emblazoned in his back, which he colored orange, and his glove lying on the ground next to him. He made his

45

decision, and he knew whom he wanted along for the ride. He looked at the big orange "S" on the back of his drawn-up self and drew a huge circle around it. He drew three branches off the circle.

To the right a baseball bat and glove, to the left a dollar sign, and in the middle, Brayden drew a cloud with a diploma inside. For the first time, Brayden felt every bit as powerful as people claimed him to be. He felt as if he finally held the whole world in his hands, and he never even entertained the thought that he might fumble it away. That business card alone did in fact represent a golden ticket to wherever Brayden wanted to go. He sat down on his bed and smiled again.

This is what living the dream feels like.

Ever since he could remember, his parents had supported his dream of being a baseball player, as all parents do, but even they probably never expected him to realize it, especially his father. Here he stood with the best opportunity to achieve that potential.

"I promise on everything," he said to himself. "I'm not going to blow this."

6

October 14ᵗʰ

(Amber)

She laid on her bed and pretended not to hear her mother calling her to come downstairs to leave to go to dinner. Usually, she didn't mind going out to eat with her mother and Michael. Tonight, however, there would be a fourth party sitting at the table with them. Her mother had met the man, Curt, at her job at the bank. He didn't work there, but as the story goes, he deposited his checks inside with the clerk, her mother, every week, every Friday. The more he showed up, the more her mother and Curt got to know each other. It didn't take long for there to be nights out where Amber would babysit her brother. Tonight was the first night that she was going to meet the mythical Curt. There was a knock on her door, and her younger brother came in soon after.

"Mommy says it's time for us to go," he said standing in the doorway.

"I know. I'm coming. Give me a minute, Michael."

She huffed and sat up on her bed.

I thought we were doing okay with just us.

It had been just eight months since her father had died. Was it really time for her mother to move on already? With someone she just happened to meet at work? Curt wasn't driving with them, instead, he offered to meet them there and pay for the entire dinner. Amber finally managed to make it downstairs and out the door to her mother's car, which was already running.

"How do I look?" her mother asked checking herself in the vanity mirror above her.

"You look beautiful as always mom," Amber answered without looking.

Her mother flipped the vanity up and drove into town to a small Italian restaurant. Amber noticed a black pick-up truck parked in the spot right in front of the place. That was Curt's truck. Amber, her mother and Michael walked in to see a man, probably around fifty or so, sitting in a booth by himself.

"Melanie!" He waved them over.

Her mother shuddered at the sound of her name being called, which caused Amber to roll her eyes as she followed her mother to the booth.

Curt stood up and welcomed Amber's mother to the inside of the booth next to him and he continued standing to greet both Amber and Michael.

"This must be Michael?" he asked crouching down in front of him and offering a handshake.

Amber got a better look at Curt. He was tall, taller than even her father was, and his hair was cut short, not buzzed, so she could see spots of grey near his temples. He wore a tan Carhartt and black jeans with boots to match it. Suddenly, he was standing in front of her with his green eyes fixed on her.

"And this must be your daughter," he said to her mother, which struck her as odd because she introduced himself to Michael directly.

"Well on account that I'm the only girl here, yes. I'm her daughter," Amber answered.

Curt laughed. "Oh, she has your wit, Melanie! It's nice to meet you, Amber." He reached in for a hug and Amber extended her hand to him.

"Likewise."

Curt took little time putting his arm around her mother right after he took his seat at the opposite end of the booth. Amber decided to try to get to know Curt and give him a chance to make an impression on her, rather than remain despondent for the entire dinner.

"So." Amber smiled. "I've heard my mom tell the story about how you two met and, I guess, started liking each other, but how do you tell it?"

Curt sat up a bit straighter. "Well, I noticed Melanie just one day at the bank, depositing my check like I do every Friday, and I was immediately captured by her friendliness and openness." Curt glanced over at Amber's mother. "From there, we got to talking about my life, her life, you kids and the idea of her and me possibly getting together outside of our small five-minute conversations."

"So, we went out for a few drinks, a dinner or two," her mother interrupted. "And now, here we are!"

"Cute story," Amber answered. "So, what is your life exactly Curt?"

Curt laughed. "I work in Shipping and Receiving at the supermarket! No kids, in case you were wondering. Married once before this, divorced."

"Divorced why?" Amber perked up.

"Amber!" Her mother seemed embarrassed.

"It's fine, Melanie." Curt put his hands on the table. "She was my high school sweetheart, and the married life wasn't all we expected it to be. You think you know a person, until you're married, you find out you don't know half of what you thought."

His honesty was remarkable. He didn't appear to deflect any question she asked and what was once a sarcastic or flippant laugh actually turned into a genuine one before the night ended. Amber remained guarded, however. She knew all too well that nobody ever was who they appeared to be the first time around. Everyone puts on their best face the first time, but it's the second, third, countless times where she starts to see people's true colors and intentions. She wasn't going to let one positive dinner let her form a final opinion.

The server walked over with the check and without hesitating, Curt pulled his wallet from his jacket pocket and slapped a credit card on the table.

"You don't have to…"

"Melanie, I invited your family out. I'll cover it. It was a pleasure meeting both of you."

Curt high fived Michael and extended his hand across the table to Amber. She reciprocated with a firmer handshake than the one from when the night began but didn't say anything back to him.

"Why don't you come back to the house, have a few drinks?" Amber's mom asked.

Amber shot a glance at her mother.

"Sounds great! I'll follow you back to your place."

Amber got up, walked out to her mother's car and waited with Michael.

"Curt seems nice!" Michael said to her, tugging on her shirtsleeve.

"Everybody SEEMS nice the first time you meet them, Michael. Dad used to be nice too."

She forgets that Michael was still young when her father began mistreating her. He didn't get to really see that side of him much before he died. The ride home was no less silent than the drive to the restaurant.

"Did you really have to invite him back to the house?" Amber asked.

"He'll be fine! It's just going to be us anyway. You kids just hang out in your rooms like you always do. We'll have a few drinks and see where the night takes us."

Amber huffed. "He's going to stay the night?"

"He might."

They pulled back in the driveway and Curt's truck followed right behind. Amber's mother unlocked the front door and Amber pushed behind her and walked up to her room. She shut the door behind her, threw off her jacket, kicked off her shoes and flopped onto her bed. She buried her head into her pillow to avoid the noise and discussion going on downstairs between her mother and Curt. She thought about texting Logan or Brayden or both to talk about how conflicted and annoyed she was about the whole situation but decided not to bother their night with her problems.

She took a step outside and knocked on Michael's door. She crept inside and saw he was lying on his bed, shoulder turned away from her.

"Hey, buddy. Are you asleep yet?"

She saw him shake his head no.

"Are you alright?"

"Mommy and Curt are loud. It's hard to sleep."

She frowned. "I know. They're being very rude, but that's what happens when adults drink a lot. They get loud and sometimes they don't always say things or do things that they mean to do."

"Did daddy drink a lot?"

"Dad was different. He was rude because that's just how he always was."

"Why?" Michael turned towards her.

"I've asked myself that a lot. I wish I had an answer for you baby brother."

"Do you think Curt would be rude for no reason?"

Amber sat down on his bed and put her hand on his face. "I don't know. I hope not!"

She pulled his blanket up over him and near his chin. "Get some sleep. It's already late." She kissed him on the forehead as she always did when she checked to make sure he was asleep at night. "Goodnight Michael. I love you."

"'Night."

She softly approached his door and shut it behind her, and she walked back to her room. She ran her tongue inside her lip thinking about all the different questions Michael asked her about their father and about Curt, and about how the two of them might be so similar. She didn't have as many answers as she wanted to have, but this was only her first night around Curt and the way he acted around her mother told her that there would be more nights for them to get familiar with one another. She wanted to go downstairs and tell them to keep their voices down so

Michael could sleep but instead, she laid there, much like she did earlier, and waited for the next day to come. Only, the conversation below her turned to silence and she perked her head up. She heard footsteps creaking the floor in the hall outside her room and there was a knock on her door.

"Yeah?" she asked from the bed.

"It's Curt. Can I come in?"

She intended to tell him no and for him to go home, but instead she said, "Yeah. It's open."

He walked in, no longer wearing his jacket, but only a button-up shirt that wasn't buttoned up any longer. He wasn't hammered by any means, but it was apparent that he and her mother had consumed a few beers downstairs.

"I just wanted to um, I guess, clear the air here," he said. "I don't want you to get the wrong idea that…"

"You're in my room, drunk. How could I possibly have a wrong idea?" she only half joked.

"You're right. I'm sorry." He moved closer to her bed. "What I mean is, I don't want you to think I'm going to be a new dad or a stepfather or anything like that. Not yet anyway. I've only been seeing your mom for a little while, and I know it's not easy for you, given your dad passing and all."

"My dad dying has nothing to do with this being easy or not," she answered.

"Your mom told me, Amber." He sat next to her, and she slid away from him.

"Told you what exactly?"

"How strict your dad could be at times to you."

"Strict?" She laughed. "If that's the word she used, then you have no idea what my relationship was with my dad."

"I can't get to know you if you don't let me in, sweetheart."

"Let me stop you right there. I don't know what you've had to do in the past with other kids of the women you've dated, but you're not going to impress me by trying to be sympathetic towards me. I don't care who you are, what you do, or what you want to understand about me. How you treat my mother and brother is going to go a lot further than you 'trying to get to know' ME." She stood up on the other side of her bed. "If you don't mind, I'd like you to leave my room and go back downstairs." She preferred that he leave the house entirely but knew that probably wouldn't happen.

Curt got up and seemed annoyed with her. "Fine. I understand. You're playing the long game with me." He walked around to where she was standing and went to reach out for a hug or something towards her shoulder.

"There is no game. This is what you get with me. Take it or leave it." She moved her shoulder and pushed his arm down. "Goodnight, Curt. It was…" she hesitated to say that it was nice meeting him. "Something. I'm glad my mom seems happy with you."

He walked out and looked at her as he stood in the doorway and she tilted her head forward motioning for him to close the door behind him. He shut it with a fair amount of force before she heard him going back downstairs. Her lip quivered, as if she wanted to cry. She shook her head to herself.

There's a long way to go with him.

7

November 22nd

(Logan)

There was a constant noise beating inside his head, like a headache. He twisted and turned trying to escape it. The more he tried to ignore it, the louder it got. Finally, he gave up and opened his eyes a moment to adjust to the light. He awoke to the face of his teacher, Mr. Pearsall smiling with his hands on his hips.

"Mr. Anderson," Mr. Pearsall sighed. "I know it's a half day and Thanksgiving break is within reach, but could you at least pretend like you're paying attention? Sleeping is just a slap in the face."

"Sorry, Mr. P." Logan replied. "I haven't been able to sleep the last couple of days."

"Well, my class isn't the place to make up for that Logan." Mr. Pearsall walked away to continue his lesson.

He wiped his hands down his face and leaned back in his chair. He drew a big breath and looked up at the ceiling, trying to wake back up. He spun around in his chair to look at Amber. She couldn't help but laugh.

"Can't you at least show him a little respect, Logan? He loves teaching this stuff. Try to at least appreciate it."

"It's so boring sometimes though. I understand it. I read it. I just don't like it much. Besides, it's not like anything right before break really matters."

She sighed as he turned around. Logan sat up straighter and did his best to pay attention to the rest of the lesson. He opened his notebook and feigned taking notes. Instead, he started writing down various thoughts that popped in and out of his head while he slept. He wrote about Amber and Brayden. The upcoming baseball season crossed his mind. His thoughts wandered towards the idea that after the next few months, he and Brayden wouldn't be together any longer. Brayden was graduating soon, and after that, he was going to head back to New York to prepare for college.

Over three pages of random thoughts had covered Logan's notebook before the bell rang, and class ended. Logan stood up to leave with Amber.

"Mr. Anderson." Mr. Pearsall stopped him. "Can I have a word for a moment? Come sit down."

Logan sighed, tossed his bag on top of a desk, and sat down.

"I don't get it Logan. You're one of the smartest kids in the eleventh grade. Yet, I feel you only give half the effort that you could. Don't you realize you could get into a good school without baseball? If you applied the same effort to your schoolwork that you do your baseball career, you'd have it all."

Logan heard the faintest sound of his father in this speech.

Do well for yourself so you don't end up doing what I'm doing for the rest of your life.

"I was a lot like you when I was younger, Logan," he continued. "I got by high school and some of college just on my own natural talent, and then I hit a roadblock in college I couldn't overcome."

"So, what did you do?" Logan asked, raising his brows.

"I almost dropped out and gave up," Mr. Pearsall admitted. "I just realized I needed to change my ways. It was either adapt or perish."

"I'm really trying Mr. P. I am. But between baseball and coursework for you and my other honors classes, it's a lot to handle honestly…"

"I know it isn't just those things, but it wouldn't feel like so much if you just managed yourself better. Just try it out. You'll be surprised what changes you see!" Mr. Pearsall smiled as he patted Logan on the back.

"I'll think about it, Mr. P. That's all I can promise you."

"I'll take that for now. Get out of here, go enjoy break."

Logan swiped his bag off the desk and started to walk out.

"And Logan?"

He stopped.

"Happy Thanksgiving." Mr. Pearsall smiled.

"Yeah. You too Mr. P."

As soon as Logan got out of the classroom, he saw Brayden standing right outside the door.

"You got your glove?" Brayden asked.

"Uh, yeah, I think so. Why?"

"I was thinking we could get a little work in before we head home."

Logan nodded. "I'll meet you downstairs."

Brayden seemed eager to get started on the journey that would be their final season as teammates. Logan walked to his locker to grab his baseball glove. He'd kept it in there all year until the season rolled around again in March. He walked downstairs and smiled entering the gym to meet up with Brayden. They began to stretch and loosen up as if no time passed between

54

the bitter cold of winter with the ending of last season in spring that saw Brayden receive his scholarship offer to play college baseball in Syracuse.

"You know, this is our last year together," Brayden sighed as he tossed a ball to Logan.

"I'm trying not to really think about that much."

"It doesn't have to be that way for long though! No bullshit this year, Logan. Scouts are gonna look at you just as they looked at me last year. Who knows? Maybe the same guy who offered me my scholarship will want you too!"

"That's a pipe dream and a half if I ever heard one," Logan responded with a chuckle.

"Think about it. Who would want to break up this dream team? We can do it all again in college."

Logan smiled at Brayden's optimism. Another realization hit him at the same time though.

He's right. Scouts are going to be looking at me this year.

Any scout who attended games this year would come with eyes fixated on the seniors of course, but Logan as well. Logan had made headlines as one of the best pitchers in Springvale's district from his very first start in his first year of high school to the game in which he had hurt his arm last year.

In that moment, Logan felt the gravity of the thought that he felt as if he lived on cruise control the last two years.

"Where did these two years go?" he said to himself so Brayden couldn't hear.

He fired every warm-up throw as if it were a game pitch. The intensity and ferocity he channeled in game surfaced during his workout with Brayden. The ball hitting Brayden's glove cracked like thunder and sent echoes through the large, empty gym.

"Take it easy man. We're just in a gym," Brayden warned.

He caught the last throw from Brayden and sat down on the floor of the gym. Logan checked out. For whatever reason, seeing Brayden today and realizing that he and Brayden would be apart next year had just taken him out of his mindset. He dropped his glove from his lap and watched the ball roll across the gym floor before seeing Brayden reach down and scoop it up in his glove.

"Hey Logan," Brayden reached out to him. "When we both go to college, maybe we'll both go pro. Who knows? Maybe we'll end up on the same team professionally too!"

Logan laughed. "Yeah, and then we can do those teammate commercials selling sandwiches, cleats, or headphones. You name it, so long as you let me do the talking and the smiling."

"Oh, you're real funny," Brayden answered. "They'll just stick me in the black and white training montage while you're talking."

"Let's go home, okay?" Logan said out of nowhere.

Brayden's mouth flinched, as if he wanted to ask what was wrong, or like he wanted to say anything helpful, but nothing came out. He just sighed, nodded and walked past Logan towards the gym doors.

Where once he enjoyed the solace of walking to and from school every day, solitude started enveloping every aspect of his life. His father had left, he and his mother almost never talked anymore, and his group of friends had shrunk down to a handful of teammates, Brayden, and Amber.

"I'm going to miss this," Logan admitted.

"Are you still thinking about the future?" Brayden responded.

"It's hard not to. Everything I walk by, think about, see, or touch reminds me that next year, I'm going to be on my own."

"You act like I'm going away forever. It's only a year Logan."

"I know," he answered. "But still, you've become like a big brother to me. I'm an only child. I never knew how it felt to have a sibling. With you here, I had that feeling and now I feel like I'm losing it and I…I just don't like it is all."

"It'll be fine. I'm not gonna be that far away. We can still talk and stuff. Just don't forget about me when I'm gone!" Brayden smiled.

"Likewise! Don't forget about me when you make all your new college friends and pull them out of fights in the locker room."

They stopped at Brayden's house.

"Hi, Logan! Good workout today?" Mrs. Lewis asked.

"The first one is always the hardest, but it felt good," Logan answered.

"Logan! Logan!" Brayden's little brother ran over to him and hugged him.

"How are you doing, buddy?" Logan asked Julian.

"Brayden is teaching me how to play baseball like him! I can't wait to start playing too."

"The kid is good. He'll probably end up better than me," Brayden admitted.

"As long as you keep teaching him, I'm sure he will be. I'll catch you later. Bye guys."

Logan's mom wasn't home when he got home from school. The middle school also had just a half day because of the upcoming holiday, so it'd make sense that she got home after him. He walked out of his room and into his parents' bedroom. He went in there from time to time to see if his mother had moved anything into the empty space where his father's clothes used to be. She hadn't. The walls inside the closet were still white, the bar still hung as if waiting for something new to find a home there, but she hadn't done anything about it.

It never felt emptier. He glanced at the closet on the right side with nothing in it except a closet bar and white walls. His dad had left, walked out and left for good, out to live a new life with a new woman. Logan punched the empty closet space.

"Go to Hell," Logan said aloud.

He walked downstairs and into the garage, sighing as he reached into the recycling can. He picked up one of several beer bottles and tossed it into the air before smashing it back into the can. He pulled another bottle amidst the newly created shattered glass and smashed that one as well.

"What did he do to you?"

Enough is enough.

He marched back upstairs and opened his mother's drawers.

"Humph. It's no wonder she's so miserable all the time," he spoke aloud.

He started rummaging through his mother's drawer. He pushed aside pictures, pill bottles, and various loose change and dollar bills. He grabbed random T-shirts and other things that he found easy to hang and he started placing them in the closet. He didn't fill the entire space, but just enough that it looked different and didn't look so empty. He stood back and looked at his mother's things.

* * *

Hours had passed and his mother should have been home by now and he knew it. He called her cell and after ringing a few times, it went to voicemail. He just hung up and lay on his bed. Not long after that, he heard the doorbell ringing. Before he had even gotten up, the bell rang five more times.

57

"I'm coming! Jesus."

He opened the door to his mother stumbling in. He caught her as she almost collapsed on the ground. He looked past her to see any sign of headlights or taillights driving away from the house, but there weren't any.

"Mom? Did you drive home?"

"It's only the bar in town Logan. It wasn't far," his mother argued.

"That bar is in the middle of town. You could have killed someone! What were you thinking?"

"I went out by myself. There was nobody there for me. You sure as hell can't drive me." She tried to push her way past, but he stood firm.

He put his hands on her shoulders. "No. No it doesn't matter! You could have asked anyone there to take you home. Instead, you decide to gamble with your life. What would have happened if..."

"There wasn't going to be any cops, sweetie. We live right there."

"That's not the point! Ever since dad left, you've been different. How can I take you seriously when you tell me to clean my room, or keep my grades up, or do dishes, or anything? When you can't even take care of yourself!" He pushed her back towards the couch and sat her down. "It's not even sundown and you're telling me you were out drinking all day after work?"

"Logan Anderson. Don't you dare speak to me that way. I only had a few drinks."

"A few? Mom, you can barely walk right now! When you start acting like my mother again, you'll get treated like my mother. I don't even have friends that act as bad as you."

"Go to your room," she muttered as she lay down on the couch.

Instead of walking away, he grabbed her hand. "I want to show you something." He led her upstairs to show her all the clothes he had hung inside the empty closet.

Before he knew it, his mother walked over to everything Logan hung up and had started ripping the clothes out shirt by shirt, hanger by hanger.

"What are you doing?" Logan yelled. "I did this for you. You need to let go and move on!"

"Maybe I don't want to move on Logan! Maybe it's too hard for me right now!" she screamed back.

"Jesus. Everything is SO hard now. Going to work is hard. Making dinner is hard. Making your bed is hard. What happened to you? You used to be so independent, so strong. Ever since dad left, you've been consumed by this self-pity. I want my mom back!"

"I am your mom, Logan. I always have been and always will be. I love you sweetheart."

"I don't need you to prove you love me. Prove that you love yourself. Prove that you can be strong again instead of just sleeping, drinking and self-loathing all the time. I can't take it anymore." He started shaking. "You take one step forward and then you backpedal about twenty feet. I'm done being sympathetic. If you can't get over it, then you're lost. I'm sorry mom. It's becoming clearer that even though he isn't here, he still finds a way to ruin our lives." He stormed out and went back into his bedroom before she could even reply.

Logan slammed the door behind him, hopped onto his bed, and unleashed a furious scream into his bedspread. He chucked a pillow across his room and pounded away at his bedspread.

She refused to move on, all for the notion that maybe, just maybe his father would return. Logan knew better. He knew what kind of man his father was. Nothing about his father told Logan that he would be back.

Multiple knocks on the door took his attention away from his thoughts. "Go away," he shouted.

"Logan I just want to…"

"Go. Away."

Without a reply, he heard footsteps walking away from the door. He sighed once more and opened one of his novels for Mr. Pearsall's class. He figured now was a better time than ever to get lost in books and fantasy worlds. He heard rummaging come from downstairs, the fridge opening and his mother sighing as she undoubtedly returned to the couch.

8

December 4^{*th*}

(Brayden)

Logan walked into Brayden's room frantic. Brayden glanced up.

"Uh, hey?" Brayden asked shutting his notebook.

"I need your help," Logan answered in between breaths as if he ran to Brayden's house.

"Do I even want to know?"

Logan sat down on Brayden's bed like it was a therapist's couch. "I don't know what to get Amber for her birthday."

Brayden laughed. "Are you kidding me? That's why you came running in here?"

Logan spread out and looked up at the ceiling. "I know. It's stupid right? I don't know what to get my best friend for her birthday that's in like two months, but here I am, at a loss."

Brayden reached behind him and grabbed his sweater. "Let's go. Depending on how much you got on you, I think we can figure something out for her."

They walked into town and went in and out of various small shops. They stopped in Mr. Brooks' shop in the middle of town. The shop didn't sell anything specific, but sold little odds and ends, trinkets. If any place in town had something for Amber, Mr. Brooks would have it. The old man was sweeping the back counter with a younger boy when Brayden and Logan walked in.

"Mr. Anderson and Mr. Lewis! How are you two young men doing today?"

"Hey Mr. Brooks! Who's the kid?" Logan asked pointing out the boy, no older than thirteen, behind the counter.

"This is my grandson, Stephen. My son went back to school to finish his degree and asked me to watch him for the time. Come say hi, Stephen!" Mr. Brooks motioned over.

Stephen either pretended not to hear him or flat out ignored him because he kept his head low and towards the counter, pretending to do work to avoid saying hi to either of them.

"He's a bit shy. Now, what brings you into my shop of all places?"

"Well, I was trying to think of something to buy a friend for her birthday," Logan answered with his eyes at the ground.

"Oh, another girlfriend?" Mr. Brooks asked with a wry smile.

"No! Not another…"

"Yep!" Brayden interrupted. "A girlfriend." He nudged Logan's ribs.

Brayden walked around while Logan browsed some of the things Mr. Brooks had in the store that he might potentially want for Amber. The old man seemed so fond of everyone in Logan's life, everyone in general really. From what little Brayden saw, Mr. Brooks seemed every bit the kindly old man he portrayed himself to be. Logan came back to Brayden empty-handed.

"You might try to jewelry store next door," Mr. Brooks suggested.

"Thanks Mr. Brooks, for all the help," Brayden said.

"Of course, boys! I know between the two of you, you'll figure out the perfect gift for that special girl in your life."

They left to go to the jewelry store and Logan walked with his head down and his hands in his pockets.

"Why are you getting so stressed out over this?"

"Because…" Logan stopped. "I think I might want to ask her out, like for real."

Brayden smiled from ear to ear. "It's about time! But what about that…uh, what's her name, Melissa? That you were gonna bring to my birthday thing?"

Logan had been seeing one of the girls on the volleyball team for a few weeks, but as Mr. Brooks alluded to, Logan never seemed to be able to stick with one girl for any length of time.

"She's nice, and funny, and smart, but I don't know…I don't get the same feeling with her than I get when I'm around Amber, I guess. Maybe I'm just overthinking everything. I'll probably still take Melissa to the thing, but I don't know where things will go after that."

Brayden just rolled his eyes and walked ahead of Logan into the jewelry store. The clerk didn't say anything to them, didn't even suggest anything or ask them about their day. He just gave a quick glance and went back to observing pieces in one of the cases. Logan's eyes widened seeing the price tags of certain items, bending over and looking at others as if he himself was an expert. He stepped back, still looking puzzled.

"Why don't you get her something with her birthstone in it?" Brayden suggested.

"I don't even know what that is," Logan answered.

"Look it up. You got a phone, don't you?" Brayden badgered.

Logan pulled his phone out and kept his eyes glued to the screen. Brayden kept looking around in the meantime and noticed a silver bracelet in the display case in front of the clerk.

"How much for this one?" he asked out of Logan's earshot. "With a stone or two."

"Probably more than you can afford, son," the clerk answered.

"Try me."

"Depending on the stone? Anywhere between one to two hundred."

Brayden thought to himself for a moment and answered, "Hold that thought."

He walked back over to Logan to see if he had an answer.

"Amethyst. It's Amethyst," Logan replied looking at his phone.

"Well, there you go! How about this?" Brayden pointed out the sterling silver bracelet in the display case. "Hey, how much for that bracelet with amethyst stones in it?"

"130," the skeptical clerk answered.

Logan fretted. "It's nice and all, but I still need like fifty bucks for it. I don't have a job or any…"

Before he could finish, Brayden pulled out his wallet. He gave Logan a one-hundred-dollar bill on the spot.

"Bray…where did you…"

"My parents gave me some spending money because of my scholarship and stuff. Take this. Get that girl a birthday present she'll glow over getting. I don't know if you deserve a girl like that one, but damn, you two have been eying each other as long as I've known the both of you."

"Brayden…I…I can't."

"You can, and you will. Take it. Don't worry; I'm sure you'll pay me back some time!"

"Th…thank you Bray. Holy shit dude. I can't believe I'm actually doing this. You sure you don't want to ask her out? This whole thing is because of you."

"Just make sure when ya'll get married, I'm your best man, alright?" Brayden teased.

"You got it. That's a promise," Logan answered leaning in for a hug.

"Man, knock it off before this dude thinks you're buying me that bracelet." Brayden laughed.

The clerk walked back into his storeroom to either assemble or pull a new bracelet with that stone from the back.

"You better not mess this thing up with Amber," Brayden warned.

Logan looked at him. "What do you mean?"

"Something tells me you need her a lot more than she needs you. Just, I don't know if you have some type of switch you flip when it comes to girls, but she isn't going to fall for your usual stuff. She's different. You have to know that, right?"

"Ever since we were kids, I've always known that. Don't worry. The day I ask her to be with me, I know it'll be the time when I can fully commit to her. I'm not gonna half ass this. I promise."

"Better not. Because if you end up breaking her heart, I don't care where I am, I'll find you and give you that beating I saved you from freshman year."

Logan only half laughed as the clerk returned with the bracelet in a black box and Logan gave him the money he had with the hundred dollars Brayden gave him and purchased the bracelet right there on the spot. The clerk looked at Brayden and Brayden only raised his eyebrows and smiled. Logan carried the bag with the bracelet in it as gingerly as Brayden's ever seen him hold anything all the way back to Brayden's house.

"Brayden, I can't thank you enough," Logan said as they stood in Brayden's driveway.

"Man, you already did thank me enough. Don't mention it. It's what friends do." Brayden extended his fist out. "I always got your back. How many times do I have to tell you and show you that?"

"I know. But just know that I appreciate it, alright?" Logan said a bit sterner than usual. "I'll talk to you in a bit."

Logan walked down the driveway and up the road back to his house. Brayden laughed to himself and walked back inside.

"Logan figure out his problem?" Brayden's mother asked upon Brayden coming in.

"Yeah, he did. Needed a little push, but he got there."

Brayden walked back to his room to see his little brother sitting on his bed with a PlayStation controller in his hand. Brayden didn't say a word and nodded, and Julian ran out of Brayden's room and into his own waiting for Brayden to follow. He put his phone down on his bed and went into the kids' room to play games with Julian until dinner was ready. Julian remained laser focused on the game, a fighting game as usual while Brayden feigned intensity but really played around until Julian got mad enough, then he'd let Julian win a round or two.

"Are you going away?" Julian asked.

"Who told you that I was going away?"

"Me and Angela overheard you talking with mommy and daddy about going away to college."

Brayden paused the game and put the controller on the ground so he could face Julian. "Yeah, J, I'm going away, but not for good! I'll come visit when I can, maybe every other weekend and for the holidays. It'll be like I never left!" He stood up and took Julian's hand to escort him to his room. "Besides, once I leave, this will be your room while I'm gone! A whole room, my room, all to yourself."

Julian's eyes widened. "Really?" He giggled.

"Yep. You're gonna be wishing I was gone sooner!"

Julian started running around the room and plotting where he'd move the bed, the dressers, his PlayStation, the TV, almost everything.

"Are you gonna want it back when I go away to college?"

Brayden laughed. "If I'm half as successful as I'd like to be, you won't have to give me this room back after I leave. It's yours after this summer."

Julian ran out of the room to tell their mother the good news that he received Brayden's blessing to take his room. It gave Brayden time to look at the ever-growing stacks of letters and introduction packages from the various colleges he'd gotten mail from over the past few months. He kept the Syracuse materials separate from most of the others, but he occasionally took time to sift through the others: Penn State, Michigan State, Miami, Cal, all different schools that wanted to court his talent for the next four years. Every school offered him the same thing on the surface, but only Syracuse offered him the same type of exposure and the bonus of being back in his home state.

As much as his father told him to mull over the decision, his mind had been pretty much made up since the day he sat with the scout, Andrew Davies, in his living room. The first scout always makes a good impression because he or she is always the first, the one most eager to meet you. Money was never an issue. Each school had offered him a full ride. Brayden had printed out an article that *The Daily Orange,* Syracuse's student newspaper, ran in a feature they had printed not long after the scouting trip.

"A once in a generation player, with a once in a generation attitude," the article read.

He flopped down on his bed and stared at the ceiling. He was in the middle of the final year of his high school life. After the next few months or so, he would be going back home to New York to play baseball at the college level. That was the plan at least, to begin the next journey in his life. He swung upright, stretched, and got up to look in the mirror.

"Four years," he muttered to himself. "I can't believe it's already been almost four years."

"Neither can I," Brayden's mother interrupted as she peeked into her son's bedroom. "Your father and I are so proud of you Brayden, but it isn't over yet sweetheart. Get through this year and then you get to go back home."

"Me? What about you guys?" Brayden replied. "Wouldn't it be easier for dad to work if we all went home together?"

"Of course it'd be easier for your father, but we want to raise your brother and sister here. Springvale is a nice place, a good place, with good people."

"You know, it's kind of funny, and I'd never tell dad this, but some people think I could skip college altogether and go pro right now." Brayden smiled.

"You're right, you won't ever tell your father that." His mother laughed.

Brayden had become a success. He had come to a place where he never thought he would fit in and became a regional, social, and near national commodity. Some professional level scouts had considered Brayden the best baseball prospect in the entire country. Brayden had security. He had forged his own future. He would go to college, play baseball, get a degree, and health permitting, start looking towards playing at the professional level. Talks of him skipping college altogether were ridiculous.

The pressure is off now, he thought to himself. *The pressure is finally off.*

9

December 19ᵗʰ

(Amber)

She gazed into her bedroom mirror and pressed under her eyes with her black eyeliner. She blinked several times. She almost never dressed herself up, but Logan planned a dinner party tonight for Brayden at Dianne's, a local restaurant in Springvale. Brayden was turning eighteen. It was a big deal. She slid her fingers through her long black hair as far as she could, as it ran all the way down near her waist. She retreated towards her bed, looked over her dress, picked it up, slid it over the top of her head, and let it fall along her waistline just over the black tights.

"Mom!" she yelled from the doorway. "Can you come up here for a minute?"

She had never gone to parties or out to eat, unless it was with her mom and brother, but tonight had given her an excuse to dress up. She sat down on her bed and smoothed out her crimson bedspread. She dangled her legs over the end of it. Her mother walked into her room and seemed rather surprised that it was in fact her daughter sitting on the bed in front of her.

"Amber." Her mother's mouth stayed agape. "You look amazing sweetheart."

Amber blushed. "I was just wondering if you could do that thing with my hair like you used to."

"Of course, sweetie, here, come here and turn around." Her mother tiptoed towards her.

Her mother started to pick at Amber's hair, strand by strand. Amber clinched her teeth and winced as her mom pulled a few strands loose from knots or even uprooting a few. She felt tightness around her head as her mom weaved in and out. She hadn't worn her hair like this since Catholic school because it took too much time now that her hair was so long. Minutes passed, and Amber's legs grew a bit tired from standing around waiting for her mother to finish.

Finally, her mother sat her hands aside and brushed the remaining strands of hair off Amber's shoulders. She looked into the mirror and smiled a bit. Her mother braided her hair around to the back of Amber's head before the two braids met in the middle and cascaded into the waterfall of darkness that crept down the rest of Amber's back.

"It's beautiful Mom," she remarked touching the braids.

"No," her mom interrupted. "YOU are beautiful Amber."

Amber reddened again as she slipped her feet into a pair of black strap sandals that she bought a couple days ago. As she walked downstairs, she came eye to eye with Curt, who had been spending a lot more time at the house since their dinner out a couple of months ago. Curt was inching closer to being less of just a guy her mom was dating and more of an eventual stepfather. The more she'd been around him, the more she started to draw parallels to her father.

"Well, aren't you a pretty little flower all dressed up tonight?" He grunted getting up out of the deep blue recliner her father always sat in.

"Thanks Curt," Amber replied trying to get away and out of the house.

He walked around her, almost entranced. Her heartbeat quickened and her breathing became more rapid. He held his hand over her shoulder and picked at one of the braids in her hair.

"Your mom do this?"

"Yes."

"She's awfully good at it."

"Thanks." She distanced herself away from him.

His eyes seemed to fixate on her.

"I gotta go."

"Don't be home late."

"You're not my dad."

Her mother rushed downstairs soon thereafter and followed Amber out the door to drop her off at the restaurant. She sat in the passenger seat of her mother's car and rubbed her shoulder while looking out the window.

"Are you and Curt getting along?" her mom asked.

"I wouldn't call it getting along exactly. Tolerating is more appropriate."

"Did he say anything to you? Do anything?" Her excitement turned to concern.

Amber hesitated. "No. It's fine. He just reminds me of dad in a lot of ways. It's weird."

"You'll see his individuality shine soon sweetheart. I know it's hard to see another man in the house, but, you and Michael will grow to love Curt like I have."

"If you say so." Amber kept her head up against the window. *How much longer will soon be?*

The car stopped in front of the restaurant.

"Have a good night baby!" Amber's mom leaned over and went to kiss her.

"No! You'll leave lipstick on my forehead." Amber laughed.

"Sorry honey." She retreated to a hug. "Don't be home too late!"

Amber rarely hung out with people other than Logan and Brayden. Almost the entire baseball team would be there, their dates, Logan, Brayden, everyone. She approached the small restaurant and stood underneath the black and gold neon sign, in homage to the high school. Amber pressed down on her skirt and before she walked in, she caught sight of Brayden.

"Hey there! I'm glad you came! Look at you all dressed up for me," Brayden exclaimed as he clinched her in a powerful embrace.

"Brayden, you're crushing my chest! I can't breathe!" she teased as she pushed him back. "Happy Birthday!" She gasped recollecting her breath.

"Sorry." He laughed. "And thank you! I haven't seen him yet, if you're wondering. He's late. Let's get inside."

They walked inside to greet everybody else who had arrived.

"Guys, this is Amber. Amber, these are the guys," Brayden said as they made their way to the table.

"Hi everyone," Amber said nervously.

Some of them seemed interested in her. She smiled, laughed, and enjoyed herself far more than she thought she would.

"Brayden," she heard one of his teammates whisper. "You didn't tell me you were friends with her. Holy shit. That the same girl you and Logan sit with all the time?"

"Stop pretending like you never noticed her," Brayden teased, but also said to defend Amber.

"And I'm certainly not stupid enough to fall for your little jock compliments," Amber mocked.

"Oh, she's funny too! You'll fit in better than you think around us."

Apparently, her dressing up caught the attention of many of Brayden's friends. She never sought attention, but she'd be remiss if she didn't feel flattered by all the eyes drawn to her.

Suddenly, a door opened, and a sharp, brown-haired boy walked in, only he wasn't alone. Logan walked in wearing dark blue jeans and a short-sleeved black polo shirt. Not a single sandy hair on his head seemed out of place. Behind him walked a beautiful girl in a midnight blue dress. The girl in heels stood almost as tall as Logan did. Her green eyes appeared to change colors as they met the lights of the restaurant. Logan had been seeing Melissa for a few weeks, and he kept swearing up and down that it wasn't anything "too serious" as he put it.

"Hey guys," Logan started. "You all know Melissa already."

Melissa laughed. Logan walked over to Brayden and Amber.

"Brayden, Amber, this is…"

"Melissa! Hi!" Amber smiled and hugged her.

"Oh, I didn't know you guys knew each other."

"We have art together. First period," Melissa said.

As everyone sat, Amber caught Logan glancing in her direction more than a few times. She felt some kind of satisfaction from that. Even with a trophy-like date, Logan's eyes wandered over towards her. Melissa interlocked her arms around Logan's right arm and rested her head on his shoulder as the kids all socialized and celebrated Brayden's night.

John Stevenson commanded attention. "I'll never forget, hold on," he put his fork down and swallowed his food. "I'll never forget the first day Brayden showed up at practice and put a hole RIGHT through the batting cage ceiling. Shit was crazy. That's the type of thing you only see, you know, in movies. And this dude comes up and WHAM, sends one clear over the street."

"Yeah, and y'all still found a way to hate me for that whole year," Brayden interrupted.

"We didn't hate you. We were scared to death of you. You're built like a god damned superhero," another kid chimed in.

Amber glanced over at Logan and Melissa just as Melissa planted a kiss on his cheek. Amber looked away. She felt full. Not that she ate too much, but the lovey-dovey-ness between Logan and Melissa was making her feel what little food she had eaten. Everyone talking distracted her from eating what she ordered. Her mom gave her money for the bill anyway, so it wasn't exactly a waste of her money.

"I'll be right back," she said to Brayden.

Once she got into the restroom, she let out a sigh. She felt as if she hadn't been able to breathe in the past hour or so because of her uneven nerves.

"Where did she even come from?" she yelled into the mirror.

It wasn't Melissa that bothered her. It was the way that anytime Amber asked Logan about her, he would promise her that it was just something he was into "for now," as if he knew things with her were temporary before they even started dating. That line of thinking never made sense. No matter how bad things got between her and her father, she knew that he and her mother would have been married still if he had never died. She had always held relationships in a more serious way than Logan did. She thought about the day they talked when they first met after all the time she had spent away.

Your eyes look even prettier now that your hair is dark, Logan had quipped.

She returned to the table to see singing servers from the restaurant rounding the corner from the main dining room. She smiled and joined everyone else in singing happy birthday to Brayden. Brayden kept his head in his hand and his eyes away from the singers, clearly embarrassed by the entire pomp and circumstance.

"No, really, that's enough," he said aloud finally. "Thank you, everyone, seriously."

"You're with me now!" John belted from across the table. "The two old guys in the room.

Rather than spend time on dessert, Brayden said his goodbyes and called Logan and Amber aside.

"Hey, what say we head out to field for a bit?" Brayden asked.

"I'm down," Logan answered.

"Sounds good to me!" Amber replied with a smile.

"Not me. This sounds like something the three of you should do," Melissa interjected.

"You sure?" Logan asked.

"Yeah! I'll wait for my dad to pick me up. Goodnight, Logan." She shared a long kiss with him before he, Brayden, and Amber set out for the field.

The three made it out back to the same park that they had shared together once on a summer evening. Brayden walked out onto the field first and hopped on the worn-down dugout, with Logan following soon after. Amber fretted, but before she could say a word, Logan extended his hand to her to help her up as well.

"Come on." He chuckled.

She grabbed his hand and let herself become weightless as he pulled her up. The three sat atop the dugout and looked out into the clear night sky.

"I never got to do this back home," Brayden whispered as if serenity took over him.

"What, sit on dugouts?" Logan asked with a laugh.

70

"He means look at the stars Logan," Amber cracked. "You can't ever see them in the city because of the lights."

Logan slid a bit closer to Amber in that moment. Her lips bent upward slightly, but she didn't move a muscle. She focused her attention on the sky.

"Hey, let me ask you guys something," Brayden started. "You guys believe in like…fate…destiny, that kind of stuff?"

Logan and Amber looked at each other and laughed.

"I do," Amber admitted.

"I guess I do too," Logan agreed. "But what's on your mind Bray? What's up?"

Brayden sighed and spoke, "I look at it like this: We always think our fate is gonna be something really special right? No matter what, we always feel like we're here for some kinda higher purpose, even if life eventually shows us that we're not. We're gonna believe it until we're proven wrong."

Amber and Logan leaned in.

"So, I've always seen it like the stars in the sky. Each star represents a different potential fate for us. There's millions of ways our lives could turn out, with millions of different possibilities, just like there are millions, well, probably billions of stars in the sky. No matter what though, when we're out here looking at them, we always selfishly pick the brightest one to be ours, just like we always dream big dreams, and think we have the best fortune life can offer us," Brayden stopped, as if questioning himself as to whether he was even making any sense.

"Keep going Bray," Amber said.

"It's like…sometimes the road isn't always gonna be clear for us. Sometimes life is gonna do unexpected things that you won't always understand, and you might think your fate is changing. Sometimes, you aren't always gonna see your star in the sky because it's too cloudy or the stars are hidden…or maybe you lose it in the sea of space, but you still know it's there, you know? You still know that you're gonna do great things, even if you don't see it at first. That star you pick out becomes your star, your destiny, and no matter what, it's always gonna be there, and it's yours forever. Nobody can take it away from you. Get it? It's yours for the rest of your life."

Logan and Amber both looked at Brayden with astounded looks on their faces. Neither of them had expected anything so deep and personal from the usually stoic Brayden. Amber looked up and gazed at the sky again. She found herself believing everything Brayden said. She looked up and found the brightest star that she could lay her eyes on.

She grabbed Logan's arm and pointed upwards. "That one's mine!" she shouted.

Logan chuckled and shook his head. "I guess the one next to that is mine then."

"Then that one, way up there, above yours, is mine." Brayden claimed an appropriately higher star.

"Brayden," Amber beamed. "That was really beautiful, what you said about the stars, life, and fate. It really was really sweet."

"Just how I always saw things really. It keeps me motivated sometimes, to know that even though I might be unsure of myself, my path is still always out there for me to follow." He clenched his fist. "And I know I'm gonna reach it one way or the other, because it's always there for me, just like that star, just like you guys."

"You're gonna make me cry dude." Logan laughed.

Brayden vaulted off the dugout roof. "Come on, let's get going," he said as he helped the other two down.

"You go on ahead Bray. I'll walk Amber home, if that's okay with her," Logan said looking over at Amber.

She smiled and nodded. She hugged Brayden. "Happy birthday, Bray."

Brayden faded away into the darkness of nightfall as Logan and Amber stood underneath the beam of light secreting from the light-post over home plate. They walked side by side off the field back towards Amber's house. She kicked up gravel with almost every step she took with Logan on her way home. She hummed to herself in an effort to kill the awkward silence of the walk. Suddenly, she allowed herself to be a child, somewhat inspired by Brayden's hopeful speech atop the dugout. She pushed Logan across the double-yellow lines and began humming louder while skipping around him in a circle as he continued to walk. He couldn't help but laugh.

"Can you stop? I'm getting dizzy!" Logan exclaimed as he grabbed and twirled Amber around by the arm.

Amber giggled. "Why don't you make me?"

He chased her back across the street and she eluded him once more as her hair swung past him and brushed across his face. They laughed loud enough for a light to flicker on inside the house they danced by. Logan finally caught up to Amber, grasped her by both arms this time, and drew her in close to him. She resisted at first before leaning backwards into his chest, forcing him to hold her up. He spun her around as if performing a ballroom dance and she indulged him by pirouetting twice before coming to a full stop.

"You ever have a pretend dance in the street with Melissa?" Amber laughed.

Logan shook his head. "No…No…I believe that's the first time I've done that with anyone." He smiled.

She sighed to catch her breath, locked his arm with both of hers, and rested her head up against his shoulder. She had felt his arm pull at first, but he relaxed after a moment and continued to walk with her close to him. She felt a little guilty being so pushy with him, but at the same time, it felt harmless. They had played together all the time as kids. This seemed no different to her. Still, she couldn't help but feel a little irresponsible for acting so affectionate to Logan. She pulled herself away from him and walked a few steps behind him.

"I was just starting to get used to your head being there," Logan said.

"Do you love her?" Amber asked out of nowhere.

"What?"

She turned Logan around and grabbed his head. "Do. You. Love. Her?"

"She's been really good to me," Logan admitted. "She's fun to be around, she's super smart, and we're both into sports. I'm happy."

"But…" Amber grinned.

"But nothing. I'm happy with her. That's basically it."

"You're afraid to love her, aren't you?" Amber questioned.

"I'm afraid to love anyone at sixteen years old Amber." Logan laughed her off.

"So, it's still nothing too serious?" She prodded him further.

Logan laughed. "What is with you all of a sudden being so interested in me and Melissa?"

"You didn't answer my question," she came back in a sing song-y voice.

"No, it's still nothing serious. To be honest, I took her out tonight because I asked her to this dinner thing a couple weeks ago when I started planning it, but I think I'm going to break things off with her." He said that last bit so quietly that she almost didn't catch it.

She had known Logan well enough to know when he felt uncomfortable. His eyes darted around, and he tended to brush his hair back several times. Even as smooth as Logan could be at times, he could not lie very well, at least not to Amber. He could never keep his feelings hidden from her. She knew that he knew that as well. She believed him though. He probably would break up with Melissa, but there was something else there that he wasn't telling her, but she had already pushed him far enough. She knew the truth. Logan wasn't just "not a fan" of commitment. He feared it. She had felt his demeanor change after his father had left. He had felt betrayed.

Even if he and his father didn't always see eye to eye, Logan had loved his father. Logan didn't confide in anyone. Logan and Melissa shared a very superficial relationship. The way his eyes had wandered away from her at dinner told Amber everything.

Of course she makes you happy. Look at her, how could she not?

But he didn't love her. She had run through all these thoughts through her head not even realizing the two were still walking together. He had walked a bit ahead of Amber, with his hands in his pockets, looking up at the stars. Her thoughts consumed her so much that she didn't see him stop and she bumped into his back. They finally arrived at her house.

"What, you forget where you live?" Logan asked.

She sighed. "No, I didn't forget silly! I was just thinking about our stars."

The two of them looked up at the sky, and sure enough, they noticed right where the three stars were. Two stood almost side-by-side, chosen by Logan and Amber. Then, the third hovered several feet above, which might actually be millions of miles. That third star belonged to Brayden.

"You think after tonight, we'll even recognize our stars?" Logan asked.

"Probably not," Amber admitted. "But it's like Brayden said, you always pick the brightest to be yours anyway. We'll just have to consciously choose the three brightest that happen to be closest to each other."

Logan nodded in agreement. "Well, I guess this is goodbye for tonight then."

She smiled. "Thanks for walking me home Logan. It was fun! Maybe one day, we can share a real dance."

"I would prefer a dance on the concrete as opposed to a dance floor. That way nobody can see how bad you make me look!"

She obliged and he drew her in close to him once more and flung her outwards, an exact repetition from the dance in the street earlier. She walked back in near Logan, and she looked up into his eyes and stared for a moment. She let out a nervous laugh before he reached out for a hug. He squeezed around her back, lifted her about a foot off the ground, and turned her back to her front door placing her on the steps to her house.

"Goodnight, Logan," she said with her head down as she opened the door to head inside.

Before she could, she heard his voice echo from the driveway, "Amber..." he stuttered.

"Logan?"

"You look amazing tonight," he spoke as he turned away, mirroring the way he complimented her several months ago.

"Don't you mean 'looked?' The nights over, Logan," she replied.

"You look amazing every day, so it's not like you ever look less beautiful," he answered as he turned back around.

She blushed. "Thank you," she whispered.

"Anytime." He smiled and winked back at her. "Goodnight."

Before she could return a goodnight back, he disappeared into the darkness. She pulled her key from her bag and slowly opened the front door so she wouldn't wake anyone. She looked down at her phone. She didn't expect to be out past midnight, but walking home from the field took far longer than when her mom drove her. She noticed the living room TV was still flickering. Her eyes opened wide to see Curt passed out on the same recliner she encountered him when she left earlier. She snuck past him while smelling the faintest stench of alcohol on his coarse breath.

You'll see his individuality shine soon! Yeah right. She mocked her mother's words from earlier.

She tried to wave the stench away as she treaded upstairs. She walked into the bathroom and flipped the light on. She turned on the sink to freshen up for bed and washed her make-up off in the process. She gazed back into the mirror and reflected on everything that happened in the night. She smiled. She brushed her teeth and finally unfurled her hair from the now frizzy braids.

She flipped her hair forward and tied it back into a messy ponytail before making her way to her little brother's room. She had made a habit of visiting Michael every night since he was a baby. He would always scream and cry at night as a baby unless Amber was around. Even at a young age, she'd pick him up from his crib and rock him as her mother would, and the baby boy would fall asleep in her arms, only for her to place him in his crib moments later. As he had grown older and his cries had become scarce, she'd always visit him, and she'd kiss him on the forehead before she turned herself in to go to sleep. She slipped into his bedroom, stood above him, and paused for a moment. She smiled as she leaned in to kiss her baby brother on the head.

"Goodnight baby brother. I love you."

She trekked backwards and closed his door, walked down the hall, and stepped into her own room. She threw off her dress and tights, kicked her sandals off, and slid into a long black tee shirt and grey sweatpants.

She made a mess of her bedspread and flopped down into a sea of white, red, and black pillows before she settled on just one of them. She stretched her legs out underneath her sheets and took a deep breath. She looked out the window once more and looked out at the half-moon staring back at her. The trees outside obscured her view of the stars.

They're still out there, no matter what.

As she turned and nuzzled her head into the pillow, she felt herself drifting asleep with a smile on her face, and with a mind full of new memories she would not soon forget.

10

January 19th

(Logan)

Preparations for the upcoming season were in full swing. Logan and Brayden had kept going to the gym after school every day since before the Christmas and New Year break. Logan watched as Brayden stacked plate after plate on each side of the barbell.

"I thought you said we were doing light training today?" Logan joked.

"This is light. You gonna stand there or are you actually gonna spot me?" Brayden fired back as he laid flat on the bench.

Light for Superman maybe.

Logan hovered over Brayden as Brayden took the bar off the rack. There was an aggressive exhale after every rep. Logan did less spotting and more just watching. Brayden finished ten reps with maybe half effort before placing the bar back on the rack.

"A few more you think?" There was a faint chuckle in his voice.

"One on each maybe. That's it," Logan answered.

Logan put the plates on, and Brayden laid back down, sweat dripping from his head and into his eyes. He huffed a few more times and gripped the bar. He put four reps up and placed the bar back for a second. His head started nodding as if he was silently psyching himself up. He gripped the bar tighter. His arms shook as he lifted the bar up and Logan put his hand over the bar, waiting for it to drop. The bar fell to Brayden's chest. He exhaled again and let out a yell as he thrusted the bar high above his head and it clanged on the rack.

"I thought I told you to get yourself a spotter, Lewis," a familiar voice said from behind them. Coach Stevenson poked his head out from his office.

"Hey! What do you think I'm doing?" Logan cracked.

"Being a cheerleader. Be honest with yourself Anderson, if that bar fell on him with all that weight, what exactly would you do? You know the thing about Excalibur and the stone? That'd be you trying to get that bar off him."

Brayden and Coach Stevenson shared a joint laugh at Logan's expense.

"You know, I didn't come down here to get ganged up on."

"Relax, Anderson. Just a joke. Jesus, you're tense today. Hey, Lewis. Take a break and come see me in my office."

Brayden hopped off the bench. Logan turned and saw Amber across the gym in the doorway.

"Aw, crap. I forgot I was supposed to go over some English thing with her after school was over," Logan said.

"Well, you get going then. I'll talk to Coach and meet up with you in a bit."

He made his way over to where Amber was. His steps were light. He was anticipating a scolding for forgetting about working on the project.

"How was the…"

"I am so…"

"Workout?"

"Sorry." He has his apology preloaded. "Wait, you're not mad at me?"

She laughed. "What, that you forgot about working on the project? It's okay! It's Friday. We have the weekend. We can work on it tomorrow or something! Where's Bray?"

"Talking over some things with Coach Stevenson. He said he'd meet up with us in a bit. Let's get going."

Logan walked slightly behind Amber, watching her hair sway across her back. It was like a metronome and his eyes followed. He thought about the bracelet that Brayden helped him pick out and her birthday in a matter of weeks. The idea of asking her out, for real, was enough to make him lose track of his pace. By the time he snapped out of his stupor, he had walked ahead of Amber.

"In a rush?" she giggled.

Instead of replying, his eyes darted. He heard voices from around the corner. There was a chorus of laughter from three, maybe four people. There was the sound of sneakers squeaking across the floor. Suddenly, there was a loud crash. A body just hit a locker. Logan glanced back at Amber and then ran forward and around the corner to see what the commotion was all about. Three of the kids, he didn't really recognize, aside from two of the boys were wearing Springvale Wrestling jackets. Two of the kids he took notice of immediately, the small brown-haired kid with glasses pushed up against the locker, and the stocky and slightly taller boy doing the pushing sporting a jet-black Mohawk.

Logan lowered his eyes and widened them just as quickly after finally putting a memory to the face of the boy against the locker. It was the "butterfly freshman" from the first day of school, who had lost his way going to class. This time, he lost his way again, but right into the grasp of Springvale's standout wrestler, Connor Devlin. Besides baseball, Springvale also had a standout wrestling program. The school had not groomed a wrestler like Connor in quite some time, perhaps ever. He stood a few inches shorter than Brayden but was frighteningly strong. Banners hung in the Springvale gym on various weightlifting records held by students in the past. Some of the records were Brayden's and some were Connor's. Logan hesitated, not really wanting to get involved in the scuffle. With Amber there though, he felt like he had to do something.

"Hey Connor! What, uh, what are you guys doing?"

Connor's hands loosened around the shoulders of the boy, and he exhaled and smiled. "Logan! How's it going, buddy? I see you brought your girlfriend, but where's, uh, uh…" he was mocking Logan's stammer. "Where's your bodyguard?"

Logan ignored both comments. "You…gonna let him go or?"

"Not really. I was just about to give this freshman here a nice little introduction to 2018. Let him know that it might be a new year, but he's still a freshman."

Logan rolled his eyes. "Just let him go Connor!"

Connor nodded his head and completely released the boy, who dropped like a potato sack and down to a knee before scrambling up to his feet.

"Well, since you're here and I'll cut you off before you hit me with the cliché 'pick on someone your own size' thing, maybe I'll get a head start."

Amber jumped in front of Logan. "Nobody is getting a head start on anything! This is stupid and childish. Grow up."

Connor laughed and it was contagious because his three friends started laughing as well.

"Oh, so instead of Brayden saving his ass from a fight, now it's you? That's too funny."

"I'm not saving him from anything other than, oh I don't know, a pointless fight, maybe a few bruises and a suspension? If I'm saving anyone, it's you Connor, from another stupid decision you'd inevitably be making in your life."

Connor huffed and moved towards Amber, who didn't flinch or even blink. Another voice came booming from behind them.

"Hey, hey, what's going on here?" Brayden approached what had become a bigger conflict.

"Oh hey, Brayden!" one of the boys, a skinnier, brown eyed kid with a shaved head, responded. "Just trying to tell Logan here to mind his own business."

"Are you seriously doing this right now, Connor?" Brayden asked with his arms between the groups.

"How do you do this every time? You're always around him, even when you're not around," Connor interrupted.

Brayden turned to Logan. "So, you gonna tell me what's going on or not?"

"Look, they were picking on this kid a little too harshly, so I said something. That's it," Logan snapped back.

Brayden looked over at the kid that Connor had his hands on. Brayden tilted his head to the side and smiled.

"It's not your place pretty boy," Connor responded. "Not yours, not your big buddy's, or your pale princess's," he said directed at Amber.

"Alright, Alright, both of you need to calm the Hell down," Brayden interfered. "None of us want any problems. I know you don't want problems Connor," he shot a glance at Connor.

Connor grabbed the statuesque freshman by the back of his shirt and thrust him into Brayden with one arm. Brayden's fist clenched and his face turned serious as if he was contemplating taking a swing at Connor himself.

"Don't forget. You aren't the only D-1 athlete in this school," Connor said.

"That's what this is about? The fact that I got a scholarship too?" Brayden couldn't help but laugh.

"That's always what it's been about. Ever since you showed up. Everyone forgot about me, forgot about my success, and everything I've done. You took my spot."

"You and Brayden play two different sports. Who gives a shit if you both have scholarships?" Logan thrust himself back into the confrontation.

"I'm sorry. This is a conversation between two real athletes. Keep your mouth shut Logan."

Logan went to rush Connor, but Brayden held him back with one arm.

"I'm not gonna fight you Connor, not here, not ever. You aren't worth it. Nobody is," Brayden said.

"That's your problem, man. That's your problem. You won't ever solve anyone's problems. You'll just put them aside and let them get worse."

Connor got close enough to Brayden until Brayden literally towered over him. Brayden looked down and right into Connor's eyes. Connor didn't look up at many kids in school, but Brayden looked up at nobody. Brayden wasn't backing down. Connor feigned cocking back a punch and Brayden didn't even flinch.

"Connor let's get out of here, man. This isn't worth it," one of Connor's wrestling buddies said from behind him.

"Listen to your friend, Connor. Trust me. You don't want to get hurt," Brayden threatened, his tone more serious than usual.

Brayden continued to stand between Logan and Connor with his arms stretched out. Brayden never sought after a fight. He had always seemed to be the one to break up fights and calm down any escalating situations. He was obviously working overtime to keep Connor and Logan separate. Though the issues stemmed between Brayden and Connor, Logan had always wanted to knock the wrestling champion down a peg.

"Fine. We're done here. Logan took the fun out of everything like usual. She's welcome to come with us anytime," Connor said with a wink at Amber.

"No thanks," Amber replied.

"Catch you later Logan," Connor walked away with the rest of his friends.

"What the Hell was that all about? That's more than you just defending some kid." Brayden asked.

"Nothing man," Logan replied. "Connor is just an asshole to everybody he talks to."

"Yeah. I guess," Brayden hesitated. "Just remember, he isn't worth getting in trouble over."

"I don't understand how you keep so calm all the time."

"I've seen things, been through things before I moved here. It taught me a lot about restraint. It's whatever. Listen, John is throwing a little party at his house tonight. You wanna come?"

"Uh, yeah, I guess. I don't have anything to do," Logan replied. "How about you, you want to come?" Logan asked Amber.

"No thanks. I have to watch my brother tonight. You two have fun!" She laughed.

Amber departed to go wait for her mother to pick her up as Brayden and Logan left to walk back home.

* * *

Instead of going home after reaching Brayden's house, Logan came in with him.

"Hey, boys, you're home pretty late," Brayden's mother said as they walked in.

"Got hung up at the gym for a bit. No big deal," Brayden answered.

Julian rushed out of the kids' room upon hearing Brayden's voice.

"Brayden! Brayden! Look, mom bought me a new game. Do you wanna play with me?

"I'm going out in a little bit Jay. How about later when I get home if it isn't too late?" Brayden answered.

"Okay! Can you ask mom if I can stay up until after you get home?"

"Yeah. I'll walk right up to mom and say, 'Mom! Julian is staying up late to play video games with me. Deal with it!'" Brayden chuckled in a mock-stern voice.

"He'll try, he means," Brayden's mom interrupted.

"Thanks Bray! I love you." Julian hugged Brayden.

"I love you too, buddy."

Brayden lifted his brother up and carried him into his room under his arm like a piece of luggage as the boy laughed. Logan followed them and laughed. Brayden pushed Julian into Logan. Logan swept Julian up and carried him over to Brayden's bed. Logan and Brayden grabbed Julian by the arms and legs and swung him onto the bed. Brayden then rolled onto the bed with him. Logan turned and noticed Angela standing in the doorframe. He tilted his head over to Brayden to get him to notice. Brayden just smiled and extended his arms out.

"I got enough for both of you!" he shouted to her.

She giggled, ran over, and jumped onto Brayden. As he often did with her, he grabbed her by the stomach and lifted her from his back. She squealed with laughter as he boosted her up and down from the ceiling back to his chest and over again like she was one of the barbells he was lifting earlier.

* * *

Logan and Brayden hung out for a few hours before Brayden stirred and started to change for the party. He swapped shirts from the one he was wearing to a black t-shirt. He threw on charcoal grey spring sweater. Lastly, he put on his black and gold Springvale baseball cap and kissed his mom goodbye.

"Don't be home too late, darling," Brayden's mother said as he went to leave.

"Never am!" Brayden replied. "Hey, I have a game night with my brother to get back to!" He pointed at Julian before he left. He patted the boy on the head, winked and nodded at him. "I promise."

Logan waved goodbye to Mrs. Lewis, and they made their way to Logan's. As they walked up the road to Logan's, a car slowed as it passed by.

"Brayden Lewis! Good luck at 'Cuse next year!" the driver shouted.

"You're quite the celebrity there," Logan said with a chuckle.

"I'm still not used to that." Brayden laughed and shook his head.

They made their way to Logan's house, and his mother barely said a word to either of them when they came in. Logan put up a half wave, and they walked upstairs to his room. Logan rummaged through his closet tossing aside various colored polos before settling on a black one and he tossed it over his t-shirt that he was already wearing. He spritzed some cologne and hustled across the hall into the bathroom to fix his hair. Brayden followed him slowly and laughed at Logan staring into the mirror, checking to see if any hair was out of place.

"You know, even your reflection thinks you spend too much time in front of a mirror, kid," Brayden teased.

"That reflection, Brayden, is the reflection of perfection," Logan snapped back with a smile.

"Oh Jesus. Can we go?"

"Yeah, Let's get out of here." They both jogged downstairs and passed by Logan's mom on the couch. "Bye mom! I won't be home late."

"See you around Mrs. Anderson," Brayden followed.

"Have a good time sweetheart," Logan's mom answered without looking at them.

"She still doesn't like me," Brayden said as soon as they got outside.

"She's…"

"I know. Tough times. I got it." Brayden walked out into the winter air.

The cold air was slapping Logan in the face, and he blew into his hands and rubbed them together. The light sweater he put on was hardly enough for the January air. Brayden could do little more than laugh.

"What? Don't you get cold?" Logan asked.

"No, man. It's a little warmer here than it is back home, even at this time of year," Brayden answered. "Besides, I kind of like this piercing cold. The air is crystal clear."

"You're a strange dude, man. You really are."

The only thing missing was snowfall. After walking awhile to John's house, Brayden and Logan were both surprised at how many people were going to the party. They saw several people walking towards the Stevenson home on their way to the party as well. As soon as they got inside, they noticed John Stevenson on the couch with Melissa, Logan's sort of ex-girlfriend.

"Hey, I thought you said this was going to be a small party?" Logan said looking around.

"Yeah, I thought it was too," Brayden said.

Logan and Brayden separated for a moment as Logan made his way into the living room where most of the partygoers were standing. Across from John and Melissa, Logan spotted Connor on a loveseat by himself. Judging by the beer bottles surrounding him, he was well into party mode. Logan looked to turn and leave after seeing Connor.

"Hey! Anderson!" Connor shouted from the loveseat.

Logan took a deep breath and just ignored him. Nothing good could come out of dealing with Connor, especially with his drinking.

"Hey, buddy. I know you hear me," Connor prodded.

Logan turned and faced Connor. "What do you want, man? Gonna harass me again?"

Connor wobbled up to his feet. "Harass? Pfftt." Spit flew and hit Logan on the cheek. "I just wanna make sure we're cool after today. You got a little sensitive and I wanted to make sure, I didn't, uh, you know, hurt your feelings or nothing."

"We're cool." Logan tried to remain calm.

"You see? I knew we were buds. Come here man." Connor went to put his arms around Logan for a hug.

Logan pushed his arm out into Connor's chest. "Not interested."

"What are you being a little bitch for? Just come here and hug me bro." Connor reached in again.

Logan's arm was a bit stiffer this time. "I said no thanks."

"What is your problem? Wait, the bodyguard ain't around is he? Just come here. He don't have to know. Amber don't have to know either."

Connor reached in a third time and Logan extended both his arms this time and gave Connor a good shove. Under normal circumstances, a shove like that wouldn't even teeter Connor, but his drunkenness got the best of him, and he stumbled backwards and couldn't catch himself before he fell through an end table next to the loveseat he was on. His head smashed against the glass top, but the table didn't break. Connor shrieked in pain and put his hands over his eyes, forcing the eyes of everyone in the room to fix on him and Logan.

Logan felt his face warm up. Connor's hands lowered for a minute and there was a nasty gash over his right eye, which started to bleed. Logan backed up towards the entrance to the living room and quickly turned around.

"You're fucking dead! You're a dead man Anderson!" he heard Connor scream from the living room. Logan saw Brayden as he made his way towards the front door and grabbed Brayden by the arm. Brayden resisted and threw Logan's arm off him.

"Whoa. Whoa. What happened?" Brayden asked.

"We're leaving. I want to go. I'll tell you on the way out," Logan replied.

11

(Brayden)

Brayden followed Logan out of John's house, but Logan was already well ahead of him. For someone who was going to explain, Logan was certainly doing his best at creating distance between himself and Brayden.

"Hey Logan! Wait up! We gonna talk about this?" Brayden yelled from behind him.

Logan didn't answer. He kept his head straight, not even looking back at Brayden. After getting to a point where John's house was out of sight, Logan started to slow down and eventually stopped and it allowed Brayden to catch up.

Brayden grabbed Logan's shoulder. "What the hell happened back there? Talk to me Logan."

Logan shrugged Brayden off. "Connor is an asshole. End of story."

"You're gonna have to give me more than that this time," Brayden sighed.

Logan stopped. "Alright, look, we were hanging out and Connor was drinking a little bit and he got in my face about how cool we were and it was really overbearing. I pushed him aside and he didn't like it, so he got back in my face and was threatening me and all this other crap." Logan's fist clenched. "So, you know me. I gave him a good shove and since he was already drunk, he stumbled backwards, fell, and crashed into John's end-table face first. He cut his eye up. He screamed and everyone started freaking out. But it wasn't even a big deal."

"You should have just walked away from him Logan."

"Jesus Brayden!" Logan shrugged him off. "I can't be like you. I can't be levelheaded all the time. I wish I could be. I wish I could take my goddamn emotion out of everything I do like you're able to do, but I can't! I feel. And yeah, maybe I'm a little irrational, but you need to let me make my own decisions sometimes! You don't always have to be there making sure I don't get into trouble."

"Logan, I'm your best fr…"

"And if I do get into trouble? I can get myself out of it."

The two walked in relative silence as snow and sleet started falling from the sky. Brayden and Logan had butted heads quite often on the baseball field due to them both being fierce competitors and both possessing alpha dog type personalities. Connor didn't help to keep that suppressed.

"Logan. You know I'm just trying to help you, right?" Brayden said again tailing him.

Logan ignored him again and just kept walking forward.

"Logan!" Brayden shouted out from behind him.

Logan stopped and scratched his head. "Bray, I'm sorry."

"For what?"

"For what? For acting like an asshole to you, for being so short tempered all the time, and for not being as good a friend to you as you are to me."

Brayden slapped Logan on the back. "Don't even worry about it. I get it," he said.

Logan smiled. "Thanks Bray. You're my brother…well, like the brother I never had, but always wanted. I'm not used to having someone watching my back all the time."

"Best believe I'll always watch yours, Logan," Brayden replied with a chuckle.

Snow started to cover and stuck to the road as they continued walking back towards Logan's house. There was an icy glaze over the road. It was beautiful in a way. Not long after, a burgundy pick-up flew past them and almost struck Logan where he stood.

Logan chased after the truck. "Hey! Watch where you're going asshole!"

He finally stopped after seeing brake lights flash. Brayden followed him. The truck came to a dead stop on the side of the road. Three kids wearing Springvale wrestling jackets hopped out. One of them got out with a bat in hand and a bandage covered the bottom of his eye.

"Hey Logan, looks like I owe you a little payback for this," Connor said pointing at the gash above his eye and the bandage underneath. He put the bat down beside the truck.

"Yeah. You could say that. Or you could say you came back to get a matching one for your other eye," Logan replied.

Brayden jumped in the middle of the two. "Look, we don't gotta do it like this. Everyone just stay cool, alright?"

"Why don't you let the jerk-off fight his own battles for once? Why don't you ever let him loose Brayden?" Connor asked. "You act like Logan can't take care of himself."

"Because I'm not like you, and I don't gotta settle everything with my fists and neither does Logan," Brayden snapped back.

"I'm not going to walk away this time, but if you knew what was good for you, you would." Connor smiled.

"What do you mean by that?" Brayden answered.

"You know exactly what I mean. You know what? I can't wait until you graduate and go back to where you came from. Hopefully you take you and your stupid family with you."

"Bray…" Logan said. Brayden felt Logan's hand on his back.

"Keep my family out of your mouth Connor. I'm not asking you either."

"Brayden. Keep cool man. Just keep cool." Logan tried to grab Brayden's shoulder, but Brayden powered away from him.

"No problem, but it'll be hard to keep me out of your mom's mouth…" before Connor could laugh, Brayden uncorked a piston-like right hand that knocked Connor flat on his back. Brayden stood over him for a moment, contemplating continuing his assault.

"Say something now! Go ahead! Say something now! I dare you!" Brayden screamed at Connor.

Brayden felt a hand on his shoulder, and he almost took a swing before he noticed that it was Logan and he lowered his hand. Brayden turned around to see Connor's two friends, the scrawny kid from earlier and a taller, but equally as skinny kid standing in front of Connor. The scrawny kid made his way past Brayden and took Logan down to the ground and before Brayden could react, the taller kid shot down and wrapped his arms around Brayden's legs to try to take him down. Brayden's hips touched the road, but he didn't go down to his back.

He grunted and got his arms into the armpits of the attacker, which allowed him to rise off the ground and toss the kid down to the ground. Brayden walked in a direct line towards the kid, who was trying to scramble to his feet. Brayden pushed him back down to the ground and placed one hand on his chest, holding him to the ground and thought about uncorking another punch like the one he landed on Connor. The more he thought about it, that kid wasn't the problem. He was probably just going along with Connor. He relaxed his fist and took his other hand off kid. He nodded his head, essentially telling the kid to get up.

He turned and saw the other kid still on top of Logan, pounding him in the chest. Brayden walked over to that scuffle, grabbed the scrawny one by the shoulders and tossed him off Logan. When the kid got back to his feet and saw Brayden, he retreated towards the truck as well. Connor had just begun to get his bearings back after the punch Brayden landed on his jaw. Brayden wiped what he thought was blood from his brow, but it was only sweat. Logan stumbled to his feet, holding his ribs, and winced a bit. Connor's jaw already swelled to such a size, that it looked like Brayden had stuffed a baseball in his mouth along with the blow he'd thrown. Brayden slapped off the snow stuck to Logan's back.

"How are you gonna spend the whole time on your back? Damn Logan." Brayden laughed.

"I'm not as strong as you. Apparently, I'm not strong as him either. Thanks for the assist."

"Anytime man. You know that."

"Hey, Bray? I don't think we're done yet." Logan pointed behind Brayden.

Connor was standing in front of his truck with the bat in hand.

"This dude man. He needs to give it up."

"Hey…hey Connor!" one of his friends said. "Maybe we should just go home, man. It's over."

Connor screamed a muffled yell and swung the bat at Brayden. Brayden reacted just in time to block the blow with his left arm, but he let out a grunt. He shoved Connor backwards and created enough space to unleash another brutal right punch to the ribs that doubled Connor over. With the full force of his nearly two-hundred-pound frame, Brayden sprinted forward, leapt with his knee in the air, and slammed into Connor's chest, once again knocking the wrestling champion flat on his back.

"I'm gonna give you three options," Brayden said somewhat calmly. "You tell him to stay down, get back up and get in that truck and go home, or he can get up and get his ass whipped again. It's his call."

Connor's friends helped him back to his feet. Connor looked vacant and he seemed lost. Connor, under the care of his friends, returned to the truck. The truck peeled off into the night. Brayden shook out his arm, but he felt along the bruise where he blocked Connor's attack with the baseball bat. A deep, dark bruise protruded from Brayden's arm. He winced again as he shook the arm.

Fuck.

"Brayden…" Logan said.

"My arm's broken. I feel it. It shouldn't have let it get that far, even for the things he said." He sighed.

"You're human, just like any of us. You can't let a guy like him get away with saying the things he said. Look at him. He whimpered away like a scared little puppy dog. He's never going to mess with us again. You saw the look in his eyes just as I did. He wasn't walking away without a fight."

Brayden clinched his fist. "I guess. I don't know. I hate being like that. Are you okay?"

Logan started to walk and winced as he dropped to one knee. "That kid roughed me up pretty good. It feels like I have a knife in my stomach with every step."

"He probably broke a rib or two. Come here, I'll help you a ways."

"Even with your arm?"

Brayden smiled. "Even with my arm."

Brayden picked his hat off the ground, wiped the slush off it, and extended his good arm to Logan. Logan put his arm around Brayden's shoulder and Brayden pretty much carried Logan down the block.

"Bray, about what happened back there...are you alright?"

"Yeah. I'm fine."

"It's just...I've never seen you that way before."

"I've seen a lot of shit back home in the city, shit that I wouldn't want you or Amber or anyone here to ever see. Even the stuff I heard, when I was posted up in my bedroom at night."

"I didn't know. I'm sorry."

"No, it's fine. I never talk about it. As for what happened with Connor? My dad taught me how to fight when I was a kid, taught me how to box. He told me I could have become a big-time boxer, but I like my brain cells too much." He laughed. He finally mustered up the feeling to smile.

Logan gathered himself up under Brayden and separated himself.

"You sure?" Brayden asked as Logan pulled away.

"I'm fine. Thanks, but I got it now."

Both were beaten up, but proud of one another. They stood their ground, even if it seemed like a foolish choice. The beginning of the baseball season loomed in a handful of weeks and the school's star player had broken his arm in a fistfight with the school's star wrestler.

"Coach is gonna be pissed," Brayden said. "The season starts in a couple months, and I broke my damn arm."

"We can tell him what happened, with Connor, with all of this," Logan answered.

"Na man. It doesn't have to be like that. We settled our problems. He doesn't need shit for something that happened outside of school."

The snow had intensified over the last hour. Brayden watched Logan walking gingerly across the road.

"I'm good," Logan said giving a thumbs up.

He heard the sound of a car engine coming towards them and saw the shadow that the car's headlights cast over the two of them. The light seemed to be approaching at a fast rate. Logan was still in the middle of the road crossing over. Brayden glanced back at the car, an SUV, picking up speed before he heard brakes fail to check and stop the car. He shot a glance at Logan and rushed over to him, realizing Logan wasn't going to get out of the way of the SUV, which showed no signs of slowing.

"Logan!" Brayden shouted.

He mustered up a full sprint and bashed into Logan shoulder first, sending him onto the lawn of the house they were in front of at the time. The car slid sideways, and its tires screeched against the icy pavement trying to get out of the way. The full force of the SUV smashed into Brayden, sending him end over end down the road. He tumbled down the road, hitting snow, pavement, and gravel. He felt his body finally come to rest. It became difficult to breathe. The pain was staggering, as if each organ inside his chest was being stabbed with little razor blades. His eyes widened. Every time he tried to breathe, no air entered his lungs. He couldn't move. His legs were so numb that it was as if they weren't there at all. He couldn't move his head, and his eyes were fixed on the sky. There were no stars, and the moon was hidden behind the clouds. The snow and sleet continued to fall to his face.

He heard a voice faintly. "Oh my God." A car door opened and closed. Footsteps approached and his vision blurred.

"Br…Bray?"

12

(Amber)

Amber hadn't taken her eyes off the phone since the text from Logan. *Brayden. Hospital. It's bad. Please come.*

The broken language was enough for her to know what kind of shape Logan was in, but her mind fluttered to Brayden. How bad was it? What happened? As all the thoughts rattled around in her head, the car came to a stop. They were there.

"Want me to go in with you?"

She could barely think, let alone speak but managed to utter out, "No. I have to see them."

She opened the car door slowly and closed her eyes tight. *Please be okay, both of you.*

When she got into the waiting room, she didn't see Logan and her heartbeat quickened.

She approached the receptionist at the desk.

"Logan Anderson? Brayden Lewis? I'm here to see them both."

The receptionist checked her computer and then a clipboard.

"Mr. Anderson is in X-Ray right now and Mr. Lewis is in Intensive Care. Mr. Anderson will be out shortly. Unfortunately, we can't let you see Mr. Lewis at this time."

Her entire body was shaking as she went over to the waiting area, but she couldn't bring herself to sit down. She buried her head in her hands and wiped her face. She tried to take deep breaths to calm herself down, but the breaths went from deep to rapid at an incredible pace. Suddenly the emergency room doors opened, and Logan gingerly walked out. She hugged him and he grunted and put his arms out.

"Logan what happened?"

"We got into a fight with Connor and his friends, and I fractured a few ribs apparently."

Bloodstains were splattered on his shirt by the shoulders, and his sweatshirt was ripped. She looked past him towards the doors.

"He's still in Intensive Care," she said. "What happened to him?"

Logan's mouth went to form words, but he couldn't bring himself to speak about whatever happened.

"He can't leave. He can't." Logan started to tear up. "He's gonna make it. He has to!"

Amber reached out and hugged him softly this time, wary of his ribs. "He will. We just need to have faith. He's strong. He'll pull through."

Suddenly, Logan's face almost turned white as his eyes were looking past her. Amber turned around to see Brayden's parents walking into the waiting room.

"Oh no," Logan said.

Brayden's father walked towards him with a wild look in his eyes.

Brayden's father approached Logan, grabbed his shoulders, and shook him. "What happened to my boy, Logan?! What happened?!"

Logan trembled with tears in his eyes. Looking away from Mr. Lewis he stammered, "I…I…I'm so sorry Mr. Lewis. I…"

"Richard, Logan is shaken up. Take it easy," Brayden's mother pleaded.

"I know…I know." He let go. "But our boy is in there fighting for his life! Logan, just try to tell us what happened. That's all, son. That's all I want to know."

"We left the party early and got into a fight with some kids from school. After that, I…I was walking across the street and there was this car coming. It was sliding down the road and it couldn't stop. I couldn't see it. I swear I couldn't. I just saw Brayden run across and knock me across onto the lawn of the house we were by. Then…Then…" Logan's voice began to crack as he recalled the events. "When I got up, I saw the car…truck…van, whatever. It was sideways and I looked in front of it and Brayden was on the ground down the road. He wasn't moving. Someone called an ambulance as fast as they could. Mr. Lewis. I'm so, so sorry." Logan broke into tears.

Brayden's father began to cry. "Come here, son. Come here. It's okay." He embraced Logan.

Logan pulled away. "It's not okay! If it weren't for me, Brayden would be okay right now! If it weren't for me, he wouldn't have to put himself out there all the time. Everything bad that's ever happened to him since he's been here has been my fault! I'm just so sorry."

Amber stood still. It felt like she got punched in the gut. She found it difficult to collect her breath. The Emergency Room doors opened again, and a doctor walked out.

"Mr. and Mrs. Lewis?"

Mr. Lewis brought Logan along and Amber looked over at Brayden's mother and quickly grabbed her hand.

"We…we did everything we could, but…we lost him."

Before the doctor could finish, Brayden's mother buried her head in her hands as his father stood still as a statue.

"The internal bleeding was too severe and the damage to his brain and skull were too much." The doctor paused. "I am so very sorry for your loss." The doctor closed her eyes.

Amber stood there stone faced. She couldn't hear the rest of the conversation. She didn't hear Mrs. Lewis weeping beside her. She only saw Mr. Lewis gripping Logan's shoulders. Nothing felt real to her anymore. Everything became a blur. Time slowed down and he couldn't do anything.

It was over. Brayden was gone.

She couldn't move. She couldn't think. She could barely breathe. She watched the surgeon walk back into the emergency room. Then, something took over Logan. He took off and sprinted towards the emergency room doors.

"Logan?" Amber followed him.

She watched Logan look around the hallways until he fixed his gaze on a room in the ICU. She followed him inside and they both stood stunned. A covered-up body lay before them under a baby blue sheet. A bruised arm hung limp from underneath. Brayden lay beneath that sheet.

"Brayden!" he screamed out.

One of the doctors gently grabbed him.

"No! Get off! That's my best friend! He's my best friend! He's my brother! Leave me alone!" He reached out to the table.

Logan knelt beside Brayden's body and whispered something, but Amber couldn't hear what he said. He stood back up shaking in place.

The doctor came from behind him. "I know how hard this is for you. The police are here. They want to know what happened so they can help you."

"Nothing can help! He's gone."

The doctor didn't respond. He just patted Logan on the shoulders and led him back to the lobby. Amber noticed a couple of cops and they pulled him outside into the cold. Amber stood in the lobby, and she walked back to Brayden's parents.

"Mr. and Mrs. Lewis," Amber started.

She couldn't bring herself to say she was sorry. She heard that far too many times when her father died to know how empty that phrase was. She first walked over to Brayden's father and just hugged him as tight as she could. She felt his arms wrap around her. His arms were as strong as

94

Brayden's were. She looked up into his reddened eyes and buried her head back into his chest and for the first time, she started sobbing. She sniffled and wiped her eyes and sat alongside Brayden's mother, whose eyes were wide.

She grabbed Mrs. Lewis's hand and squeezed. The two never shared a look, but Amber felt everything in the squeeze. Logan plodded back inside and couldn't stop shaking. He fell into Mr. Lewis's arms.

"Mr. Lewis…I am so sorry." Logan started to cry again.

Mr. Lewis's eyes were red. "It's okay, Logan. It's okay. We'll get through this. We will."

It wouldn't be okay. And she wasn't sure if any of them would get through it. The officer who interviewed Logan followed after.

"Mr. and Mrs. Lewis, I'm Officer Roberts. I want to offer my sincerest condolences for the loss of your son," the officer said with his hat in hand. "The driver who struck your son turned himself in after the incident. We just needed Logan to corroborate the story."

"Thank you, officer," Brayden's mother responded. "But my son is lying underneath a sheet right now."

"I understand. Just know, the person responsible will be fully prosecuted." Officer Roberts looked at Amber and Logan. "Would you kids like a ride home?"

Amber struggled to answer, not wanting to leave Brayden's parents or Brayden back at the hospital.

Mr. Lewis nodded. "It's okay, go on home kids. Try to get some sleep."

Mrs. Lewis walked over squeezed Amber tight and whispered, "It's going to be okay."

Amber looked down at the ground and nodded. Amber watched as Officer Roberts led Logan out of the hospital and into his squad car. They were leaving the hospital without Brayden. So many things ran through her head on the car ride home. The worst thing was that this was only the beginning. Instead of using saved up money to send Brayden off to college, now the family needed to use that money for a funeral.

The car slowed as they approached Logan's house. Amber got out also.

"You live here too?"

"No." Amber shook her head. "But I'm going to stay the night with him."

Officer Roberts rubbed Logan's back. "Stay strong through all this, okay Logan?"

Logan looked down at his shirt and pants and Amber saw Brayden's blood drying up on his clothes. He stumbled wide-eyed towards his front door. She walked ahead of him to open the door for him. Instead of going through the door, he just collapsed in her arms and started sobbing. She buckled as she attempted to hold him up, but she managed to hold him. She led him inside and brought him upstairs into his room.

"Logan…"

He didn't answer her. He just remained wide-eyed and silent. She followed suit. What else could she say? Any words at this point were useless. They were both in shock. She felt a weight in her chest. She walked across the hall into the bathroom and ran warm water over a washcloth. She returned to his room and began wiping his hands and face clean of the dirt and blood that had dried on his skin. She pulled out a new t-shirt and sweatpants after rummaging through his drawers for something for him to wear. She wanted to take off his bloodstained clothes. She removed his shirt and put her hands over her mouth seeing the bruises on his chest and the bandages around his ribs. She carefully examined the welts and ran her hands across them. She started to tear up a bit. She untied and removed his shoes and slid his jeans off. She tossed the dirty, bloody clothes aside to the corner of the room. She laid him down on his bed and put a few blankets over top of him.

"Thank you," he whispered. He reached out and put her hand over his heart. She put her other hand over top of his and hugged him.

She pulled his desk chair beside the bed and sat down. "I'm not going anywhere, okay?"

He rolled over away from her.

"Try to close your eyes."

Neither of them had ever experienced anything like this. Amber had lost her father, but this somehow felt different. She truly loved Brayden. She loved Logan. Brayden was gone. Logan was suffering and no words or actions could fix it.

"I promise. I'm not leaving," she reassured him.

He closed his eyes tight. He must have been exhausted. He kept his hand clasped in Amber's as he drifted off to sleep. She gently released his hand and put it near his head. She grabbed a throw blanket off the end of his bed, tossed it on top of her and tried to get comfortable in his desk chair. She leaned backwards. Her bottom lip was quivering. When she closed her eyes, all she saw was Brayden's body underneath the sheet in the hospital and her eyes snapped open. She kept her eyes fixed on the ceiling until they became too heavy to keep open. She rested her head on her arm and drifted to sleep. She heard Logan stir but couldn't open her eyes anymore.

13

(Logan)

He couldn't see anything. He didn't see who or what hit him. It must have been Brayden. He heard him yell right before the impact. It didn't change the fact that he couldn't see. Tires screeched. There was a crash. Then, silence, a deafening silence that stilled the air around him. He picked his head up and saw nothing except a body in the street. He stumbled to his feet and across to the scene.

"Br...Bray?" he whimpered.

Brayden was supine, his head to the sky. He was gasping for breaths that weren't there for him to take. Logan dropped to a knee and felt wetness near Brayden's abdomen. He pulled his hand back, now wet with Brayden's blood.

This isn't happening.

He cried for help, but nobody came. He cradled Brayden's head as he saw life leave his eyes.

He woke up screaming. His heart felt like it was going to burst through his chest. A hand rubbed his back.

"Shhh. It's okay sweetheart. It's okay," he heard his mother's voice. She wrapped her arms around his head, just as he did to Brayden in the dream.

He was broken out in a sweat. His eyes became wide; he ran his hand through his hair and began to sniffle. Another person sat on his bed beside him. It was Amber. Her hair was tied back by a rubber band and there were traces of make-up on her face from the night before. He rested his head on her shoulder, and she followed suit by tilting her head down onto his. His mother got up, picked up his bloodstained clothes from last night and walked out into the bathroom.

"Logan..." she stammered. "I don't even...I don't know what to say."

Logan still couldn't speak. Amber grabbed his trembling hands and just as she'd done last night, she turned and hugged him tighter than ever. He didn't want her to let go, hoping that if she never released him, that somehow, everything would be okay. He began to stir from up under her and he rose up off his bed. His eyes turned to the TV, which was already on before he woke up from the nightmare.

"The town of Springvale wakes to somber news as Brayden Lewis, the young 18-year-old baseball superstar from Springvale High School, was killed late last night, when he was struck by an out-of-control SUV amid the freezing rain and snow that fell in the area overnight. The star was set to attend Syracuse University, where he would play baseball next spring,"

The TV clicked off after that. Brayden was gone. Logan sat down in the middle of his floor and still hadn't said a word since he woke up. So many thoughts ran through his mind, but he didn't have the strength to even verbalize them.

Why was it him? Why did it have to be him?

More images began to flood into his mind: Brayden lying there, unable to move, bleeding onto the ground. He couldn't say goodbye to Brayden. It was too soon to think about. He'd never be able to see him again. He struggled with that aspect the most, the finality of it all.

We were supposed to be together for the rest of our lives.

Amber walked over to him. "Do you want to go?"

He nodded and the two walked downstairs and out the back door. The birds were chirping. The sun was out, and the air was cold. If it wasn't for the chill in the air, he'd swear it to be a perfect summer day. There wasn't a cloud in the sky. Amber stood beside him, and they walked in silence. He stomped ahead of her into the woods. It didn't take them long before they came to a small, tattered cabin. Logan had found the cabin over the summer. It was only one room, with a stone fireplace in the middle.

"How long has this been here?" she asked.

Logan didn't answer. The porch was rotted, a few of the windows were blown out and the roof was partially caved in. Logan walked in without a second thought. He curled up inside the still intact fireplace. Amber sat down on the floor across from him. Neither of them said a word, but in a way, he felt that she knew exactly what he was thinking. The way she looked at him told him. Her brows were furrowed, and her eyes seemed lower than usual, even the blue in them seemed a few shades darker than usual. He buried his head on his knees and began to cry. That's when he heard something slide across the floor. He moved his eyes over to see Amber's phone, and on the screen was a picture of the night sky.

"He sent that to me a few days before Christmas," she said. "Told me to look really closely at it. Notice anything?"

Logan picked her phone up and looked at the picture again. Maybe he was just imagining it, but he could swear he saw three stars pop out of the picture, brighter than all the others in the frame.

"The stars," he answered. "Our stars."

Her lips lifted to form a slight smile. "He never stopped believing in that."

"I just don't understand," he cried. "Why is he gone?

"Logan...I"

"It wasn't supposed to end like this. He saved me and...and..." he couldn't finish. *He saved me and paid the ultimate price for it. That's not how a hero is supposed to be paid back.*

"He died doing the thing he'd do if we all lived to be old and withered, Logan. He died looking out for you."

He couldn't draw up the strength to argue, or to even say anything else. He wiped tears out of and into his eyes and laid his head back into the fireplace, looking up at nothing but stone. Amber slid next to him and put her head down on his shoulder. Logan put his hand on her head and gently moved her aside as he stood up and went outside the cabin. He found a softball sized rock and hurled it into the woods with an aggressive exhale. He picked up a few smaller rocks and did the same before falling onto the withered porch.

"Why am I still here and he isn't, Amber? It isn't fair," he bawled. He saw her arms wrap around him over his shoulders and he felt her kneeling behind him. "His family, his brother and sister, his future? It's all gone. HE'S gone."

"Logan! Stop. Please," she cried out. It stopped him.

He pulled from under her. "I'm sorry. I didn't realize...," he stammered between breaths. In that moment, something spooked him. This was only the beginning. Brayden's future was never in question. Now those opportunities and that life would be forever waiting, as Brayden lay forever young.

I'm never going to see him again. His laugh. His voice. He's gone.

The scariest part of it all to him was that he had just seen Brayden alive and well last night, which felt like it was an eternity ago. Suddenly, sadness rushed over him, and he felt as if he were drowning between the waves. He looked over at Amber, who was now in tears herself. It was the first time he had seen her cry like that. She had been keeping so strong through the last 24 hours that her sudden vulnerability took him by surprise.

"Are you...okay?"

"I feel sick," she sniffled.

"I just...never asked you how you were holding up. I've been so wrapped up in me that I just..." he paused. "I just hadn't thought about how you're feeling. I just don't want you to go just yet."

"Well, I wasn't planning on leaving you anytime soon," she said with another half-smile.

He felt the lump in his throat return as he looked at her. He wondered how this compared to her losing her father. Did she feel the same sadness? Or was this worse because she was probably closer to Brayden than she ever was with her father. His brain was scrambled but the images of the night before were burned there. The nightmare returned. Suddenly, he was back lying on the lawn after Brayden shoved him out of the way. The screeching tires, the sound of the car and Brayden's body colliding and the silence, it all came back to him again except he wasn't asleep. This wasn't something he could just wake up from.

"Logan?" Her voice snapped him back to the moment.

He looked at her with a vacant expression.

"What happened to him was an accident. You know that don't you?"

Her words rang around in his head, but he couldn't form a response. He only stood up and walked off the porch and away from her. He turned around in a near trance and went out of towards the line of the forest outside the neighborhood. He sat cross-legged where the gravel met the dirt and grass. He started tossing small rocks into the forest further than his eyes could see. He was in a stupor. He could hear Amber's footsteps not far behind where he decided to sit down.

"Logan, nobody could've stopped what happened last night. You have to know that," she said.

"I know," he answered sharply. "I think that's what I'm struggling to grasp the most. No matter how many times that scenario has played out in my head all day. I keep seeing it but not seeing everything because I couldn't have known. Brayden made a decision and what kills me," he started sniffling. "What kills me is I'll never know if he knew he was going to die. There's nothing I could have done and that feels worse than feeling like I could have done anything at all."

"Brayden did what he felt he had to do in the moment. I don't think he could have known either."

"It's like a weight wrapped around my waist and I can't move forward or backward, I'm stuck in this in-between place, and it's torturing me."

She walked closer to him, wrapped her arms over him, and rested her head on his shoulder again. She didn't say anything else. She just kneeled over him. He grabbed her hand and squeezed tight. He began to sob again. Nothing either of them said had made him feel any better. They couldn't walk far enough away to escape the idea that Brayden was gone.

"What are we going to do without him Logan?" she asked.

"I can't even think about that right now. I still don't want to believe he's gone."

"Me either. It's not real to me yet."

It was the same feeling as when he woke up this morning after his nightmare. He refused to believe that Brayden was gone. Part of him expected him to sneak up behind them, slap Logan on the back and put Amber in one of his signature bear hugs. Only the wind ran across him, and he swallowed hard at the emptiness of the moment. He waited with bated breath for something, or someone to pull them both from this, but it never came. He felt his arms leave him. Then, he saw her hand out in front of his face with her phone in it. Staring back at him was himself, Amber and Brayden all smiling. They took that picture at the park during the summer.

"This was the only time we all smiled together," Amber said, but he heard Brayden's words through her.

"It's only going to get harder, isn't it?" Logan said staring out into the vastness of the woods.

Amber sighed. "It is. So much harder."

"You're going to be here for it aren't you?" He turned and faced her. She kept her phone clinched to her heart.

"Just as long as you are Logan."

"I won't be able to get through this without you."

"This isn't something you, or me, or anyone has to do alone. You shouldn't expect to be able to do it alone."

They both turned back to watch the trees sway in the wind. She rested her head on his shoulder and placed her hand over his heart as he put his arm around her. Neither of them knew where to go from here.

He heard her whispering to herself, "I know we haven't talked in a while, but just if you could, give us some direction away from the pain, the sadness, the unpredictability." She prayed. "Anything. Take this sadness away from Logan before it consumes him and give him the strength he needs to endure this."

"He already did," Logan said overhearing her.

"Huh?"

"He did give me the strength. You are my strength." *I don't know if I can do this without you Bray.*

He felt a little guilty in a way, putting so much on her. It didn't seem fair. He made a silent promise to himself that he wouldn't lean on her too much. Neither of them deserved to carry too much and he realized that.

I'll get my legs under me eventually.

She stood up. "Logan?" she said to get his attention.

"Hm?"

"Promise me something, okay? I want you to promise before I tell you what I want you to accept."

"I promise," he answered, weakly.

"Promise me that no matter what, you'll stay here for me, and you'll stay here for you. We get through this together, okay? We never leave the other's side, no matter how dark things get, and no matter how much we don't think we can. We have to know that we can get through this, okay?"

"Amber...I..."

"Promise me!"

"I promise."

He reached out for her. The wind howled and sent a chill coursing through his body, but his grip on her remained as strong as ever.

"I promise," he muttered into her coat.

"And I promise to help get us through this, no matter what."

She peeked up at him, glanced away, and darted her eyes to the sky, as if waiting for a signal that everything would work out the way she envisioned it, but received no such confirmation. Her arms tightened around him, and it made him feel safer and more confident, because he knew that in the coming days, both of them would need all the strength they could muster. He knew the hardest parts were still to come. Logan watched Amber pull her phone out and she pressed a button. She put it on speaker, and the phone rang a few times, and then a familiar voice came across the other side.

"What's up? It's Brayden. Leave a message. I'll get back to you when I get it. I swear," followed by a shallow laugh and a beep.

Amber stretched her arm out to Logan.

"I can't," he said.

She stuttered, "Hey Bray...um, I'm here and Logan is here too. We're okay. I just...I wish you picked up, so I could know this was all just a bad

103

dream. But here I am, talking to nobody, because you aren't here Bray."
She started to break down. "It hasn't even been a full day, and we miss you
so much. We love you, Bray. I can't believe you're gone. Rest in peace and
harmony, Brayden. You're forever in our hearts." She hung up and buried
her face in her hands as she wept.

Logan hugged Amber. It was a reversal of roles from earlier in the day.
He knew that it wasn't up to one or the other to be strong. They had to be
strong for each other, even now when it didn't seem like it was possible.

"I got you," he whispered to her, "I got you. Don't worry."

She collected herself and wiped a tear from her eye. "I got you too."

14

January 26th

(Amber)

She gazed at herself in the mirror and ran her fingers through her black hair, which was starting to show signs of lightening back to her natural brown. Her palms were sweating as she reached for a glass of water perched on her end table. She'd see Brayden for the first time since doctors had covered him up with a blue sheet after he died. She feared this day like no other. A wake and a funeral tomorrow morning, time was moving too fast. She grew short of breath. The days felt as if they'd melted together since that night. She hadn't gone to school since the day of John's party and hadn't gone outside since she and Logan took a walk to the woods the morning after. School, friends, and any other responsibilities of life seemed so unimportant.

What's the point in even going back? she thought to herself.

It had been a week. She sat on her bed waiting for her mother to ready herself, and as she's done so many times, stared at the blank ceiling. The school district made the call to close the school for Brayden's wake. Brayden had left such a massive impact on the school. Every single soul who attended Springvale High knew Brayden Lewis in some way. Whether they knew him as most did, as the superstar baseball player, or as a classmate, a teammate, or as Logan did, a brother and a friend, everybody wanted to say goodbye in their own way.

"Amber honey? Amber are you ready to go?" her mother called from downstairs.

"In a minute. Yeah."

She finally lifted herself off her bed and trekked downstairs. The car ride to the funeral home didn't last as long as she hoped. Amber watched trees, buildings, other cars and people whisk by in a blur of color. When she arrived, she opened the car door, shocked to see so many faces. Almost all of Brayden's teammates from the baseball team gathered outside the door. John Stevenson and his father stood outside the front door.

"Hi, John," Amber opened. "I know we only met the one time…"

"Amber, right?" John said giving her a big hug that mirrored the ones Brayden often gave her. "How are you holding up? I know you and Brayden were close."

"I'm...I don't know. I'm okay, I guess. What about you and everyone else on the team?"

"I just can't believe it. You know? We were supposed to graduate together and now we're all here and we're saying goodbye. I don't know. It doesn't feel right."

"Because it isn't." Amber frowned. "Have you seen Logan by any chance?"

John pointed towards the door. "Yeah, he, uh, he headed inside with Mr. Pearsall not too long ago. I'm sure he'll be happy to see you."

Amber walked towards the funeral home's door, but she turned to see John and the rest of the team gather out front.

. "Everyone get over here. I have something to say." John was a senior like Brayden. "Everyone take a knee and grab a hand."

The entire team circled and joined hands.

"On and off the field," John began, "Bray was the strongest kid I knew. He wasn't always accepted at times, but he never stopped fighting, never stopped trying, and never stopped caring...never once. We'll miss you Bray, more than you know. You left a mark on every single one of us, on our community, and on our school, and you're the type of kid most of us only meet once in our lives." John looked around at the rest of the team, and told them to bring their hands in, "One clap, one time, Bray on three, Bray on three. One! Two! Three!"

"Bray!" The team echoed.

Amber smiled and walked in. She turned the corner to where the coffin was and was amazed at the sea of people that had already gathered in the room. She went over to the guestbook to sign her name, scanning it for Logan's. She found it a few spaces up, right above Mr. Pearsall's. She paced around the room, glancing over at the casket several times, and gazing at pictures that various members of Brayden's family had brought and pinned on several boards around the room. She stopped upon seeing a picture of Brayden after one of Springvale's games holding his baby brother and sister on his shoulders. He looked like a giant holding the two kids up. Amber never saw a bigger smile on Brayden's face than in that very picture.

In the same moment, she turned around to the front of the room and saw the same two young children sitting in chairs, gazing at the coffin. She saw Logan with them already. He was kneeling in front of the coffin with Brayden's baby sister. She stood in the doorway and just watched him, praying, talking to Brayden, whatever he needed to say.

106

"Thank you for coming, Amber," a voice said coming off from the side. It was Brayden's father.

"Mr. Lewis, I...I'm," before she could apologize, Brayden's father cut her off.

"Shhh. No more apologizing. Thank you for coming sweetheart. You were like a sister to Brayden, which makes you a daughter to me and my wife, and a sister to Julian and Angela as well. You're like family, Amber."

"I don't know if I can see him," Amber admitted almost in tears.

"You'll be alright dear," Mr. Lewis hugged her and kissed her on the head.

Amber continued to watch Logan from the doorway until he got up and their eyes met. Logan smiled a bit and walked over to her. The two shared a long embrace.

"How are you holding up?" Amber asked from the comfort of the hug.

"I...um...I just saw him," Logan answered with his face buried in her shoulder.

She brushed her hair out of her face. "I want to see him too."

"I'll come with you, if you'd like," Logan requested. "Angela helped me go up, so, I'm passing along the same courtesy."

Amber nodded and Logan extended his hand to her. He felt her stop as they approached the casket.

"I don't know if I can do this," she said.

He said nothing but his hand met her back and he eased her on towards the casket. Amber ran her hands across the maple-grain, and then to the soft white cloth and her hand stopped when she saw the body. Amber wiped a tear from her eye and uttered a breathless laugh.

"He looks so peaceful," she said looking at his slate-grey suit jacket.

Various trophies sat beside Brayden's body. His Springvale baseball cap, still somewhat stained with a touch of blood around the brim, lay next to his head. Amber looked over his whole body, silently recreating that night in her mind. She pictured this same body lying broken and battered in the road. She closed her eyes tight and shook her head of those kinds of thoughts. She looked up again at the dozens upon dozens of flowers colored across the visible spectrum with tags from countless donors. She knelt on the kneeling stand and gazed at his face. She waited for Brayden's dark brown eyes to open one more time. His hair looked shaved, his skin, though paler than she remembered it to be, still appeared to have some semblance of life.

107

"He looks like he's asleep," Amber said running her hands across Brayden's.

"Yeah…Yeah he does," Logan replied.

Except he wasn't going to wake up. She remembered her father's wake hazily. There hadn't been nearly as many people at his wake. She hadn't said anything to him when his body was laid out. She didn't even kneel over him. She just stood for a few minutes and then walked away with barely a tear in her eye. This was different. This is what it felt like losing family.

Amber reached her arm out and ran her hand up and down Brayden's broad shoulders.

"What I would give up to get one more hug from you, Bray."

She kept her hand over Brayden's heart, waiting for it to beat, before reaching back and clasping her hands together.

"I want to say all the usual things about you being in a better place, but you're not," she whispered. "Your better place is here with us, with your family. There's nothing better about this." She kept her hands clamped to avoid shaking as she spoke. "How is this fair? I wish you could see how many people you touched Brayden. It seems like the whole town is here to say goodbye."

She was beginning to break down in front of Brayden, and she felt Logan's hand rubbing up and down her back.

"I hope He takes really good care of you because he took you away way too soon. Rest in peace and harmony, Brayden. Amen." She finished her prayers, wiped her eyes, leaned over the casket and kissed Brayden on the forehead.

Logan rose beside her, and she rested her head on his shoulder as they looked down into the casket at their best friend. Even after saying goodbye face-to-face, Amber still refused the reality of Brayden's death, despite looking at him lying in casket.

This has to be a bad dream.

They drifted back to the middle rows of chairs and caught up with various classmates. Amber sat and listened to all the fascinating stories told by kids she only just knew. All of them spoke glowing words of Brayden, despite never knowing him. Never once did they misinterpret who he was. It astounded Amber that even though Brayden didn't open himself up to anyone, the students felt like they knew him.

"He was scary," one kid said. "As soon as you talked to him though, he was probably one of the nicest kids I've ever met. He commanded attention, even when he never asked for it, you know?"

Amber felt a bit better after hearing people share such kind, moving words about Brayden.

Her head turned when he heard Brayden's father. "I want to thank you all for coming. It means the world to our family to see how many lives our son touched. I want to give the opportunity to anyone who'd like to share anything about Brayden with everyone else."

The room sat still for a moment. Whether out of discomfort, fear, or sadness, nobody could muster up the will to speak. Despite hearing several anecdotes over the last few minutes, everyone fell silent when prompted to speak in front of everyone in the room. Logan looked at Amber and stood up. She watched him pace to the front of the room, between the coffin and Brayden's father, and cleared his throat.

"I um...I honestly don't know what to say that you guys don't already know," he began. "Brayden was like my brother." He began to tear up. Mr. Lewis put his hand on Logan's back He tried to form words, but nothing was coming out.

Oh Logan

She wanted so desperately to run up there, grab him and tell him everything would be okay. She was watching Logan collapse in the middle of the room in front of everyone. She felt a lump develop in her throat.

"I'm sorry...I just can't do this right now." He ran off and out the door.

Amber looked at Mr. Lewis, who nodded his head to her, and she got up and followed Logan out the door.

"Logan..."

"I couldn't. I can't do this!"

Amber wrapped her arms around him. "It's okay! Logan, it's okay. Everyone understands."

"I just keep letting everyone down. I let his family down in there." He broke away from her. "I'm sorry but I just need to go outside for a minute."

She watched Logan go outside as Brayden's family came out together from the parlor.

"Is he okay?" Mr. Lewis asked.

"He feels terrible about what happened in there."

109

Mrs. Lewis interrupted, "Do you think you could take the kids to him? I'm sure seeing them will put him in better spirits.

Amber nodded and motioned for Julian and Angela to follow her outside. Logan was around the corner from the front of the funeral home, on one of two benches. Julian sat down on the bench next to Logan as Angela and Amber sat on the other bench. Logan looked down at Julian and then glanced over at Amber, almost as if he understood what was going on. Amber lifted Angela up and seated her on her lap.

"You miss your brother, don't you?" Amber asked Angela.

The girl nodded.

"It's okay to cry, you know. I've cried a bunch. Sadness is just a way of expressing how much you love your brother."

The girl lifted her head. "You cried for Bray?"

"I cried a lot for Bray," Amber replied.

"I thought bigger girls like you aren't supposed to cry."

"Big girls cry all the time. It's part of being a big girl."

"Or a big boy," Logan chimed in looking over at Julian.

"Look, you guys don't have to be tough for anybody. If you want to cry, you cry until you can't anymore, okay?" Amber turned her eyes right towards Angela's.

Without a response, Angela doubled her head into Amber's chest and began to sob. Amber wrapped her arms around the girl, rocked her, and rubbed her back.

"It's okay. It's okay. Let it out. Just let it all out sweetie."

In the same moment, Julian looked up at Logan, and they hugged as well before Julian hopped off the bench he was on to sit with his sister and Amber. He hugged his younger sister and the two children cried together. Logan looked over at Amber, almost as if asking what they should do. Amber tilted her head and shrugged. She put her arms around the children. Her experience taking care of her younger brother helped in the effort to keep the children somewhat calm.

Amber heard footsteps behind him. Brayden's father and mother had come out of the funeral home.

"Thank you for watching the kids," Mr. Lewis said to Logan and Amber.

"Don't thank me. Thank Amber. She's the one who had all the right things to say and do. She's the one with the younger brother. She's better equipped to do things like this than I am."

"Logan," Mr. Lewis stopped before leaving. "Don't become a stranger, okay? You're like a son. Remember that, always."

Logan got choked up. "Thank you, Mr. Lewis. I know. That means so much to me."

"And Amber? You don't be a stranger either, okay sweetie?" he directed to her.

"Of course. We love you as much as we loved Brayden," Amber answered.

"Thank you, kids, for everything…for helping our family through this," Mrs. Lewis opened, "You two are incredible young people. Brayden knew how to pick his friends. You two are so special."

"Remember, big boys and girls are allowed to cry whenever they want." Amber smiled, putting her hands on Angela. "Okay?"

"Mhm." Angela nodded.

"I'll see you soon," Logan whispered hugging Julian.

Amber exhaled, feeling as if an hour's worth of tension released with it. She sat back down on the bench and Logan soon followed her. She bowed her head to the ground to recover and reflect on maybe starting to move on from this nightmare.

"I don't know how I'm ever going to get back to normal without him," Logan stuttered.

"You'll get through this, Logan. I know you will. I'll make sure you do."

Logan looked at her a bit surprised. "How? I mean…where do we even start?"

She fretted. "I don't know. Maybe we start by trying to start our regular routines over again."

"You mean school, don't you?" Logan joked.

"Yes. I mean school, silly."

"I don't know if I can."

"You have to. We have to. Monday. We go back Monday."

"Amber I…"

"Don't say anything. Don't thank me. None of that. Not now. Just come here. Big boys are allowed to cry." She grabbed him and brought him close.

He rested his head on her chest. She closed her eyes and squeezed. Neither of them spoke. Losing Logan would crush her, and it was at that moment, she started to tear up. She heard sniffle as well and he rose up from under her embrace.

He put his hands on her shoulders and stared into her eyes.

"Thank you, Amber," he said.

"I told you not to…"

"I know, but you need to hear it. And you need to know how important you are to me. The thought of losing you…"

"I know, Logan, I know. I can't afford to lose you either, not after this." She got up and started walking towards her mother's car. "I'll see you in the morning?" she asked alluding to the funeral.

"You will," he answered.

She hugged him tight, and he reciprocated with a firm embrace of his own. She found it difficult to separate from him and felt her fingers wisp from his hands as he withdrew to the passenger door of his mother's car. In contrast to the ride to the funeral home before, the drive home felt agonizing. When she got home, she ran upstairs and washed her face. She splashed the water and looked in the mirror. Her face lost its shine; sizable dark bags began forming underneath her eyes. There wasn't enough make-up in the world to cover them up. Her fatigue never appeared to fade. Her skin looked paler than usual. She felt weak, but not just her body. She was falling apart, piece by piece.

She walked back to her room and quickly changed into comfortable clothes and collapsed onto her bed. All the images from the day had lit up in her head, from seeing his friends, classmates, and teachers, to seeing Brayden's family, his younger brother and sister, and Brayden himself. She ran over to a small trashcan by her desk and threw up into it. She wiped her mouth and stumbled into the bathroom again and washed the chunks out of her hair

"Oh forget it." She undressed and hopped in the shower.

The water calmed her down like nothing else could. The warmth of the water seemed to touch her soul. She pressed her head up against the shower wall and closed her eyes.

"I miss you so much, Bray," she mumbled to herself. "And I'm not ready to say goodbye for good."

15

January 29th

(Logan)

For the first time since Brayden's death, Logan awoke in a daze, rather than with a shriek from a horrible nightmare reliving that night. His eyes still felt heavy, but he looked over at the clock to see it read at 7:02. He glanced at his end table to see the pack of sleeping pills half empty. He had started taking them a few days after Brayden's death to get him into deeper sleeps at night. He wasn't hungry. His mom had forced him to eat every day since that night. He sat up on his bed motionless, waiting for time to go by. Then he walked over to his mirror and glanced at various newspaper clippings and headlines from the last two seasons. Much of them had shifted from his individual performances during his freshman season to headlines detailing the tandem success of both he and Brayden. Some articles had already begun writing about the future of the two this year.

"With Lewis entering his swan song at Springvale, and Anderson entering his third and possibly most successful year, could this be the year Springvale ends their championship drought?" one article questioned.

Logan took various clippings about the two of them and placed them atop his dresser. He rummaged through drawers and under his bed before he came across an almost empty silver binder. He took a folder from his backpack and dumped loose papers out of it. He forced the folder through the three rings of the binder. He put all the clippings inside the folder, closed it and placed the binder atop his dresser. Picking through his drawers again, he found a black marker with which he wrote simply, "Bray" on the binder's cover. He smiled for a moment as he ran his fingers across the name. The binder represented Brayden's living legacy. It would serve as a constant reminder of who his best friend was, and to Logan, a symbol that Brayden was never that far away.

By the time he reached Brayden's house that morning on the way to school, he stopped. "This was a mistake."

He looked across the street at the dormant house, waiting for the front door to open and it never did. Brayden wasn't walking out to greet him, wasn't going to walk to school with him, and he wasn't going to slap fives or tell a joke. Every day, there seemed to be a new reminder that he wasn't coming back. He felt his heartbeat increase. Sighing, he finally pulled himself away to keep walking to school. He watched kids flutter into the halls. He pulled his phone out of his pocket and checked the time.

"Shit." He was running later than usual.

It almost seemed like two different years to him. Kids he knew and even those he didn't stared at him as if they had never seen him before, seemingly unsure of how to approach him or what to say to him. It was like the first day of baseball practice in his freshman year where he had scanned the locker room and found no familiar faces aside from Brayden. Now even the most familiar of faces was gone.

He threw his hood over his head and walked down the hall. For the first time in a long time, Logan preferred to fly under the radar instead of appearing at the epicenter of attention.

"Hey! Hey Anderson!" he heard a familiar voice yell. He swiveled his head to find the source.

For a moment, the two locked eyes. Logan squinted before making his way over to where the voice bellowed.

"Anderson, Jesus man. Where have you been?" Connor asked, with a bit of a stilt in his speech. His jaw was probably still recovering from the punch Brayden landed that night.

Logan shoved Connor against a locker, catching the attention of kids in the hall. Connor seemed taken back with Logan, but rather than retaliate, he stayed up against the locker. He didn't even so much as tense up.

"Where have I been? Where have I been?! How can you even ask me that?" Logan yelled as he felt his lips quivering. "My best friend was killed, minutes after you and your buddies tried to jump us. Where have I been, Connor? Brayden is gone."

"Look And...Logan." He sighed. "I am so friggin sorry about Brayden, honestly. Listen, we weren't friends, but I wouldn't ever want that kind of thing to happen to anyone, okay? I'm sorry."

Logan's eyes softened as he looked back at Connor. He scanned Connor's face and saw swelling where Brayden's fist had fractured part of Connor's jaw. Logan relaxed his grip on Connor, though, in truth, Connor could have tossed Logan aside if he really wanted to. Logan didn't say anything back.

Connor shook his head. "Nobody knows what to say to you to make this better, man."

"Make it better?" Logan snapped. "Nothing can make this better. I just...I just want to be left alone, alright?"

Connor extended his hand. "You're gonna have to get over this eventually, kid. But until you do. If you, I guess if you need anything, just let me know, alright?"

Logan looked away. He walked away leaving Connor's hand extended.

As Logan went to walk away, Connor grabbed him and Logan almost swung at him. "I wasn't at the wake or the funeral because." He looked around to see if anyone was listening to them. "Because I couldn't help but feel everything that ended up happening was somehow my fault."

Logan couldn't believe it.

He ran his tongue inside his lip. "It's got nothing to do with you. It's got nothing to do with anyone else. Everyone thinks they're making it better by taking responsibility for what happened to Brayden, but it's not helping. It was an accident okay? It could have happened to any of us. So, do yourself a favor Connor and stop blaming yourself for it."

As he walked away, he turned back around to notice Connor turning to his friends and shrugging. After making it over to his locker and pulling out books he hadn't used in over a week, he made his way to his first class. When he walked in, nobody said a word.

"Logan?" his teacher broke the silence. "Have a seat. Welcome back."

Her sunny disposition did little more than annoy him. He sat and fell in and out of attention as the rest of the class continued.

* * *

After laboring through his first class, he returned to a classroom that he maintained certain closeness with, Mr. Pearsall's English class. Finding his seat in front of Amber, he tossed his books onto his desk. Mr. Pearsall whisked into the classroom as usual and walked over to Logan soon after and exchanged a glance with him.

He leaned over to Logan. "I'm glad to see you Mr. Anderson." He smiled.

"Same."

Mr. Pearsall patted him on the shoulder and moved forward with taking attendance. Logan opened his notebook and started drawing and scratching out random words or phrases just to keep him distracted. He tuned in and out of the lesson.

"Mr. Anderson?" Mr. Pearsall interrupted. "The hood please?"

Logan huffed, removed the hood and put his head down on his desk.

"Logan…" Amber whispered.

He turned slowly to look at her. His eyes felt heavy. His hair sat flat and messy. He exhaled after looking at Amber and turned back around to put his head down back on his desk. She reached in front of her and rubbed his back. The familiarity of that act alone made him feel somewhat calmer. He looked at her again without her noticing. She had seemed so strong through the entire process of Brayden's death and burial. He had only seen her cry a few times, far less than he did.

"What? Is something wrong with my face?" She laughed as she caught his continuous gazes.

He smiled for the first time all day and answered, "There's nothing wrong with you at all," he turned. "Especially with your face."

"That's the Logan I needed to hear," he heard her respond.

The bell rang.

"Logan? A word?" Mr. Pearsall called him over to his desk.

He turned around to Amber. "I'll catch up later." She hugged him and he walked over to Mr. Pearsall's desk.

"How are you doing, Logan?" Mr. Pearsall asked. "I know the transition to coming back can't be easy for you. Is there anything I can do for you?"

"If I had a dollar for every time someone asked me if there was anything they could do…"

"You'd be a fairly wealthy young man," he cut Logan off.

"I think it was a mistake coming back so soon, Mr. P."

"Really? Because I think it was a mistake not coming back sooner."

"What?" Logan asked.

"Don't get me wrong. You have every right to grieve. I know how much Brayden meant to you. I know how much you meant to him. He was a great student of mine, just as he was a great friend and teammate to you, Logan. But what do you think he'd say if he saw you like this right now?"

Logan took a moment. I never thought about that.

Anytime Logan got down about something, whether it came from bad game or lamenting about issues going on at home, Brayden had always put a positive spin on it.

"You're always in your own way man. You have to let shit roll. Tomorrow is another day." Brayden's voice lingered in his mind.

Brayden possessed an optimistic mind. He had never complained. He never once got down. Everything about Brayden revolved around what he felt he needed to do next to break through anything in his way.

"He'd probably whack me upside the head if he saw me like this," Logan admitted. "But he's not..."

"He's not here. I know." Mr. Pearsall bit his lip. "Look, I know what you're going through."

"Nobody knows what I'm going through," Logan replied.

"I lost a good friend in college and I...I did a lot of things I'm not proud of. Remember how I told you I almost dropped out of school? That's why. I lost a good friend, and I wasn't sure how to move on from it. I don't want to see you fall into the same trap that I did. You're a great kid, Logan, with limitless potential. I just don't want to see that potential sour because you're trapped in your own mind."

"I just..." he stopped. "Why am I even telling you any of this? You're my teacher. I just lost my best friend. What can you possibly do for me?"

"Nothing if you don't let me, Logan. Listen, I'm not going to tell you how to figure yourself out. I can't. That's part of being a teacher. That's also part of being someone who has gone through something like this before; I give you the blueprint and you do with it what you will. Just promise me something. If you ever come across something you don't think you can handle, come find me, okay? It doesn't matter if it's before, during, or after class. I'll make time for you."

Logan felt the intensity in his voice; unlike anything Mr. Pearsall had said to him before. He felt sincerity radiating off every word his teacher said to him.

"Okay. I promise. Thanks Mr. P."

"Take care of yourself, Logan. You can get through this. Just remember what he would want from you, okay?"

"Yeah. Thanks. I got it."

* * *

The walk home was lonelier than the walk to school. The chill in the air didn't help. Snow had started to fall before school let out and intensified a bit about halfway through Logan's trek back home. Even the snow annoyed him now. It also brought back horrific memories. He thought about Brayden lying still that night, how his blood had mixed and muddied the snow that had already fallen and covered the pavement.

He walked into an empty house. His mom worked later because of after school activities at the middle school. He sat down on the couch in the living room and couldn't shake a pounding migraine. Sleeping felt like the only way to ease the pain. He walked upstairs to his room, pulled the sleep medication off his desk and swallowed two pills with a small cup of water. He walked back downstairs into the kitchen searching for food or drink to alleviate his headache. Scanning the refrigerator with his eyes, he came upon four bottles of beer on the middle shelf behind the orange juice. He extended his hand for a moment and then pulled back.

He thought for a moment about his mother, remembering how he had said so many disparaging things to her regarding her drinking habit after his father left. He picked the bottle up and gazed at it for a handful of seconds.

"It seems to help you cope," he said aloud.

He wanted to do the same thing, just to see if it worked. He shook his head and put the bottle on the counter, popping the cap off in the process. Logan had never taken a sip of alcohol before. He'd been to parties and around it, but he never found the intrigue in it. He grabbed the bottle by the neck and took a sip. He winced as it ran coarsely down his throat. Choking back a bit, he put the bottle back down and wiped his lips dry.

"It's not…horrible," he remarked to himself before picking the bottle back up.

He took another sip and the beer felt as if it had gone down his throat a bit cleaner. A few more, larger sips followed the first two. Before he knew it, he emptied the bottle. He took a step back. He tossed the empty bottle up in the air and caught it behind his back. He pulled another bottle out of the fridge.

"You can't keep track how much beer is in the house anyway."

The second bottle felt much easier to drink than the first. He did feel his headache start to lift. He went to toss the bottles into the trash before considering what his mom might say finding empty bottles in the garbage.

He stepped into the garage and out the back door to his backyard. He held one bottle in each hand and fired the first into the depths of the woods behind his house. After hearing the bottle smash into the leaves behind the veil of the forest, he tossed the second bottle. He flipped one of the bottle caps like a coin, caught it, and put it in his pocket. After plodding back inside, he fanned his face, feeling hotter than usual. He wobbled into the bathroom and washed his face. He almost felt a sense of paranoia. What would happen if she found out Logan had taken alcohol from her? What would he say? He felt too tired to work up any kind of lie now. He stumbled into his bedroom and sat down at his desk.

He tried to focus on his homework, but his mind kept straying. His mind kept shorting out on him whenever he tried to put a thought towards his work. He felt himself drifting off. His head tilted back in his chair, his eyes closed, and suddenly, he was out.

* * *

He awoke in his bed, wondering how he'd gotten there. What woke him, however, startled him more. Rapid thuds against his window made him wince. He rose up to find what caused it. He opened his window and heard rain pounding away at his house. He rubbed his eyes, slipped into a pair of sneakers, and tossed a hoody over his head. Stepping downstairs, he unlocked and walked out the front door. The rain suddenly dissipated. He stood on his front stoop. He walked down his driveway and into the street, and he heard thunder rumbling. Slowly, he walked up the street and the thunder grew louder, and it began to drizzle. He made his way around the corner, and the storm started to intensify again. He put his hood up and ventured further into the storm. The wind started to howl as he made his way down the block he turned onto from his own. Once he reached the middle of the street, the storm reached an apex.

That's when he felt something else. Heavier thuds pounded the back of his head and on his back. He saw a body lying in the middle of the street. Then, it occurred to him. This is where Brayden had died.

"Bray...Brayden?" he stuttered looking at the body.

The body seemed to be nothing more than a shadow.

He collapsed to his knees in almost the same spot he did when he had tried to keep Brayden focused and alive.

"Wake up. Brayden, wake up!" he pleaded.

Brayden's body sunk into the ground. He ran his hand behind his head and pulled it forward to see the familiar sight of blood staining his hands. He turned his face up to the sky and shrieked.

* * *

He gasped and snapped up, back in his room, on the chair that he'd passed out in hours ago. He looked down at his phone to see 3:12 A.M. illuminating the top of the screen. He pinched his collar between his fingers feeling sweat keeping his shirt glued to his body.

Took the pills too early

They couldn't keep him sleeping through the whole night. Now he sat at his desk wide awake and feeling drowsy and sluggish.

Maybe I can get some work done.

He fumbled around for his desk lamp and flipped it on. Rummaging through his book bag, he pulled out materials from all his classes. He

119

looked at the clock again and sighed. His schoolwork felt easier. For the first time, he felt almost focused.

It only took him about an hour and a half to finish all his schoolwork. He looked at his bed.

"What's the point?" he said as he only had to be up for school in a few hours.

Despite feeling wide-awake, he put his head down on his pillow anyway and tried to fall asleep again. He tossed and turned but couldn't get comfortable.

He pulled his phone off his end table and found Amber's name at the top of his recent messages.

Hey, he sent.

He didn't expect her to be up, but she was the only person who made him feel like himself anymore.

Suddenly his phone vibrated against the wood. *Hi,* the response read.

Can we talk? I had a nightmare.

Of course. What's up?

I dreamt about Brayden dying again.

He told her everything about his dream from almost two hours ago. He slid back down under his blanket. He put his phone back on the end table and rolled over on his side. He heard the phone vibrate again, yet his eyes felt far too heavy to roll back over and check the message. However, he felt like he should. He turned over and picked his phone back up.

I'm going to sleep, goodnight Amber. He moved back over on his side and seconds later, the phone buzzed again. He sighed, growing frustrated and looked at the time before checking the message, nearly 5:15 now. He needed to be up for school in less than two hours.

Goodnight Logan <3

He smiled. He felt stupid for smiling so much after just reading words on a screen in the early hours of the morning. Only Amber could manage to make him feel so embarrassed and happy at the same time in the middle of the night when he knew he should be asleep. He decided he wanted the last word when it came to their conversation.

He reached behind him to get his phone, refusing to turn back to his end table. Feeling the cord of the charger run across his neck he opened the message thread back up.

<3, he replied before putting his phone by his pillow and drifting back to sleep for the rest of the early morning.

16

February 12th

(Amber)

Ever since her father died, birthdays had seemed less important. He'd been gone a year already. Tonight was her seventeenth birthday. Her mother, brother, and Curt had already celebrated with her with a cake in the kitchen and she took her slice up to her room. She ran the sterling silver necklace her mother bought her through her fingers as she sat on her bed. She missed him around her birthday, if only because at least he seemed to care about her birthday, unlike Curt. He didn't sing with the others. He stood there, as if his presence were a gift in itself.

She heard a slight knock on her door.

"It's open!" she yelled from her bed.

The door cracked open, and Michael crept into her room with his hands behind his back. He was a spitting image of her dad: sandy brown hair, and deep green eyes, which contrasted her night black hair and baby blue eyes, which she'd inherited from her mother.

"I got you something!" he exclaimed.

"Oh did you?" she laughed. "I didn't know you had a job!"

"It didn't cost me money! I made it at camp last summer and Mommy helped me finish it!"

From behind his back, the boy pulled a wooden frame haphazardly glued together. Inside, a picture sat behind glass from one of the many trips to the park they had shared over the summer. The picture had caught Michael in mid-swing on the playground with Amber behind him, pushing.

"When did this…who took this picture, Michael?"

"Brayden did! He gave it to mommy a few months ago!"

Of course it was Brayden. Why wouldn't it be? Brayden was there with his younger brother and sister. Logan was there too, and he was much happier then. It seemed like it was forever ago. She held it out in front of her and a tear ran down her face.

"Michael, this is the best gift I've ever received," she stuttered.

"You like it?" he replied.

"I love it. I love you. Thank you so much." She squeezed him as hard as she could and kissed him on the forehead.

"Happy Birthday, Amber. I love you too!"

"It's going right here by my bed, so I can look at it every morning and every night."

The boy nodded. She hugged and kissed him again. Suddenly, she heard a large amount of shouting from downstairs.

"Michael, I need you to stay here, okay? I'm going to go see what's going on."

"I'm coming with you."

"No. Just stay here. Promise me," she answered.

"I promise," he groaned.

She opened her bedroom door to try to hear what her mom and Curt were arguing about this time. Their arguments always seemed so menial to her and their fights always escalated to shouting matches. The honeymoon phase of their dating had run its course. She followed the handrail down the stairs and into the living room. They argued about Curt not wanting to be at the house for Amber's birthday.

"You didn't have to come if you didn't want to be here for her!" Amber's mom yelled.

"I wanted to be here for you, and for her!" Curt screamed back.

"Well, you could've at least acted like it then! My children are the most important people in this world to me, the most important things I have in my life, and they're more important to me than any man will ever be!"

Curt reached for her. "I'm sorry, just calm down, baby."

"Don't touch me!" She slapped his arms out of the way.

He grabbed her arm and turned it to restrain her, which prompted Amber to jump into the middle of it, and amidst the chaos, Curt swung his arm back and knocked Amber against an end table.

"Don't put your hands on her!" Amber shouted, rising back to her feet

"Amber, please! Go back upstairs, honey," her mother cried.

"Yeah, listen to your mother and go back upstairs, sweetheart," Curt followed.

"Don't talk to me like you're my father! Don't talk like you're anyone important to me," she snapped back. "And if you put your hands on me or anyone in this house again, I'm going to call the police." She picked up the phone fighting back tears.

"Okay! Okay. Look, I'm not gonna hurt anyone, dear. Just calm down." He backed away.

"I want him to leave, Mom, and I want him to leave now."

"You should leave, Curt," Amber's mom echoed.

"Melanie, you can't be serious," he growled. "Can't we just talk about this?"

"You heard what my daughter said. Leave, now."

He stood as Amber continued to grip the phone in her hand. She massaged her hip. Curt finally snatched his jacket off the recliner and walked towards the door.

He stopped as he grabbed the doorknob. "Happy friggin' birthday," he snarled and slammed the door behind him.

"Are you all right, Mom?"

Her mother sighed. "I'm fine, honey. Are you okay? Are you hurt?"

She ran her hand along the bruise. "No...no I'm not. I'm fine. I'm just glad he's gone. I don't want him here anymore. Please, mom. He's not right for you!"

"Amber...sweetie, it's complicated," she answered as Curt's truck could be heard peeling out of the driveway.

"No it isn't! Mom, I know that you've been hurt since Dad died, but rushing into things with him is only going to make things worse!" Tears streamed down her face.

"You don't know what it's like having lost the only man you've ever loved!" her mother shouted.

"You're right! I don't. I do know what it's like to feel guilty about wishing Dad was gone all the time but never thinking in a million years that he'd ACTUALLY be gone. I never got to say goodbye to him, and I never will. Despite all the yelling and all the times he smacked me around for doing things he didn't like, I never wanted him to die!"

"I'm sorry, sweetheart. I didn't want your birthday to be like this...I'm so sorry." She sat down on the couch and buried her head in her hands.

"Amber?" she heard a gentle voice from the staircase.

"Oh God," she gasped. "I thought I told you to stay upstairs."

"I wasn't gonna let him hurt you..." Michael whimpered.

"Come here, buddy." She extended her arms out and ran over to him. "Let's get you to bed. It's late." She looked over at her mother. "I love you, Mom. Goodnight."

She walked Michael to his room and got him ready for bed. After tucking him in, she smiled and left briefly. She brought the slice of cake from her room to Michael.

"Usually, Mom and I both don't like you having sugar before bed…but! It's my birthday, so if I say you can have cake before bed, you can have cake before bed!"

"I knew there was a reason why I kept you around," the boy replied.

"Thank you for the picture, Michael. It really was the best gift I've ever received."

"You're the best gift I have too, Amber," the boy answered.

She kissed him on the head. As soon as she closed his bedroom door, she felt her arms shaking. She walked to her room, closed her door, collapsed against it and began to sob. Her hip throbbed from how she landed, and a bruise developed near her shoulder. She threw a light sweater on and fell back again. She just wanted to cry for the rest of the night. She ran her fingers through her hair and down her face as the tears continued to flow. A knock startled her.

"I really don't want to talk right now, Mom." She sniffled from the floor.

"Amber, it's Logan."

She gasped. "Logan? It's really not a good time. I'm sorry."

"Then when is a good time? Your birthday's almost over."

"Logan…I'm sorry. It's just…it's been a hard night."

She heard him grunt and felt the floor shake as he hit the ground.

"Well, I'm gonna sit out here, until it's a good time for me to come in," he answered.

She knew he wouldn't go away anytime soon. She sat curled up with her head resting on her knees as she continued to cry from earlier in the night. She could feel Logan on the other side of the door, waiting. Finally, ten minutes after telling him to go away, she rose up off the ground. She took a deep breath, wiped the remaining tears from her eyes, and opened the door. She poked her head out and found him nodding off on the wall beside the door. He came to rather fast, shuffled up to his feet, and brushed his hair back. He looked a little better than he'd looked the past few days. His hair had spiked up like it used to, and he looked put together with a collared shirt and pressed jeans.

"I…um…Happy Birthday!" he blurted as he pulled a tiny box from behind his back.

"What's this?"

"Just…open it!"

She stood with her mouth agape. Inside the box sat a sterling silver bracelet that matched her necklace. At the forefront of the bracelet sat a brilliant violet stone.

"I had to do a little research to get the right stone." He laughed.

"Logan...how did you...where did you get the money for this?"

"I had a little help from a friend. Let's just leave it at that."

Thanks, Bray.

"It's...Logan it's beautiful, but why?"

"Well...I know your dad's anniversary just passed. I wasn't sure how good of a birthday you'd have and seeing how you wouldn't let me in your room for almost half an hour." He ran his finger down her cheek. "And that make-up smudged by your eyes, I'd say I was right."

She blushed. "I'm sorry about...well, this." She waved her hands in front of herself.

"What happened tonight?"

"It's a long story." She sighed.

"All your stories are long, but I still want to hear it." His eyes darted past her. "And I have an idea."

She raised an eyebrow and watched him. He moved towards her window. He opened it, popped the screen out, placed it underneath and sat on the windowsill.

"Yep! This'll definitely work," he spoke to himself.

She laughed. "What's going to 'definitely work?'"

He waved her over to him.

"Here, take my hand, I'll prop you out. Grab that branch and from there grab the edge of the roof and climb up."

"Are you crazy?! What if I fall?"

"If you slip, which you won't! I'll catch you."

She grabbed Logan's hand and reversed positions with him. She stretched her arm out and squeaked as she grabbed the branch. She hopped out onto it as she felt his hands leave her. She took a deep breath and looked up at her rooftop. She reached out to the edge of the rooftop and took a leap of faith. Her foot slid on the side, she screamed, but felt Logan's hand beneath her propping her up, and she climbed the rest of the way.

"There! That's wasn't so hard, was it?" He laughed.

"Shut up and get up here!"

She moved away from the edge of the rooftop and watched as Logan scaled the roof effortlessly. It was cold, but not a single cloud floated in the sky and the stars shone in abundance.

"It's beautiful." She smiled.

"You gonna tell me what's wrong now?"

"Sure, but first, come here." She lay on the rooftop.

She put her head on his chest and placed her arms under his back and across his abdomen and proceeded to explain to him everything that happened earlier in the night with her mother and Curt.

"He's lucky I wasn't there," Logan said.

"What would you have done?"

"Given the mood I'm in? Who really knows? But he'd regret putting his hands on you or your mom."

Amber laughed it off. After she finished telling the story, she turned her head to the sky.

"See that?" Logan opened out of nowhere.

She looked at him.

"The stars. See them twinkling? They're talking to each other."

"Logan...they-"

"About us. They're gossiping about us!"

She laughed. "Oh, and why would the stars be talking about us?"

He got up from underneath her. "They're jealous of us."

"Why would the stars be jealous of us, Logan?"

"Because..." he stopped. "Because despite their brilliance, they can't ever replicate the light and beauty between you and me."

"Logan!"

He curled his tongue inside his lips. "Amber...I." He leaned closer to her.

When his lips met hers, her eyes shut tight. She wrapped her arms around him, pulled away, gasped, and reopened her eyes. He flopped down and she followed him. He rolled her on top of him. Placing her hands alongside his shoulders, she stared into his hazel eyes. She leaned in for another kiss and he reciprocated by tilting his head up.

"The stars are really going to have something to talk about now!" She laughed.

She flipped back over by his side, snuggled up close to him, and glanced down at her wrist. The moonlight bounced around through the amethyst stone on her bracelet and appeared to transform it into a dark red as she raised her arm to the sky. For the moment, everything the two of them had endured over the last month seemed years away. She felt as if her heart were about to burst out of her chest from it beating so fast. The electricity from the kiss went through her, radiated through her chest, and felt like it would burst out of her fingertips. There was no weight of despair. She felt like a kid again.

"Look," he said pointing up to the sky once again.

She looked up and spotted two stars, seeming as if they shined brighter than the rest.

"Our stars," she said in awe.

"I think so. If not, it doesn't matter because they're ours now."

"Always pick the best and brightest to be yours, right?"

He nodded. "Yep. Those are our stars, and our destinies."

"We should find a third for him." She felt sadness stirring in her chest.

"How about that one?" He pointed up and it took her a moment to find the one he singled out.

Then she found it, sitting up and off to the right of the two they picked out for themselves.

"It's perfect," she said closing her eyes to fight back tears.

He looked over at her and wiped the tears out of her eyes.

"Looks like you were wrong," she said. "This is the best birthday I ever had."

She leaned over, kissed him on the cheek, and rested her head on his chest again. He turned in towards her and looked at her.

"I've waited ever since I crashed into the hallway with you that day last year..." He paused. "I've been wrestling with my feelings ever since that day, trying to figure out if I would be making a mistake trying to allow myself to fall for you. The more I asked myself, the more the answer kept coming back the same. It's like...I don't know...it's like I was waiting for a reason to talk myself out of it, but sitting up here with you, and looking into those beautiful blue eyes, I know there is no reason good enough to keep me from showing you how much I care about you."

"You did a good job," she replied. "I wasn't sure I would or could ever be good enough for you, so I just did my best to be the best friend I could to you, and then all this happened with Brayden..."

"I know," he cut her off. "I just realize now that you're more than a best friend. You're the best person in my life, period. You're beautiful. I don't just mean your eyes that I can get lost in for weeks, or your hair, which is as elegant as it is long, or the most stunning smile I've seen on any girl I've ever met. You're gorgeous. I mean your mind, body, spirit, and your soul. You're the most caring and generous person I know, and I'd be an idiot to try to find a reason not to be with you. Brayden helped me realize that."

"Logan...I-"

"The only thing I want to know, is…if you have a reason to not be with me?"

She bit her lip. She knew what she wanted to say but wasn't sure how to say it. She choked on her words and felt her throat dry up.

Finally, she gained her composure. "There's not a reason in the world I can find to not be with you, Logan."

He smiled as wide as she could ever remember. "Thank God. 'Cause then I would have had to throw you off the roof." He laughed as he stood up.

"Logan Anderson! You take that back!"

He wrapped his arms around her and backed her towards the edge of the roof.

"It would have gone something like this…"

"Logan!" she shrieked.

"But then again." He picked her up and turned her back towards the middle of the roof. "You didn't say no."

She nudged her head against him and looked up. He shrugged and they shared another kiss under the stars. She stood up on her toes, wrapped her arms over his shoulders and looked at the bracelet again. She rested her head on him, never wanting to let go. Logan was where she felt he belonged, right by her side.

"Okay, how do we get down?" she asked him.

"Easy. I'll help you this time."

He guided her back to the branch. She climbed through the window and Logan followed soon after.

"Hey, Logan?"

"Yeah?"

"It's late. Why don't you just spend the night here?"

"You sure your mom would be okay with that?"

"My mom loves you. You're sleeping on the floor though!"

He laughed. "Okay. Fair enough."

He kicked his shoes off as she pulled a crimson throw blanket from the end of her bed, a black comforter from her closet and placed them on the ground. She grabbed a handful of pillows off her bed as well.

"Sorry! It's the best I can do," she lamented.

"It's more than enough. Do I get a goodnight kiss at least?"

She smiled. "You get a kiss anytime you want one."

"Sounds like quite a perk. I knew there wasn't any good reason not to try this."

She leaned off her bed and planted another long kiss on his lips.

"Goodnight, Logan, and thank you again…for all of this. It's all so perfect."

"Goodnight, Amber. Trust me. Nothing in life is perfect, but you sure make it hard to keep thinking that."

She pushed him down onto the floor and stepped over him to get ready for bed. She walked to Michael's room to find her brother sound asleep. She pecked him on the cheek. Soon after, she went into the bathroom to wash the rest of the make-up off her face, temporarily reminding her of all the drama that surrounded her earlier in the night. Then, she looked at the necklace from her mother and the bracelet from Logan. After walking back to her room, she pulled a white t-shirt from her drawer and threw it on. She looked down at Logan.

As she put her head down on her pillow, she glanced over at the picture. Logan mentioned earlier about how bright her spirit was. Her little brother gave her that light. The simple, messy wooden picture frame from her brother stood as the best birthday gift she received. She looked at the picture and into Michael's eyes in the photo and then to her own. She brushed her jet-black hair out of her face and clutched the picture in her arms before putting it back on the nightstand.

"I love you baby brother."

She took one last look at Logan, who was already asleep, which surprised her. She knew Logan kept having problems sleeping ever since Brayden had died, so she figured the emotion he rode on must have knocked him out once he came down from it.

"Goodnight beautiful boy," she said in his direction before putting her head down to sleep.

17

March 27th

(Logan)

His vision blurred. He had skipped final period in favor of heading to the locker room for the first game of the season. He pulled a half-empty water bottle out of his locker and took a swig, wincing as it went down his throat. When he fully opened his eyes, he saw a shadow towering over top of him with a hand out.

"You gonna take my hand or are you just gonna lay there like a punk?" the figure boomed.

"What?" Logan's eyes widened as the figure revealed more of himself.

"Well, you gonna sit on your ass, or take my hand and get up?" the broad-shouldered boy demanded.

"You…you can't be real," Logan whimpered.

He rubbed his eyes, yet the figure remained. His hands trembled by his side as he scanned every inch of the person in front of him. The shadow stood a bit over six feet and stared a hole through Logan's soul with pitch black eyes. That body was recognizable at any time. It was Brayden, who retracted his arms and crossed them.

"You're not real. You're dead Brayden," Logan cried.

"Am I? The look on your face says something totally different."

"What…why…why are you doing this to me?" Logan snapped.

"Look at you, Logan. This isn't you, man. Skipping class, drinking, using meds to sleep…You gotta start letting go, kid."

"How?"

"By knocking this shit off before you go down a path nobody will be able to follow, and by getting off your ass and taking my hand."

Brayden extended his arm out again. Logan looked up and down and noticed bruises on Brayden's face and cuts all along his arms, where his body skidded down the street. It was almost as if the corpse got off the ground and animated in front of him.

"This? Nah, these are just cosmetic," Brayden said pointing to the cuts. He pulled his shirt up to reveal a stomach-turning bruise and deeper cuts on his abdomen. "This is the one. It took my breath, and I couldn't get it back. Not to mention my brain getting scrambled."

"I miss you, Brayden. This is always gonna hurt," Logan said as a tear fell down his cheek.

"I miss you too, man. Trust me. This wasn't the plan. I miss everyone…my mom, my dad, Julian, Angela, Amber, everyone." Brayden looked down.

"They all miss you too. I wish you could come back," Logan answered.

"It doesn't work like that, kid. It's a one-way trip."

"You booked a flight way too soon, Bray. Why'd you have to go?"

"Yeah…sorry about that. The big man in the sky bought the ticket in advance. Look man, you're gonna snap out this. I'm gone, okay? I'm never coming back. So just take my damn hand, get ready for the game, and kill it like I know you can. I hope you find peace soon, little brother. I just don't want you to mess up everything you have right now."

Logan didn't answer.

"You can, and you will. I love you, Logan. I'm never too far away, I'm right here." He pointed to Logan's heart. "And you already know I'm in the stars," he said looking up.

As he went to reach for Brayden's hand, he found nothing but thin air, and Brayden's figure vanished. He stumbled and crashed into a locker behind where Brayden's figure stood. He pounded the locker several times and screamed so loudly that anyone in the gym might hear him. With tears in his eyes, he turned around and stood against the locker before slumping down on the ground.

His teammates would be arriving soon. He tried to shake the headache and the nausea. He walked over to his locker and his number 24 Springvale jersey hung there. The arm injury from last year seemed like years ago.

"Gotta start off strong," he said to himself.

It would also be his first game without Brayden. As he began changing into his uniform, Coach Stevenson walked into the locker room. Logan slammed his locker shut upon seeing his coach enter.

"Anderson, you're super early, aren't you?"

"Excited to start the season, Coach," Logan lied.

"Well, I suppose there's no point in putting this in your locker. Catch." He tossed Logan the game ball for the start of the season.

Logan tossed the ball up and caught it before putting it in his locker. Coach Stevenson retreated to his office and Logan stood alone once again. He looked across the locker room at Brayden's locker, which wasn't empty. The team had left tiny mementos and notes to Brayden. His number 12 still hung in the locker. Logan took it out and laid it over his lap. He pulled various newspaper clipping out as he had done each of the prior two seasons. He started putting them in Brayden's locker and dropped to a knee.

"I know you're not here, but I could really use your guidance out there today, man. I miss you. I love you," he said to himself.

The rest of the team began to file in shortly after, and Logan perked his head up. He started seeing familiar faces and felt the team's energy starting to fill his body. With everything that had happened to Brayden, Logan wasn't in as good a shape as he usually wanted to be by the time the season started. Kneeling in front of Brayden's locker, though, instilled confidence in him. He smiled.

"Hey, Logan," a scrawny, shaggy haired kid said.

"Hey Jake. What's up?" Logan answered.

Jake Mitchell had been Brayden's back-up for the last three years. He'd never played much because of Brayden's durability and reliability. He only stood a few inches taller than Logan did. He kept brushing his thick black hair out of his face while talking to Logan.

"What's. Up. Jake?" Logan asked again more sternly this time.

"Oh, oh, nothing. Just wanted to make sure you were okay with, you know, me being behind the plate," he said with a lilt in his voice.

"Don't have much of a choice," Logan said with an empty laugh. "Don't worry. Everything is gonna be fine, as long as you call the game the way I want you to."

He patted Jake on the back. The rest of the team circled around Brayden's locker.

"We lost a captain and a brother over the winter," John Stevenson said. "But we're gonna go out there today and win one, no, win them all for Brayden."

The team roared with approval and ran out onto the field. Jake stayed behind as well.

"Hey, Logan, everyone is going out. Let's go!" Jake slapped Logan on the back.

Logan glared.

"Yeah, sorry," he said as he took his cap off.

Logan huffed. *How am I going to do this without you?*

He shook himself and took a deep breath before putting his hat on. He picked up Brayden's jersey and rushed out onto the field. Once he reached the field, he felt right at home again. He looked out into the sea of cheering people and found Amber front and center behind the Springvale dugout. He smiled at her and she reciprocated his look with a wave and a confident nod.

Before taking the mound, he noticed another group of people in the stands. Brayden's mother, father, brother and sister were all in the crowd as well. Logan felt his heart flutter because they were there to see him play, to see him carry on. He ran over into the crowd. Upon entering the stands, he waded through the sea of people to Brayden's family. He patted Julian on the head and shared a long hug with both of Brayden's parents before kissing Angela on the forehead.

"Logan?" Brayden's father interjected before Logan ran down.

Logan looked back at Brayden's father, and they locked eyes for a moment.

"Go out there and do what you do best," he said with a confident smile.

Logan nodded and mouthed the words, "Thank you." He smiled as he trotted back to the field.

He took the mound as if he'd never left it. His face turned into his familiar scowl, and he began stretching before throwing warm up pitches. His fastball felt a touch slower than last year, but it felt good to throw again. The first batter stepped into the batter's box to start the season. Logan looked into the dugout to see Brayden's jersey and in a way, felt as if Brayden was there with him, guiding him. Jake threw down the familiar one finger to the inside, indicating Logan's set-up fastball. Logan wound up and fired the fastball near the chest of the batter, who stumbled out of the way. After one pitch, he found himself in a rhythm.

He threw a curveball on his second pitch that hung over the plate. The batter put a good swing on it and lined it into right field for the first hit of the game. Logan grimaced as he took the ball back. He walked the next batter on five pitches and suddenly, found himself in a first inning jam. Coach Stevenson and Jake jogged out to the mound to check up on Logan.

"You okay, Anderson?" Coach Stevenson asked.

"I'm fine," Logan answered. The same, "I'm fine" he'd been using for months.

He felt a weight on his shoulders.

"Alright, well, get your head on straight and get out of this." He patted Logan on the shoulders and walked back to the dugout.

Logan managed to strike the next better out on four pitches.

The strikeout calmed him a bit, but he shook his arm. He fired the first pitch of the next at bat too far inside and it hit the batter in the back, loading the bases with only one out.

"God damn it!" he yelled drawing smiles from some opposing players.

On the very first pitch of the next at-bat, the batter smashed the ball past the shortstop and into left-center field, allowing two runs to score. Logan snatched the ball from John before taking the mound again.

He fired another pitch inside to the next batter and hit him in the leg, loading the bases once again.

"24! That's a warning," the umpire scolded.

Logan barely gave the umpire a nod before the next batter stepped in. Out of the corner of his eye, he saw Coach Stevenson talking to one of the relief pitchers on team.

"Are you fucking kidding me?" he said to himself.

He looked into the stands and saw Amber's face. He tried to regain focus.

Jake put down two fingers for a curveball to start the next at-bat, and Logan acknowledged it. Instead of throwing the curve, Logan fired a fastball that struck the batter in the head and knocked him flat on his back drawing a collective gasp from the crowd. Before the umpire could even say anything, Logan threw his glove up in the air and started to walk off the mound.

"That's it! 24! You're done!" The umpire motioned to eject Logan from the game.

Logan just waved him off without looking at him or saying a word.

"What a baby!" one of the opposing players shouted from the dugout.

"Looks like the superstar can't handle a bad game," said another.

Logan kept his head down as he walked back to the locker room, not even taking a glance at the kid he struck with the pitch.

"What the hell were you doing out there, Anderson?" Coach Stevenson roared. "We'll talk after the game is over. Hit the showers."

Logan said nothing, grabbed his bag and walked off the field towards the locker room. A loud thud followed as he flung his glove into the side of the lockers.

He kicked his locker and put a small dent in the front of it. He sat down on the bench in front of his locker, buried his head in his hands, and started to sob. He heard footsteps through the halls.

"Get away! I'm not talking right now!" he screamed into the emptiness.

To his surprise, Amber walked in from the shadows of the hallway. She sat down beside him.

"What happened?" she questioned.

"I don't...I don't know. I lost myself out there. I lost my mind," Logan replied.

She leaned in closely. "Logan, your breath, it stinks. Were you drinking before the game?"

"I..." he sighed before opening his locker and showed her the bottle he had sipped on earlier.

"Logan! You need to stop, before you do something you're going to regret!" she yelled snatching the bottle out of his hand.

"I can't just stop, Amber! Don't you get that? This...it's the only thing that makes me feel somewhat better!" He tried to grab it back from her.

"No. You don't need this to make you feel better," she snapped pulling the bottle away. "What would Brayden think if he saw you right now?"

He laughed, remembering the encounter with "Brayden" earlier in the day.

"I don't know what's happening to you, but I don't like it. I don't like it at all." She started to cry.

He had seen her cry, but never because of him.

"Can I have the bottle, please?"

She shook her head and walked past him. She walked into the bathroom and dumped the rest of the bottle's contents down the sink. After she tossed the bottle in the trash, he leaned in for a kiss.

"I really don't want to kiss you right now."

"Kiss on the cheek then?" he asked.

"I'm sorry. I can't." She backed away. "But, promise me you'll call me later and we'll talk about all of this? About you?" she pleaded with him.

He sighed and nodded. "Yeah, sure. I can't leave the locker room, but you go enjoy the rest of the game, okay?"

He watched her hair sway and merge with the darkness in the hallway, leaving him alone once again. He itched for a drink. He sat back against his locker, which he just put a fresh dent in and leaned his head backwards. Once again, though, he heard footsteps approaching again.

"What now?"

This time, an elderly man limped his way into the locker room. Logan stood up recognizing Principal Stewart. He walked in with a freshly pressed charcoal suit. The light bounced off his bald- head as he made his way over to Logan. Logan only met the principal a handful of times, but never in a situation like this.

"How are you doing Logan?" he asked rather warmly. "We have some things to discuss young man."

"Yes…yes sir," Logan replied from a distance.

"What happened out there, son?" the principal inquired.

"I lost my cool, sir. I don't want to use my current mind state as an excuse for my actions. I acted inappropriately. I realize that. I realize I also represent more than my team and myself; I represent the school. I get that."

"I'm glad you recognize that, son. We all know you're still trying to find a way to overcome the loss of Mr. Lewis. Our whole school grieved that brilliant young man, but you did touch upon that your loss does not excuse you from unacceptable actions." He sat beside Logan. "Of course, it's up to your coach to decide the best course of action. If it were up to me, and if you looked deep inside yourself, the baseball field may not be the best place for you right now."

Logan wanted to argue, but realized he had no grounds to. "What are you saying?"

"I think you need to consider sitting the season out or at least taking the next few games off." He stood back up. "You need to sort out what's going on inside you. You know we have counselors available if you need them, guidance and grief. We have some of the best."

"I know. Thank you."

Logan had only seen the grief counselor once, more or less as an introduction at the behest of Mr. P. Maybe Principal Stewart was right. As much as he thought baseball could be a sanctuary, maybe it was just driving him down a darker path. Every time he looked behind the plate at Jake, he saw a hole where Brayden used to be. Every pitch, every look was a reminder of who he lost.

"Let this be a lesson to you, young man," the principal reprimanded. "You represent our school out there on that field. You cannot act out the way you did today. I'm aware of what tragedy you've gone through in the past few months. You are one of our best and brightest student athletes, Logan, and you represent both of those words so well. I don't want your potential to disappear."

"I'm sorry sir. It won't happen again," Logan replied.

"You're right. It won't. Or you won't be playing for this school any longer," Principal Stewart admonished. "My sympathies for your loss, but you need to get your head on straight, young man."

"How many people are going to tell me I need to get my head on straight?" He pounded the bench as the principal left the room.

The team started to fill the locker room with a sour mood. Springvale had lost the game by eight runs.

"Hey man," Jake said.

"Not a word," Logan snapped back.

"Dude…" John Stevenson said.

"You saw just as well as everyone else. I talked to the principal already. It's a done deal. He told me I should sit out the season. As far as I'm concerned, he's the only one I need to explain anything to at this point."

"Wrong," Coach interrupted. "Come here, Logan."

He never called him that.

"Did Stewart talk to you yet?" Coach asked.

"Do you agree with him?"

"It doesn't really matter if I do or don't, Logan. What matters is if you agree with him," Coach Stevenson answered. "But for what it's worth? I think he went easy on you."

"What?"

"In my ten plus years coaching this program, I've never seen a player blow up like that Logan. You could have done some serious damage to that young man."

Logan never even thought about the kid that he struck with the ball.

"That kid was out for a pretty long time. He came to eventually, but it was scary there for a second."

"Holy shit," Logan said stunned.

He didn't even look at the kid he struck, laying in the batter's box. He was too absorbed in his own frustration to think about it. It didn't help that he was being heckled by the opposing players, with no idea of what he was going through. It went beyond a tantrum. All the anger, sadness and confusion that the last couple of months had filled him with came out at that moment. It went beyond a few wild pitches and a couple of hits. In a weird way, that baseball was the only thing he could control. He just took it all out on the last person who deserved it.

He glanced over at Brayden's locker.

"I am so, so sorry Coach," Logan said.

"Don't apologize to me. Apologize to them."

Coach Stevenson introduced the young man's parents into the locker room. Logan bit his lip as he looked up at the boy's family.

"Logan, this is Mr. and Mrs. Grant. Their son, David, was the one you hit with the pitch."

"Mr. and Mrs. Grant..." Logan stuttered. "Is your son okay? I am so sorry. I didn't mean to...no, that's not right. I..."

"It's okay, Logan," Mrs. Grant said.

Logan perked his head up.

"Coach Stevenson talked to us about what happened to your friend," Mr. Grant said. "And if it were me, I wouldn't even be playing baseball or going to school."

"My grief isn't an excuse to hurt other people," Logan interrupted. "With all due respect, sir, I appreciate your sympathy, but I don't need it. I hope your son isn't hurt. I lost my cool. It was unacceptable and I'm sorry. I know I can't take it back, but this is the first and last time I'll do anything like that ever again."

"It's okay," Mrs. Grant said as she patted Logan on the shoulders.

"Guys," he said to his teammates. "I'm sorry I let you down. Coach, I'm sorry I put you in this position and again, Mr. and Mrs. Grant, I am so sorry about Dave. Let him know, okay?"

David's parents nodded almost in unison and left the locker room. Logan changed back into his regular clothes and left soon after. Wading into the parking lot, he stumbled upon Brayden's family again.

Speaking of letting people down.

Seeing Brayden's father made him want to cry after all the confidence Mr. Lewis instilled in Logan before the game started.

"Logan..."

"Before you ask me what happened, I just lost myself out there Mr. Lewis." Logan cut him off.

He looked down at Julian, who, now with his head shaved, looked like a smaller version of Brayden.

Mr. Lewis placed his hands firmly on Logan's shoulders. "It's just one game, Logan," he reminded Logan much as Brayden used to after a bad start.

"I know. I just...I lost control, and it scares me, Mr. Lewis," Logan replied.

"You'll get there son. It takes time. Believe me. It wasn't easy for us to come here, but we want to support you more than anything else. It'll take some time to figure out, but you'll get through this stronger than ever."

"Everyone seems so sure about that, but I don't know how."

"Because we all know what he would expect from you, and deep down, you know too."

"Thanks, Mr. Lewis. I'm going to do better. I'm sorry for letting everyone down."

"You aren't letting anyone down, Logan. We're all here for you."

Julian and Angela jogged over to hug Logan as they used to embrace Brayden after a game, win or lose.

"Sorry you guys lost, Logan," Julian said.

Logan smiled. "It's okay. There's always next time, right?"

"Right!" the boy replied.

Though Logan knew there was no way he'd play the next game, maybe even longer.

I'll fix this.

Staring into that little boy's eyes ignited something inside Logan. Deep down, he knew that he couldn't stay trapped in his own mind. The more he looked at everyone around him, the more it felt like he was the last one to start moving on. Everyone kept telling him what he needed to do to move on. But how was he supposed to do that?

18

April 14th
(Amber)

Logan had taken the advice of the principal, the coach, well, almost everyone around him and stopped playing baseball after his blow-up a few weeks ago. Amber knew it was eating him up not being on the field, but it gave him more time to heal. She managed to help him substitute the time away by having him come over a few days after school to play catch with Michael. It gave Logan the chance to have a ball in his hand and have a sense of normalcy without the pressure of being on a field and looking towards a catcher that wasn't Brayden. It also gave Michael another older sibling in a way.

"Okay, so, a curveball. You want to put two of your fingers along the seam like this," Logan said guiding Michael's fingers on the ball. "You put your thumb here and when you throw it, whip your wrist to make it spin!" Logan tossed his glove to Amber. "Would my lovely assistant like to catch?"

She smiled and rolled her eyes. "Sure." She walked across from her brother and stuck the glove out in front of her face.

"You know if he bounces it, it's gonna hit you right in the shins, right?" Logan said standing behind her. He put his hands on her shoulders and guided her to a crouching position. "Let it rip!"

Michael nodded and wound up. He did exactly as Logan said as the ball left his hands. He bounced it, but it curved just as Logan promised. Amber's eyes widened as the ball careened towards her, but she stuck her glove out in just the right spot. She didn't catch it, but she did knock it down before it hit her.

"And you didn't even flinch." Logan sounded amazed.

"I can handle a baseball," she joked back.

"Did it curve?" Michael asked excitedly.

"It sure did! Not bad for your first one," Logan answered.

Amber tossed the ball back to Michael and he continued throwing back and forth with her as Logan watched and coached them both as if they were on the baseball team themselves.

"How about you give it a shot?" Logan asked Amber.

"Oh no, no. I can't do that!"

"If your ten-year-old brother can do it, I think you can manage. You heard what I told him right?"

He tossed the ball to her, and she handed the glove back to him.

Two fingers on the seam

"And your thumb." He guided her hand. "Underneath like this…"

"And whip the wrist when I throw." She smiled.

He nodded and crouched down next to Michael. She did her best to mimic Logan from all his games. She giggled a bit trying to obtain his familiar scowl and she squinted her eyes as he gave her makeshift signals from his crouching position. She even came set as Logan would on a mound. Then, she took her hand off the ball to brush her hair out of her face.

"Balk!" Logan shouted.

"What?"

"Balk. You can't take your hand off the ball once you're set. Runner?" He pointed to Michael. "Advance."

Michael ran around Amber and stood behind her.

"Well, now you have a runner on second, bottom of the ninth. Two strikes. What is Amber Donovan going to do?" He smiled as he dropped back into the crouch.

She settled back into her stance and ran her fingers over the ball again, remembering each step. She wound up and flicked her hand over her head. The ball curved nicely and didn't even hit the ground before landing in Logan's glove.

"Striiiiiiike THREE!" Logan yelled acting as catcher and umpire.

He ran over, gave her a big hug and kissed her on the forehead. Michael joined in also. Amber broke away from Logan to sweep her brother off his feet and to the ground.

"Are you guys in love yet?" Michael pestered. He constantly asked Amber if she and Logan were in love.

Amber let off a wry smile. "I like him a lot, that's for sure."

"She's okay," Logan said rolling his eyes.

She pushed him away and laughed.

"I'm gonna head home now. Talk to you later?" he said standing up.

"Always."

He hugged and kissed her again. He gave Michael a one armed hugged and waved as he trotted into the road to walk back to his house. As cheesy as it seemed, she really did hate seeing him leave after they spent time

141

together. She always tried to make the most of their time and did everything she could to make life seem a bit more normal. Not being able to see what he was doing at home or when he was home alone kept her anxious. Even though he gave her his word that he'd start working on his problems with drinking and taking the sleep medication at night, she always had to wonder about how much ground he was making up.

Just as she and Michael were turning in to go inside, her mom's car pulled into the driveway.

"Long day at work?" Amber asked before seeing her mom wasn't her usual jovial self. She seemed stern, or rather, upset by something. "Mom?"

She followed her mom into the house and watched her sit all her things on the table. She kept her head down and her eyes focused, never once looking at either of the kids.

"I broke things off with Curt," her mother said.

Part of her wanted to scream and jump for joy, but she knew that wasn't the best thing to do. "Mom, I know you really liked him…"

"No, I know what you're thinking honey," she interrupted. "You're happy. You're also not wrong. I don't think he was quite as right for me as I might have thought. The last couple months have showed me that."

Ever since the blow up on the night of her birthday, things hadn't quite been the same with Curt. He didn't come around as much and whenever he did, the whole nice, "aw shucks" guy routine was all but over. He was bitter most of the time, angry the rest of it. He didn't pretend to be nice to Michael or Amber anymore. He grew just as tired of them as Amber had grown of him.

"Well, I'm glad you figured that out for yourself. I really am sorry it didn't work out though."

"It's probably for the best, Amber." She sat down on the living room couch. "Maybe you were right all along. Maybe I was rushing too much into things after your father."

In that moment, it felt like her heart stopped. She thought about herself and Logan. Was this a similar thing? Were they only getting close and getting together because of where their emotions had been the past few months? She hated thinking it, but she didn't realize it until just now how easily her mother had fallen for Curt coming off her father's death. Then she thought about the night on the roof and how everything had fallen into place so perfectly for them, right down to a gift Logan had given her with Brayden's help.

"Do you think Logan and I are making a mistake?" She blurted out from her thoughts.

"What? Sweetheart, no! You two kids are match made for each other. I think you two were going to be with one another regardless of the circumstances that brought it about. You think it's the same thing, don't you?"

Amber sat down next to her mom. "It's hard not to, based on what you said about Curt and about dad. I just think that, would we be as willing to be as close if Brayden hadn't have died? Doesn't that kind of deface his death in a way?"

Her mother hugged her. "Sweetie don't think that those two things have anything to do with one another. Brayden always knew you two would end up together. He tried orchestrating it on more than one occasion. He wanted it and deep down, you and Logan both did too. The timing may not have been ideal, but there's a key difference between what you and Logan have and what I thought me and Curt had."

Amber perked her head up.

"You know one another and always have. Even though you spent some time apart. You trust each other with everything. Trust and knowledge are two of the most important things in any relationship. And damn it if you kids don't have chemistry that just radiates off you."

Amber smiled. "Thanks mom. I'm sorry. I just, with everything going on…it makes me confused sometimes."

"I'm just glad you're comfortable talking to me."

"Me too." She kissed her mom on the cheek and went upstairs to her room.

It was true. The last couple of years had made Amber and her mom closer than ever. They always had shared a bond, but when her father died and Amber started becoming more independent, she became more comfortable talking to her mother about anything and everything. She was thankful that Curt would no longer hover over her or her family. She also knew how those things worked out and she doubted it was the last time any of them would see him. Too often, her mother wavered on her convictions. She thought back to her birthday and her mother had never stood to Curt or anyone in her life in quite some time before then.

You're turning a corner mom.

She tossed her phone onto her bed and grabbed a notebook from her dresser. Brayden had spent many lunches teaching Amber how to draw

143

better. Brayden liked art, so she made him draw a picture of himself, Amber and Logan this past year. Brayden had answered by drawing three simple stick figures of them and putting them in a cartoon-looking house. After he passed, that silly picture possessed so much more meaning.

Rummaging through her folders and books from school, she found the stick figure picture and put it next to her notebook. She started a brand-new image, using everything Brayden had taught her about art and drawing.

"Faces aren't that hard if you know what to look for." She heard Brayden's words in her head. *"People altogether aren't that hard. Just pick the feature that stands out most and start there."*

She tried to construct a more complete image. She drew herself first. She even glanced across the room in her mirror to capture an accurate image of herself. She decided to recreate the night of Brayden's birthday at the park. Every stroke of the pencil felt as if she were bringing the memory back to life. Gazing at herself in the picture transported her back there. She had sat with her legs crossed hanging over the beat-up dugout ledge looking up to the sky and the moonlight had bounced off her eyes. Her hair had cascaded in a braid past her shoulders, and she smiled recreating the black and white dress she hadn't put on since that night.

"It doesn't matter."

Next, she tried to draw Logan. She started with his face. Long before his sleep problems, his face was flawless. She recreated his spiky auburn hair almost strand for strand. She even gave him a signature smile that he had once carried. She drew the black polo shirt and the dark blue jeans he wore that night underneath his Springvale Baseball sweatshirt. Instead of drawing him facing her, she positioned Logan looking at Brayden.

"You used to be so happy."

She drew Brayden sitting upon the dugout with his arm over the top of his knee. She used two different shades of brown to differentiate his skin from his deep, dark brown eyes.

He always wore his hat backwards, she remembered. Instead of looking up at the sky, she positioned his head looking down, deep in thought.

She took a deep breath and looked at her creation.

"Not perfect, but it's something," she muttered to herself.

Before she put the drawing away, she pulled out her pencil again. On the bottom, she wrote, "For Bray," before going back to the image of Brayden. She started to sketch angel's wings for him. The right wing spread far over Logan's head and the left touched the edge of the paper. One of the first objects Brayden had taught Amber how to draw with detail were wings.

"You'd think wings were easy," his voice rang in her head. *"But there are different kinds. Birds, monsters, and of course, angels."*

She remembered all the layers of feathers to create the most realistic wings possible. The wings possessed such detail by the time she finished; they seemed far more accurate compared to the rest of the picture.

"My angel," she said running her fingers across Brayden in the picture. "I'll see you again someday."

She clutched the picture in her arms and put it on her end table. It helped her cope more than anything did. She liked to imagine him as a guardian of sorts watching out for both her and Logan. She could think of nobody better to keep her safe than Brayden. He had every trait she could want in a guardian: attentive, caring, big and most of all, strong.

"You make sure you keep him safe too, okay?" she asked looking up at the ceiling.

Her phone buzzed. It was Logan telling her that he got home okay.

I had fun today with you guys

I'm glad

I need that kind of stuff sometimes. It helps keep my mind off everything else.

I know. It helps me too. Michael really likes you <3 Mom and Curt broke up.

You're prob happy about that lol. Is she okay?

I can tell she's a bit hurt but it's better for her in the long run, ya know?

Yeah. Your mom is great. She deserves someone better than that guy.

Not everyone can be as lucky as me I guess

You can say that again ;)

I'm gonna go help mom with dinner. I'll text you in a bit. <3

Ok. Talk later <3 Bye! Tell your mom I said hi!!

He sounded good through texts. He smiled and laughed more today than he had in quite a while. She was grateful for the days that he walked, talked and acted as he did before Brayden's death. As much as she wanted to believe in Logan, she knew that he'd need just a little extra push to get back to being himself. She still wasn't sure how he'd react getting back onto a baseball field or seeing little things that reminded of him Brayden. He still had a long way to go. She got off her bed and walked to her door to go to help her mother get dinner ready.

She touched the doorknob and looked up again. "Please, please keep him safe."

145

19

April 24th

(Logan)

Before going into the locker room, he reached into his bag and took a pack of two pills out. He stood for a second before tossing them in the trash outside of the gym. Nights had become longer, sleep became scarce, headaches had rampaged on through his psyche, and nightmares became more terrifying than ever, which often resulted in him awakening in a shriek. He endured, however, and since the day he stepped away from the team, he refused to ease his sleeplessness with pills or cure his sorrow with alcohol. He walked into the locker room as if he were a freshman again. He stood before his teammates, bag in hand, all the while scanning the floor.

"Hey coach," he said walking past his teammates, most of who paused at him entering.

"Anderson! How have you been?" Coach Stevenson asked looking at Logan dressed in his uniform minus the jersey.

"I was actually thinking about coming back in and playing today, if that's okay with you guys."

"That's funny," a voice said from behind him. It was John Stevenson. "We had a little heads up that you'd be back today. It's good to have you back. Why don't you check your locker?" he said with a wry smile.

"My locker?"

When he made his way to it, he took a deep breath and opened it. He gazed at his jersey hanging and the game ball placed underneath it. Beneath the game ball, however, he found a small slip of paper. A few of his teammates peered over his shoulder.

Dear Logan, it began.

I won't see you before the game, but I wanted to let you know that I'm proud of you for taking the time to try to better yourself for the past few weeks. Everybody sees it. Your friends and teammates see it, your teachers see it, your coach sees it, and I see it. Just know your hard work isn't going unnoticed and now it's time for you to reclaim everything you once had. I told you that you're one of the strongest and brightest people I know. Despite everything, I still believe that, and I never wavered, not once. Before I get silly and too sentimental, I just want to say one more thing: Strike a few people out for me; try to win, and more importantly, HAVE FUN!

Love, Amber.

"She told me to put it in there before you showed up." John came from behind Logan. "You two have quite the thing going, eh Anderson?"

Logan's face got hot as he folded the note up and put it beside his glove. "Yeah. She's alright. Hey, listen up everyone. I have something to say," he paused. "Every time I look at you guys, I expect one more face to be here, and he isn't." He sighed looking at Brayden's locker. "At the same time though…he is here. He's here in how we perform out there. Most of us played with Bray, learned from him, and channeled his spirit and energy for every game we played. I lost sight of that when I lost him, but I get it now. So, that being said, let's go get back on track for him, because we both made a promise to win a damn banner and as long as I'm still here, I'm going to fulfill that promise for both of us."

The team chanted and roared. Everyone rushed onto the field and Logan took a moment. Before walking out to the field, Logan swung by the coach's office and swiped a marker off his desk. On the outside of the wrist of his glove, he scribbled "AD" before flipping the glove over to the inside and writing "BL" underneath the palm. He pulled his phone from his locker, snapped a quick picture sent it to Amber, and ran to the field before ever receiving a reply. He met Amber by a fence down the first baseline and received a quick kiss much to the delight of the rest of the team who showered the two with whistles and cheers.

Logan met Jake on the mound. "This time, it's different. I'm gunning for control. No messing around. Okay?" he said to Jake.

"Yeah. I got you Logan. No worries."

He bowed his head and muttered to himself, "Bray, I need all the strength you can give me right now. Please. I gotta get through this game."

Suddenly, he felt a shiver shoot down his spine that forced his eyes to snap open.

"Thanks Bray."

After stretching his arm out, he began to toss back and forth with Jake before taking the mound for warmups. His pitches felt crisp coming from his hand. It felt far different from the last time he took the field. He felt as if he finally had control.

"Play ball!" the umpire shouted following the final warm up pitch.

The eyes of the first batter told Logan everything. His eyes darted from the plate, to Logan, to his team's dugout, and back to Logan again, wavering. Before Logan even came set to pitch, the batter stepped outside the box and wiped his sweat on his grey and purple jersey before tightening his batting gloves and returning to the box.

Jake ran out to the mound after getting his signals mixed.

"What's wrong?" Logan asked.

"This kid is scared to death of you. Word gets around. They think you're a headhunter."

"Well, okay. Let's use that! I'll put one right down the pipe. He won't even think about swinging."

Jake returned behind the plate. Logan came set and fired a fastball right down the heart of the plate for a strike.

"Strike!" the umpire yelled.

The strike call from the umpire felt like beautiful music to Logan. He needed that first pitch to be a strike. Two more pitches followed; he threw one fastball and followed with a devastating curveball that the batter waved at and missed.

He heard the crowd erupt. Following the strikeout, a fly out to left field and a line out to the first basemen on just five additional pitches ended the inning.

"Good friggin' inning Anderson!" his coach cheered.

Springvale plated three runs to jump out to an early lead. That lead took more pressure off. He felt more and more like Logan Anderson of old. He struck out two more batters after surrendering a weak hit to shallow right field. He peered over his shoulder at the runner, flipped around and fired into the waiting glove of his first baseman, picking the runner off and ending the inning. He pumped his fist before pointing to the sky and shouting at the top of his lungs.

As the top of the third inning began, a violent slider completed Logan's fourth strikeout in less than three innings of work so far. He called Jake back out to the mound.

"What's up?"

"Why don't we go back to the old way?" Logan asked.

"But, this seems to be working. You sure you want to change it up now?"

"I'm sure. Just go with me. The old way. Fastball, high and tight."

Jake nodded and ran back behind the plate again.

He flung the first fastball far enough inside to back the next batter off the plate. He followed up with a slider biting away from the hitter just kissing the outside corner of the plate.

148

"Strike one!"

He shook off a few calls for a fastball and slider before settling on throwing a curve, which, despite bouncing in front of the plate, fooled the batter enough to force him to swing for strike two. Logan stared in for what he anticipated would be his fifth strikeout of the game. Jake put down one finger for a fastball, but Logan shook it off. Following that came two fingers for a curve, which again Logan shook off. Logan twirled his hand asking Jake to reset the signs.

Jake threw a one, a two, a one, and finally a three. Logan nodded after he saw the three, deciding to attack with another slider. Logan wound up and fired.

Something went wrong. It felt like a rubber band stretched and snapped inside his elbow. The slider sputtered off the mound before bouncing into the ground and settling near the first base line as Logan yelped. His right arm dropped to his side and his eyes widened. Breathing rapidly, he dropped to a knee as his coaches and teammates ran to him.

"Logan? What happened son? What happened?" Coach Stevenson shouted.

"I…I don't…I don't know." Logan said biting his lip between breaths. "It felt like something just popped…I don't know coach."

"Can you hold a ball?" Coach Stevenson signaled for a ball.

Logan gripped the ball and tried to raise it, but his arm went numb, from his hand to his elbow. Coach put his arm around Logan and walked him to the locker room with Logan's glove in his hand.

"No. Let me hold it," Logan said waving with his left arm.

Logan sat down in front of his locker gasping for breath, trying not to cry. It wasn't the pain, which subsided for numbness when his arm remained still. It was the waterfall of images flooding to him and the frustration more than the pain. He wiped his eyes with his left hand. He wasn't crying, not yet at least. Logan's mother followed him off the field into the locker room.

"What happened to him?" his mother asked.

"Best guess? He tore something in his elbow, but it's hard to say for sure," Coach Stevenson answered. "But you ought to get him to a doctor as soon as possible."

"But, what about the rest of the game?" Logan said almost in tears.

"Don't worry about that son. Go get that looked at."

"Mind if I take a ride with you?" Amber's voice came from behind.

Logan nodded and got into the back seat of the car with Amber, who held his left hand. He wanted to cry. He noticed small bruising developing on the inside of his elbow.

He let out a breathless chuckle. "This would happen when I decide to play again." He sniffled.

"Don't worry about baseball right now," Amber chastised him. "Let's just get through this first, okay?"

He felt nauseous from the pain and from feeling as if someone punched him in the stomach.

"Logan…you're hurt. You're upset. I underst…"

"It's the whole one step forward, two steps back thing, you know?" He pulled away from her a bit. "I just don't know how I can keep bouncing back from this shit."

"You can! And you will! And I'll help you! But please, let's just get past this first." She gripped his hand tighter.

He looked down at his injured arm.

"Maybe you weren't ready to fly just yet," she said. "But you'll fly faster when this is all over."

He sighed and let his head fall against the window; his lip continued to quiver. The last time he had stepped foot inside the Springvale Medical Center he followed Brayden who lay upon a gurney as paramedics rushed him to surgery to try to save his life. He winced walking through the entrance of the emergency room. He backed away towards the doors.

"No, no. Come on," Amber said rubbing his back.

A nurse took Logan aside in a separate room.

"What happened?" she asked.

"I was, um…I was playing baseball. I threw the ball and felt like, a um, a pop," he said between staggered breaths.

"Any allergies to medication we need to know about?"

"Not that I know about."

"Have you had a history with smoking?"

"No."

"Do you have a history with alcohol?" she asked again. "Sorry just a cautionary thing."

He paused. "No."

"Okay. That's all we need. The doctor will be with you in fifteen or so. Have a seat and keep your arm elevated until he can see you."

150

Returning to the lobby, he sat beside Amber as his mother sat across from him. Amber gave him her sweater to rest his arm on until the doctor called him back. He struggled to get comfortable, but every time he moved his arm, pain would shoot through him. He felt the same chill that shot up his spine on the mound earlier and snapped his head around, but nobody stood there at all. He rubbed his eyes.

"Losing my mind," he said to himself.

"What?" Amber asked.

"Nothing."

"Logan Anderson?" he heard a voice bellow from the emergency room doors.

He stood up, kissed Amber on the forehead and followed his mother towards the doctor.

"We meet again, young man," the doctor said.

To Logan's surprise, the same doctor who had treated his ribs the night of the accident greeted him now. Seeing the steely-eyed old physician again raised his anxiety. He exhaled a small laugh and nodded following the doctor back to the examination room.

"So, you heard a pop? Okay. Well, let's get an X-Ray done and see if you broke something. It'll hurt a bit, but I need your arm at certain angles to get the right photos."

The doctor led Logan into a room and gave him a lead apron to put on.

"I just need to sit still for a handful of minutes while I take the pictures, Logan. We've been through this before. You'll do fine."

"With all due respect, this is much more painful than my ribs," Logan said.

The machine whizzed and beeped and before he knew it, the X-Rays were over. The doctor instructed Logan to sit and wait once again.

"Alright, let's take a look at these pictures!" The doctor opened. "Well, the good news is, there isn't any bone damage or dislocations."

"Bad news always follows good news."

"The bad news is I want to get you in for an MRI tomorrow because I believe the damage to be in your ligaments. You can schedule that with the receptionist when you leave."

"What do you think? Just based on your knowledge," Logan's mother asked.

"If I had to guess, I would assume there's some sort of tear in your elbow. The MRI will give us a scope of how severe it is. For now, I want to immobilize that arm to keep your pain at a minimum Logan."

The doctor put Logan's arm in a sling.

"Try not to move that much tonight, okay?"

He looked at his injured arm. Tomorrow, he'd find out for sure just how much damage he did to his elbow.

* * *

A torn Ulnar Collateral Ligament, that's what the MRI showed. In other words, a ligament in his elbow came right off the moment he threw that ill-fated slider. The only way to fix it, the doctors told him, was with surgery. He wasn't sure how long he was out for the surgery, but it was the most peaceful sleep he'd had in months. There were no bad dreams. There was no waking in a sweat or with rapid breaths. There was nothing. His eyes opened. He glanced around the room at the team of doctors with Dr. Armstead, the surgeon, front and center.

"Take it easy." He heard the voice of Dr. Armstead. "Just stay still for a little."

He felt a pulsing, throbbing ache in his elbow, which caused him to glance at it. He looked at the bloody rags on a tray beside where he laid. He looked over at the covered wound on his elbow, resisting the urge to move it much. He also noticed stiches in his left wrist.

"All done Mr. Anderson!" Dr. Armstead remarked. "It went as well as we could have hoped!"

Logan flinched from the pain while trying to regain himself.

"If you can sit up, we have to get you molded for a cast that you'll have to wear. It's going to be uncomfortable and bulky, but we need to give those tendons time, and we can't risk any unnecessary motion, because then you'll be right back here again, and I'm sure you don't want that."

"Just do what you have to do." Logan replied.

Dr. Armstead wasn't lying. The cast kept Logan from moving his right arm.

How am I supposed to do anything in this thing?

"I sent over the scripts for Vicodin and Percocet to the pharmacy you have on record. Take them as needed, okay?"

The pain now felt sharp, but he tried his best to put up with it.

"You did really well, through all this Logan. You're a strong young man." Dr. Armstead remarked.

Not as strong as you think, he thought. "Thank you, Dr. Armstead."

Hours after making it home, he took to one of the painkillers Dr. Armstead prescribed him to ease the sharp pain in his elbow. He almost tried to move it, but due to the monstrous cast, it wasn't possible.

He punched his desk with his good hand. "I can't move with this thing on. This is stupid."

"It's only going to be for a week. I can help!" Amber had come over after he settled in at home.

He dumped one of the white Vicodin pills out of the bottle and swigged a cup of water behind it. He wanted to rip the cast off and move his arm but knew he couldn't.

"Logan..." Amber started to say something.

"Don't start. I'm fine," he snapped back.

"I know. I just..."

"You just what?"

"I worry about you sometimes. I have worried about you."

"Worry for what? The pill thing? The drinking thing?"

"I know you're still hurt, and I don't mean your arm."

"Look at me Amber." He waved his arm in front of himself. "I'm broken inside and now outside. I keep telling myself everything that you tell me. 'Things are gonna get better Logan. Just keep trying. You'll get better.' But you know what?" He stood up off his chair. "Nothing is getting better. In fact, things are just getting worse. My nightmares got worse. I don't sleep. I barely eat. Now I screwed my arm up. How exactly are things getting better? My best friend is dead. I won't even be able to throw a baseball for probably a year."

"I care," Amber interrupted. "Stop acting like nobody cares Logan."

"You're the only one then," Logan replied.

"No. Mr. Pearsall cares. Brayden's family still cares. Your mom cares!"

"Good one," he chuckled.

"Why do I feel like you're shooting everything down before even considering it?"

"Because I see what's going on in my life every day, and as much as you're a part of it, you don't, and you sure as Hell don't know what I'm thinking all the time."

"Stop feeling so beaten before you even hear what it might take to get better!" she yelled.

153

Amber almost never raised her voice with Logan. This was their first real argument.

"You know what? I just want to lie down for a couple hours. I'm tired," he said.

"So, what, you want me to go?"

"You do whatever you want. Stay. Go. It doesn't matter to me."

She tilted her head. "I'm going to stay for a while. I don't want to leave you right now."

"Suit yourself."

He tried to get his shirt off but struggled. Amber walked over to try to help him.

"I got it!" he yelled.

She stepped back.

Holding his shirt in his hand, he sighed. "Amber...I'm sorry. I just..."

"Don't worry about it. It's fine," she cut him off.

He reached out for her. "Amber I'm sorry. I don't mean to take it out on you. I don't."

"Then don't. It's pretty simple."

"Tough love?"

"When you need it."

"Well, what I need is to get this tank top on. Can you help me, please?"

"You're not going to snap at me this time?"

He shook his head. She helped him on to his bed and set up a bunch of pillows to not only make him comfortable in bed, but to keep his arm elevated.

"Anything else?" She used a mock-nurse voice.

"Oh, no, I can take it from here nurse," he responded. "On second thought..." He reached up with his good arm and pulled her next to him. "I still have one good arm at least."

She snuggled up close to him. "You'll have two soon enough."

He kissed her forehead. The Vicodin hit him hard. After his head hit the pillow, drowsiness soon followed. He looked at Amber and her eyes seemed to sparkle. His fingers from his good arm interlocked with hers and he looked at the bracelet he gave her for her birthday, their first night together. His mind flashed back to the day at the jewelry store with Brayden. Brayden was "the friend" Logan mentioned the night he gave it to her, which to this day he never revealed, even though she probably knew. He wasn't sure he would ever tell her Brayden had helped him buy it. That

154

silly promise he made Brayden seemed to carry so much more weight with Brayden gone now. Brayden did so many things for Logan that Logan could never repay.

"Logan?" Amber woke him up from his stupor.

"Hm?"

"I love you, never forget that."

"That's...the first time you've ever said that to me."

"I know, but I was saving it for a time when I felt you really needed to hear it, and I think you really need to hear it right now."

"I was wrong before. You do always know what I'm thinking. I definitely needed to hear that right now." He smiled and kissed her. "I love you too."

"Oh yeah? That's the first time you've ever said that to me too." She gripped his hand tighter.

"I know. I've never said it to any girl I've dated. I was saving it for the girl that it was meant for."

"I'm that girl?"

"Amber. You've been that girl since third grade."

They kissed once more, and she rested her head on his shoulder. He looked down at her and then glanced over at the binder with the memories he packed inside between him and Brayden.

"Thank you," he whispered to Brayden as he closed his eyes.

He held a sleepy Amber with his one good arm.

"I promise," he said quietly. "I'm going to take care of her. I'm going to take care of your family. I'm going to take care of myself."

The three most important things in Brayden's life.

"I won't let you down anymore," Logan whispered aloud as both he and Amber drifted to sleep.

20

May 16th

(Amber)

Amber's mom rushed into her room, looking all dressed up and in a panic. Amber was lying on her bed reading.

"Do I look okay?"

Amber's head perked up. "You look fine as always!" She smiled. "What's the occasion though?"

Her mother hesitated.

"Don't say it."

"Curt's coming over."

Amber rolled onto her back and sat up. "Are you kidding me? I thought things were JUST starting to get back to normal with you, and us. After the stuff that happened on my birthday, you're just going to bring him back?"

"We have been talking here and there, and I think he means it when he says he was sorry, and things got out of hand that night. He's apologized over and over but I told him the person he needs to apologize to is you."

Amber froze for a moment. "What makes you think I'm going to accept his apology? Or accept him back into the house for that matter?"

Her mother sat down on her bed. "I know it's not easy. You're my daughter and I know what you're thinking. I know you think this is the same pattern as your father. That I never saw him for what he was and kept letting him come back."

Amber scooted back.

"But... and I can't explain it to you, but something about Curt feels different. I truly don't believe he comes from a bad place. Maybe you're just…"

"You're actually defending him." Amber laughed. "Fine. Whatever. I'm sure he's already on his way, so I don't have much of a choice. You just told me out of courtesy. I get it."

"Just try to keep an open mind about it?"

"No promises!"

After her mom left, Amber had half a mind to call Logan and talk to him about it, but he had his own things to worry about with his arm healing on top of everything else that was going on in his head. No, this was something she had to handle on her own. She thought back to her birthday and how Curt seemed so aggressive and angry. Her mom was wrong. It wasn't just her birthday. It was the nights of shouting over small things, and they weren't even living together. It was the occasional glances he would throw Amber's way whenever she walked by that didn't quite seem right with her. Now, she was stuck between making her mom happy and protecting her family's best interests. Curt was no doubt a charming man. He had a way of sounding confident and kind.

Instead of talking to Logan, she walked down the hall to talk to the only other person she truly trusted. She knocked on Michael's door.

"Hey, can I come in?"

"Mhm." His eyes were fixed on the TV.

"Did mommy come and talk to you?"

"No. Is everything okay?" He was observant for such a young boy.

"Um, Mom invited Curt over tonight. He'll be here in a few minutes I guess."

"I thought him and Mommy had a fight."

Amber laughed. "They've had a few fights, but I remember the one you're talking about. Do you want him to come here?"

The usually boisterous boy was quiet for a few seconds longer than Amber expected. She had a feeling of what he was going to say.

"Is he going to hurt you again?"

Amber bit her lip thinking about the words she was about to utter. "I don't think he meant to hurt me that night. I think it was an accident."

"So, he won't do it anymore?"

"I'd like to think that he wouldn't."

"I think it's okay for him to come over."

Amber smiled and nodded. "Okay. Thank you, Michael."

As she walked back to her bedroom, she heard the doorbell ring. She made her way to the stairs and treaded down. She watched from the stairs as her mom opened the door and sure enough, Curt was there wearing his disarming smile. He looked past her mother and looked right at Amber. Instead of a tense moment, he waved to her and smiled. Almost without thinking, she waved back, which spooked her.

What are you doing?

He kissed her mother on the cheek and sat down on her father's recliner. She didn't stick around long enough to hear them talking or doing. It didn't matter. He was there. It was only a matter of time before he made his way to her room to try for his apology that she was prepared to listen to

157

but likely wouldn't accept. Apologies don't mean anything without actions behind them and there was nothing he could prove to her at that moment that could show her his apology could be anything more than words.

Almost like clockwork, there was a knock on her door. She waited for a few minutes. The knock came again.

"Come in."

He walked in with his Carhartt and black jeans.

"Didn't you wear that same get-up the first night you and mom went out?"

"You remember that?" He laughed. "I figured it was a lucky outfit for me."

"What do you want?" She said in an ice-cold voice.

He took a deep breath and sighed. "How do I even navigate this without making you upset with me?"

She stayed silent.

He popped his lips. "Right. Uh." He rubbed the back of his head. "What happened on your birthday, I am so sorry that things escalated that way. I'm sorry you got caught in the middle and I sincerely apologize for you getting knocked down. I never wanted everything to get so out of control."

You're sorry for me getting knocked down? "Thank you, Curt. But you make it just sound like this unfortunate thing that happened. You practically caused the whole situation."

"You're right."

That answer took her by surprise.

"I had too much to drink, which I hadn't done in a long time, and it made me think about my ex-wife and the fact that I had no kids of my own to celebrate birthdays with. I took it out on you and your mother, and I am sorry for that."

His sudden vulnerability resonated with her. "Wow, Curt, I…I didn't know."

"I'm sorry I put my hands on you. I know how much that probably upset you and reminded you of your father."

She winced slightly at him even mentioning her father.

"I don't see any pictures of him around. He was that bad, was he?"

She nodded. "Worse than that bad, yeah. He did his best to ruin my life before it even got started. At least, that's how it seemed."

He walked around her room but didn't repeat the mistake of sitting on her bed. She watched him carefully, with less of a guard, but still carefully.

"Curt, I don't want you to think that I feel like you're on the same level as my dad." She bit her lip. "I never prayed for you to die." A stray tear leaked from her eye.

He took that moment to sit on her bed, but she didn't move away from him. He pulled a fast-food napkin from his jacket pocket and handed it to her. She whispered a thank you.

"I hope you understand though," she paused. "I appreciate you coming up here and apologizing and I think you really do mean it, but I can't fully trust you, not yet. I'm sorry."

He tried to put his arm around her for a hug.

She pulled away. "No, still no. We're not there."

He rolled his tongue inside his mouth, seemingly put off by that. "I get it. I get it." He rose off her bed and stood in the doorway. "I hope in time, you will see less of him in me, and we can make something of our relationship yet."

"Have a goodnight, Curt." She didn't answer him directly.

When he closed the door behind him upon his exit, she breathed deep. He was sincere. There was no doubt about that. She still didn't feel completely comfortable with him being around. It was almost like going back to square one. She looked around her room, at all the pictures on her wall and on her desk. It was her mom. It was Michael. On her nightstand, it was Logan and Brayden. There was no space for a father figure.

She hopped off her bed, dropped to the floor and rummaged underneath it. She pulled a picture frame out. Trapped in the frame was the only photograph Amber took with just her father. She couldn't have been older than five years old. It was Christmas and she wouldn't take a picture with Santa by herself. She cried and held up the line at the mall because she was so scared. Her father came up, took her hand and told her that it was okay to cry, that *big girls are allowed to cry*.

She put the picture down. One of the pieces of advice she gave to Brayden's sister after his funeral came from her father of all people, and she didn't even realize it at the time. He took her hand that day and led her to Santa and there were no more tears. That may have been the last time that he stopped her from crying instead of making her cry. Another knock on her door broke her out of her reminiscing.

"Amber, it's mom."

159

"Come in." She slid the picture back under her bed and wiped her eyes.

Her mother walked in and sat down on her bed. "Did everything go okay with Curt?"

"I mean, what do you mean okay? He apologized and I believed him, but I still don't fully trust him. It's hard to get rid of certain things. You should know that about me more than anyone."

"Amber?" Her mom must have noticed her eyes. "Were you…crying?"

"Just a loose tear. It wasn't Curt. Believe me," She laughed. "You would have known if it was."

"Then what?" her mother prodded.

She glanced down. "It's nothing, really. Just thinking about stuff. You know, Logan and dad, different things!" She smiled. "I'll be okay. Don't worry."

"Okay. Thank you for trying to give Curt a chance again. I promise I won't have any tolerance for him hurting you or Michael."

"Or you, mom." Amber cut her off. "You can't let him hurt you either. I won't let him."

Her mother hugged her tightly. "You are a strong young woman, Amber. You've been strong for this family, for Logan, for Brayden and his family. Don't forget to be strong for yourself too though."

"Thanks mom." Amber squeezed tight.

Her mother kissed her on the forehead. "He's not staying the night." She walked towards the doorway. "Goodnight sweetheart. Love you."

"Love you too. 'Night."

She got off the bed and shut the lights off, only leaving the lamp on her nightstand on. She reached back under to look at the Christmas photo of her and her father.

"One day I'll say goodbye properly," she said to herself. "But I can't, not yet."

-21-

June 2nd
(Logan)

It had been a little over a month, the hard cast was off, and he looked down at his arm in a sling, looking lifeless. He had skipped out on the game today. Day after day, going to practice and sitting, going to games and sitting, it had worn him down. His arm twitched and he winced. He pulled the painkillers from his drawer and walked into the bathroom to wash down a couple pills. His phone rang from his room, and he raised his brow. When he looked down at the name that flashed, he hesitated. He let the phone buzz in his hands a few times before he finally accepted the call.

"Hello?"

"How are you doing, son?"

"I'm fine, dad."

"Your mom called and told me about what happened. Are you sure you're okay?"

Logan pulled the phone from his ears and rolled his eyes. "Yeah, I'm fine. Dad, I got hurt a month ago, and you're calling me now?"

"Just wanted to see how you were. I figured I'd give you some time, some space to recover a bit."

Logan chuckled away from the speaker.

His dad released a heavy sigh. "Logan, we never got to talk about, you know, what happened with me and your mom. I just wanted to know if you had any questions or anything to say."

If only his dad knew what he wanted to say. "Nope. I came to peace with that a while ago. You and mom went your separate ways. I get it. Don't worry about it. It happens."

"You're sure?"

"Yeah, dad. I'm sure."

"When did the docs say you'll be back out there?"

"Don't know."

"How's school?"

"Fine."

He felt his father pause. "Well, alright. I, um, I guess that's about it."

"Alright."

"Love you, buddy. Never forget that alright?"

"Yep. Love you too dad."

The call ended almost too fast. Logan sat down on his bed, not blinking. He looked down at his phone and shook his head. The first time his father had reached out since his parents' divorce and the call ended after a few minutes. Brayden never came up. It had been a national story. There's no way his dad wouldn't have known. The only two things that ever seemed to come up between them were school and baseball. He picked his phone up and walked out of his room.

"Mom! I'm going out for a bit. I'll be home a little later."

She didn't answer.

"Okay, see you then."

The breeze was light, and the Sun shone high above his head. Sometimes he walked into town and back. Other days, he'd walk all the way to the school and back, anything to get out of the house and maybe out of his head. Many days though, he spent time in the woods, at the abandoned little cabin. He had managed to keep the alcohol out of his life. The painkillers made him feel good. Maybe he had taken a few more than he needed to on certain days, but he had kept it under control. He hadn't seen a sleeping pill since he tossed the last pack last month. He turned towards his backyard, thinking about the cabin again. He stopped in his tracks. It wasn't the time for solitude. He turned towards the street and headed down.

Cars passed by. Some of the drivers honked. It seemed like the whole community was watching him at times. He was a star and a name in his own right. After Brayden died, the community tried to rally around Logan, not knowing they might be losing him as well, or maybe they already had. He passed by the house every day. Sometimes he said hi to Mr. or Mrs. Lewis if they were outside, or he'd wave if he could see them in the window, but he hadn't gone inside since the day after the funeral.

He knocked on the door and kicked the stoop. Nobody came to answer. He peeked inside the window and saw a shadow move through the kitchen. Maybe nobody heard him. He looked over to the side of the door and rang the doorbell instead of knocking again. He heard footsteps heading towards the door and it opened. Mrs. Lewis stood with as bright a smile as Logan could remember.

"Logan! How are you sweetheart? Come in please." She waved him inside the house.

He walked in and looked around. The house was clean as always and he heard the TV on in the kids' room.

162

"What brings you by Logan? Is everything okay? Sit please."

He sat on the couch, using his good arm to guide him down to it. "Everything is fine, really. I just, um, I wanted to come by and see you guys."

"Kids! Come out here! Logan is over to visit!" Mrs. Lewis shouted into the hall. "Richard isn't home from work yet. You're more than welcome to stay as long as you'd like though."

Only Angela ran out into the living room and hugged Logan. Logan grunted as she knocked his arm.

"Angela! You know Logan is hurt still," his mother scolded.

"Sorry Logan!"

Logan laughed. "It's alright. Hey, where's your brother?"

"He's not feeling so good. Come play with us Logan!" Angela grabbed his hand and led him down the hallway.

He looked back at Mrs. Lewis. "Is he alright?"

"He misses Brayden. Go on ahead. He'll be happy to see you."

As he approached the kids' room, he glanced to the left and saw Brayden's room, with the door still open.

"Hey, I'll catch up with you guys in a minute, okay?"

"Did you want to go in?" Mrs. Lewis asked.

Logan nodded. He walked into Brayden's room and looked around. He had been in Brayden's room a couple of times, but never really LOOKED at it. His mother kept the bed neat, as if waiting for him to come home and sleep in it. There were posters all over the wall of Derek Jeter, Ken Griffey Jr. Barry Bonds, and a baseball behind glass, in a case high up on a shelf that only Brayden or his father would be able to reach. The ball was decades old, and the nearly faded ink read, *Best Wishes. Jackie Robinson.*

"Brayden's grandfather got that ball at a Dodgers game many years ago."

"Brayden, he, he never told me about this! This is amazing."

"That ball hasn't left that shelf since the day Brayden was born. It sat up there at the old apartment and only left that spot when we broke the case down to move here."

"There's so much cool stuff here that I never got the chance to really look at."

Logan kept walking around Brayden's room as if it was a museum. He was careful not to move anything out of place or disrupt anything. He looked at the papers stacked on Brayden's dresser, not unlike the mess he

163

left back home. Logan noticed the letter from the manager of the Syracuse baseball team welcoming him to the team next year. On top of that was a letter of condolence from the university to Brayden's parents. His bat sat tucked up against his bookcase, which admittedly didn't have very many books on it, but tons of memorabilia and baseball almanacs.

Brayden's closet was half-empty.

"We were thinking about putting Julian in here when he gets a little older and when he's comfortable."

Logan let out a breath. "What are you gonna do with all of Bray's stuff?"

"Oh, we'll put it away. Some of it we might sell or donate. These are things Logan. Yes, they're Brayden's things but all the memories we have of our son are in the photos, the memories. Those are the things you can't replace. We'll keep his jersey, his baseball things, keep his clothes so hopefully Julian grows into them."

"How are the kids? How are you?"

Mrs. Lewis sat on Brayden's bed and ironed the blanket with her hand. "There was a good period of time where either Richard or I couldn't even come into this room. We could hardly look at family photos, even the sight of the children filled us with grief."

A tear rolled down her cheek. "We miss Brayden. That will never go away, and in times like this, when you lose a child, Logan, it's hard to believe everything happens for a reason. And maybe God doesn't have a plan for us, but I believe he had a plan for my son and that's why he was taken from us."

He was taken saving my life, Logan thought.

"The kids, I think, I think the kids didn't quite understand it at first, but they knew pretty quickly that he wasn't coming back home, even before the wake and everything, before they saw him, I mean. They knew something had happened. They knew he wasn't coming back."

"It's hard thinking of him…I'm sorry. I don't mean to interrupt." Logan pulled back.

"No, go ahead honey. I don't get the impression you talk about him much."

"He was just so strong, so big and had this huge presence that…" Logan felt himself breaking down like he did struggling to find words at the wake. "It's hard to know that he can't come back. I've struggled with the finality of it, I guess. I always thought we'd be friends until we got old."

164

"Everyone at your age feels that way Logan. That's normal. Even adults think that way sometimes."

"He came and went so fast. It's not fair."

"Perhaps not sweetheart, but we still have each other, Richard and I that is. We still have the kids. And you, Logan. We still have you. We still have Amber and this entire community. The people have been so kind to us."

"Thank you, Mrs. Lewis." She reached out, embraced him and kissed him on the forehead.

Logan got up and wiped his eyes, but there were no tears. He walked into the kids' room and sat down on Julian's bed. The boy never turned his eyes away from the TV he was playing video games on.

"Wanna play?" Logan asked trying to get through.

"Angela's no good at this game," Julian answered. "I don't like two player games!"

"I'm not sure I'm much better than she is! I'm not much of a gamer but sure, I'll try." He laughed.

Julian was just as intense when it came to beating him at Street Fighter as Brayden was winning a baseball game. Naturally, as it was with Brayden, Logan couldn't quite match the talent of a Lewis, even to the young boy at video games.

"Man, you kicked my butt. You gotta be cheating!" Logan rubbed Julian's head.

"I'm better than Logan is!" Angela shouted.

"Brayden was the only one who could beat me sometimes." Julian's voice fluctuated a bit when he said Brayden's name.

"Come here, both of you." Logan patted the bedspread.

The kids nodded almost at the same time and sat down on the bed with Logan.

"How often do you guys talk about your brother, to your parents, to anyone?"

Neither child seemed too eager to answer.

"I'll tell you that I don't get the chance to talk about him much, you know, how much I miss having him around, how much I miss talking to him. Do you guys still talk to him?"

Julian nodded.

"Angela?"

"I talk to Bray every night before I go to sleep."

"And what do you tell him?"

She inched closer to Logan. "I tell him that mommy and daddy miss him. They said he's watching over us, that he's an angel in Heaven now."

Logan choked back tears. "That's great. He's…yeah, he's an angel now for sure. He's one of God's strongest angels."

"I ask him to come back," Julian said. "I asked dad why he can't come back, and he told me because he has a new job protecting us like he couldn't before."

"Come here." Logan hugged both kids. "I miss him too. I wish he could come back too, but your parents are right. He's still right here, watching our every move. He's making sure that we're safe."

"How do you know?" Julian asked.

"I just know. Sometimes, there are feelings I can't explain. I feel like someone is in my room with me, but I turn and nobody is there. Have you ever felt that?"

"Mhm," Angela almost whimpered.

"That's your brother letting you know he loves you and that he misses you. He visits you more than you think. He loves you so much. He always has and always will."

Julian hugged Logan and Logan rubbed his back. Angela hopped down and into the living room.

"Kids! Dinner is almost ready!" Mrs. Lewis shouted from the kitchen.

Logan walked out with Julian.

"Are you staying?" Mrs. Lewis asked.

Logan smiled. "What are you having?"

"Burgers and mac and cheese."

"If you'll have me."

Mrs. Lewis nodded and set another plate at the table as the front door open and Brayden's father walked in from work. He set his things down on the couch.

"Logan!" He walked over. "What a surprise to have you here."

"This place feels more like home than anywhere else." Logan smiled again.

"As it should son, as it should."

* * *

As Logan prepared to leave after dinner, Mr. Lewis stopped him.

"Hang on, I'll be right back."

166

Logan waited at the front door and Mr. Lewis came back almost as quickly as he left. "Catch!"

Logan caught a balled-up shirt and unfurled it. It was Brayden's practice T-shirt.

"You should have this."

Logan held it out in front of him and looked at Brayden's last name emblazoned on the back.

"Thank you," he said as he clutched it. "Thank you so much."

"Now instead of just feeling like he's there, a part of him will always be there with you, whenever you need it to be." Mrs. Lewis put her hand on Logan's shoulder.

"Thank you, Mr. and Mrs. Lewis. This means the world to me."

Mr. Lewis hugged him tightly. "You get that arm healed up quickly, okay son?"

"Yes sir."

"And take care of yourself."

"Yes sir."

Logan waved goodbye to the kids. "I want a rematch soon!" he yelled to Julian.

"It won't help!"

Logan laughed and left Brayden's house as the Sun began to sink past the trees. He kept the shirt tight in his hand until he made it home.

"I didn't cook," his mom said as he walked in the door.

"It's okay. I ate at the Lewis' and I have everything I need right here."

"You could have called."

"Sorry." Logan hurried upstairs.

He didn't quite have a frame, but the shirt would hold a special place on his shelf, much like the signed baseball held a spot on Brayden's. He ripped one of his collared shirts off a hanger in his closet and put Brayden's shirt on it. He hung it off his shelf, and while it wasn't the most stable, it would work for now.

"You're always with me," he said towards the shirt, and towards Brayden.

The jersey swung back and forth, without anything binding it besides the metal hook. Logan cracked open his notebook and started catching up on his homework due the next day. He looked at his desk at the painkillers, poured a few out and looked at the handful of pills. He put all but one back into the bottle and knocked it back without any water. He coughed and got back to work.

"I'm working on it," he said in the direction of the swinging shirt. "Goodnight, Brayden."

22

June 24th

(Amber)

Where did the time go? she thought to herself as she ran her finger across the "100" Mr. Pearsall had given her on her final paper.

Inside the classroom, it had been just another year. Outside, it had changed her forever. Brayden hadn't survived the year, Logan was improving, but his bad days terrified her. He had been shutting himself away completely. It wasn't that she didn't trust him, but she just couldn't tell sometimes how committed he was to try to feel better. To top it all off, her mother had brought Curt back into the fold of the family seemingly full time. She tried to call Logan, but he didn't answer. He was probably sleeping.

"Amber, come on hun! You're going to be late for work!" her mother called from the hall.

Logan's neighbor, Mr. Brooks, had given Amber a summer job at his convenience shop in town after Logan had declined the offer.

"Coming!" she answered. She tossed the paper on her bed and hurried downstairs.

"How are you doing sweetheart?" her mother asked, a question that had become far too routine to answer with any depth anymore.

"Fine, mom. Logan is fine. Everything is fine," she replied with her head pressed up against the window.

"It was nice of Mr. Brooks to give you this job at his shop!"

"Yeah, it was. I'm glad I can be out of the house for a few hours every day."

The car came to a stop up the street from the shop.

"Is it Curt?" her mother asked.

Amber opened the door and peered back inside. "For once?" she said thinking about Curt coming over a few weeks back. "It's not. I'm off at 6. See you later, mom." She shut the door.

She walked into the small store. Several tiny stores and shops lined the road in the heart of Springvale. When the bell rang upon her entering, Mr. Brooks stopped sweeping the floor to greet her.

"My favorite employee! Amber my dear, how are you this morning?" the kind old man said as wrinkles formed on his face after a smile.

"I'm wonderful Mr. Brooks!"

Being around Mr. Brooks put her in a better mood.

"Always a cheery disposition with this one," he remarked to his grandson, Stephen, standing behind him. "Can you do me a favor and help tidy up the back counter sweetheart?"

She nodded and walked behind the front display case waving to Stephen in the process. The young boy's eyes darted away from her.

"You know, being here kind of reminds me of doing chores at home!" she said from behind the counter.

"How so?" Mr. Brooks asked.

"Cleaning, being around a real family. It's like being around my mom and my brother."

"Well," Mr. Brooks stopped sweeping. "Not many people to sell things to these days."

She frowned. "They keep putting up new stores and knocking down trees."

"Big business is easy business."

While cleaning the back counter, she stumbled across a pendant tossed aside in a shoebox. A silver star hung off an elastic string.

This is perfect! Logan's birthday was in a month.

"Mr. Brooks?" Amber walked from behind the counter.

"Yes dear?"

"How about I play both employee and customer today? How much do you want for this?" she asked swinging the pendant in front of her face.

"Oh that? Where did you even find that?"

"In this box over here, with some old frames with no pictures in them."

"I haven't seen that pendant in years. I'm glad you've found it!"

Mr. Brooks hobbled over to Amber and looked at the pendant.

"My father gave me this when I was a little boy. He bought it at a fair. He called it a 'rare' find." He laughed. "I don't know how much it's truly worth..."

"Worth more than anything I can pay. It's a memory for you! I'm sorry I even asked."

"Nonsense! If it's been in this box for years, it never truly meant much I suppose. You, my dear, will find a far better use for it. Fifteen dollars and not a penny less!" he replied with a wink.

"Oh, it must be worth much more than that!"

Mr. Brooks shook his head and laughed. "Perhaps, but that look in your eye tells me it's worth more to you than any amount I could ask. Fifteen and that's my final offer young lady!"

She pulled her wallet out of the back pocket of her jeans and handed Mr. Brooks a fifty-dollar bill.

"Keep the change!"

"You're too kind Miss Donovan. Thank you," he said with a sigh.

"I know things have been hard for you and the store lately." She frowned.

"How could you possibly know that?" He sounded surprised.

"Just a feeling," she answered. "All the newer, bigger stores…it must be hard for stores like yours to stay open."

He chuckled. "It's God's way of telling me to hang it up and enjoy the rest of my years with my wife at home."

"That sounds lovely. I'm sure she'll be happy with that too! You deserve it. Won't it be sad to close this down?"

"Oh, I'm sure it will be. I've worked many jobs in my 74 years of life, but this I'm most proud of. To say I owned and ran my own business and did so for nearly twenty years. That, apart from my family, is my proudest accomplishment." He beamed from ear to ear. "That pendant, that wouldn't happen to be for Logan Anderson, would it?"

"How did you…"

"Just a feeling!" He cut her off and flashed a smile.

He walked into the back storeroom. Upon hearing the shuffling of shelves, she walked back to check on him.

"Mr. Brooks? Are you okay?"

"Out! You'll ruin the surprise." She heard his voice from the stockroom.

She laughed, walked out, and waited.

"Close your eyes young lady!" he yelled from the back room again. "No peeking."

She put her hands over her eyes and paused until he came out.

"Okay. You can open them now."

She did so with a gasp. In Mr. Brooks' hands sat a long black box. When she opened the box, she smiled wide. Not only did the pendant sit inside the box, but instead of the elastic string that once held it, a bright silver chain necklace now ran through the star.

"Oh, Mr. Brooks it's beautiful. Thank you!" She reached and hugged him around his waist.

"That boy does some stupid things, but finding you is either a stroke of luck or a grand master plan. You're welcome Miss Donovan."

"He's going to love it. We have a thing for stars." She laughed.

"He knows stars when he sees them, I suppose. He picked the brightest one."

She blushed and put the pendant down next to the register.

"Thank you so much again, Mr. Brooks."

"You are a pure soul, Miss Donovan. I have never known such a bright, optimistic girl that could remain so after such tragedy in her life. You are a joy to have in my shop. You still see the good in the world. There is no greater skill than that."

"It's all that keeps me going. We all have a bit of good in us, sometimes…" She looked at the pendant. "We need a little help to wake it up."

She hoped Logan would rediscover his light soon. She hoped seeing the star would remind him of the possible future over the negative past.

She spent the remainder of the day going through the backroom with Stephen trying to organize it and tidy it up.

"So, how do you like working with your grandpa?" she asked trying to get the boy, no older than thirteen, to say something, anything. He was always so shy.

"It's fine," he answered keeping his eyes averted from her.

"When did you start living with your grandparents?"

"A few months ago. My dad went back to school."

"What about your mom?"

"She didn't live with us."

In a way, she sympathized with Stephen. When her mother shoved her back into public school after her father died, she didn't know anybody. After all, she spent four years prior with the same group of kids.

Before long, she huffed and turned him around, extending her hand to him. "Don't be shy. Take my hand."

His face turned red.

"Come on!" She dragged him outside the store. "Close your eyes," she said with her hands on his shoulders.

He turned and looked at her.

172

"Don't look at me! Close your eyes. Take some deep breaths. Focus on all the things in this world that make you feel safe, secure. The things that make you feel good inside." She let go of him. "Food, family, your favorite TV shows, anything. Think of it all!"

The air went still. She could hear his breathing. When he reopened his eyes, she saw a smile on his face.

"My dad and grandpa. That all makes me feel good."

"That's good! See? If you hold on to all those things, you'll always feel secure, and you won't be so nervous!"

"You're so friendly to everyone. I see it with grandpa all the time. Why?"

"I think everyone deserves to be treated with kindness. Some of us don't get a chance, even when we need it most, and…well, it brings out the best in people I think!"

"Thank you. I always get so nervous around people. I got real nervous around you when you started working with grandpa at the shop."

"Really? Why?" She laughed.

"I don't know. You're so bubbly and positive. It's kind of intimidating." He sighed.

"Well. I hope I'm not scary anymore." She laughed again and extended her hand to him again, which he took. She led him back inside.

"Mr. Brooks! I have cracked the mystery of your grandson," she boasted.

"I'm not the least bit surprised," Mr. Brooks answered.

Stephen's body language seemed loose, as if he felt he could laugh and be himself now.

"Thank you for being my friend and being so nice."

She hugged him again. "Thank you for letting me!"

Amber spent the rest of the day entertaining a handful of customers and cleaning some more.

"Time's up Miss Donovan! Don't forget your gift."

Her eyes went wide, and she grabbed the box off the back counter.

"Have a wonderful night, Amber," Stephen said from behind his grandfather.

"Goodnight Stephen!" She waved as she watched her mom pull up in front of the store.

"Mom, look what I got for Logan for his birthday!" She pulled the silver star and swung it front of her mother.

"It's beautiful, hun. It's a perfect gift."

I hope so.

For whatever reason, she felt the things she did for Logan seemed inferior to everything he did for her. In a way, she felt as if she was failing him.

She hadn't heard from Logan all day. Logan wasn't the type to initiate conversation. If he had time to himself, he always took it. The only times he ever contacted Amber first were certain mornings just to say good morning, nights to wish her a good evening, or whenever he felt panicked or upset. She texted him a few times throughout the day but hadn't heard back from him yet. Her heart always beat a bit quicker whenever he didn't answer her throughout the day. If it turned into an all-day affair, she became worried about him.

After getting home, she hugged her brother, who was playing in the front yard by himself.

"What are you up to Michael?" she asked.

"Winning the World Series," he replied with a plastic bat in hand. She envisioned it along with him.

"You sure hit it far Michael!" She watched him round invisible bases.

"I did! You want to know who I hit it off of? Logan!"

She frowned. "Now why would you do that? I'm sure he wouldn't be happy!"

"No. He's won a bunch of championships and he's an old man now. So, that's the only reason I hit it!"

"You have quite the imagination my lovely little brother." She kissed him on the forehead.

She walked upstairs to the bathroom and washed her face. She pulled the black box housing Logan's pendant from her bag and placed it on her nightstand next to the picture frame Michael had given her for her birthday. Before going downstairs for dinner, she heard her phone buzzing. Her heartbeat quickened when she saw Logan's name come on the screen. He only ever called her for a select number of reasons, none of which were ever good ones.

"What's wrong?" she answered the phone.

"Why do you have to assume something's wrong when I call you?" he answered.

"You don't usually give me much of a reason not to think that. Sorry."

"I'm sorry. Honestly...nothing is wrong. Just wanted to see...you know, how your day at work went."

"It was fine. Logan, are you sure you're okay? You sound tired."

"Yeah...I took a couple meds earlier. My elbow was bugging me again from therapy. That stuff gets me groggy sometimes. I don't know. My arm feels better though..."

"Logan...I told you..."

"Amber? I love you."

"Where...is that coming from?"

"I just feel like I don't tell you enough. That's all."

"Well, I love you too, Logan. You know that."

"I do, but it's always nice to hear you say it. I gotta lie down. I'm dizzy. These meds...."

"Are you sure you didn't take anything other than the medication the doctor gave you?" Her heart started beating faster.

"What? Yes. That's all. I swear. Don't worry. I'm gonna lay down. I'll text you later. Love you, Amber."

"Love you..." He hung up before she could get it out.

She looked at her phone. Logan didn't sound good. He sounded groggier than usual, and she heard his voice cracking, like he wanted to cry. She gazed at the box again. Behind the picture frame was the drawing she made of her, Logan and Brayden. She ran her fingers across the drawing of Brayden.

"I don't know how to fix this," she said to picture. "I don't know what steps to take, or what to say to him when he gets like this. I can't just shake him and make him see that what he needs is here with him, and not some memory."

She started to sniffle.

"I know that...I know I have to stay strong for him, but who's there to stay strong for me? It was you, Bray. It was always you. You were there for both of us, even though the things we dealt with then aren't as heavy as they are now, you always treated our problems like they were the most important thing in the world. Now...now I have nobody to fall back on when I need it. I'm afraid if I fall back on Logan, that we'll both break."

Her sniffle became the beginning of a sob.

"I just wish there was a way for you to give me a signal, a sign, anything at all that tells me that I'm doing the best I can and that I'm doing and saying all the right things because anytime I hear him like that, I feel like

I'm failing." She wiped her eyes and let out a breathless laugh. "And you know how much I hate failing."

She kissed the drawing. "Just give me a little bit more strength and, if you can, a little more knowledge so I know what to do when the time comes to do it. I love you, Brayden."

She placed the drawing back on her end table behind the frame and got off her bed. She walked towards the door and stopped in the doorway.

"Thanks for listening, Bray. You're the best."

23

July 18th

(Logan)

The days all seemed hazy. Looking at his phone and seeing the time gave him pause. It was mid-afternoon.

"God damn it." He'd slept through his physical therapy appointment, and his mom never said a word.

She had left for her summer job at the grocery store late in the morning without reminding him.

"Thanks mom."

He grabbed a ball off his nightstand and started to squeeze it. He started to try to rotate his elbow. He could start tossing a ball in a few weeks. He was on his second prescription for the Percocet. He slept better, but more often. His nightmares subsided to flashes. He had settled on substituting sleep medication with the prescribed medications.

The school year ending was a blessing in disguise. He quickly remembered the last few days of the semester. Going to class every day and seeing his teammates annoyed him. Even though he couldn't heal any faster, day in and day out, everyone was asking how he was doing. Meanwhile, his arm was still in a sling, and he had to keep telling everyone that he was "getting there," which was a lie both physically and mentally. Everyone, from teachers to friends, told him how proud they were for finishing the year strong. He had everyone fooled. Life knocked him down. He kept getting up. He kept answering the bell. His phone buzzed. It was Amber.

Stay down, he heard a voice tell him.

He shook his head.

You're stuck with me. You're losing. You don't need to text her back, the voice persisted.

"You're wrong. That love keeps me going. You're wrong."

I'm not here to hurt you, I'm your friend.

"I'm fine."

You keep telling yourself that as your grades keep falling.

"I'm still here."

For now.

Every time he saw Amber, he felt normal again. He didn't need to rely on his painkillers to get him through spending days with her. Her eyes and presence hypnotized him, and her laugh made him feel calmer. She hugged him at the most random times, and he never wanted her to let go.

The "I love you" she had given him the night he came home from surgery lingered in his mind. She refused to let him be beaten, but he wasn't being proactive enough in his recovery. She had shown him the way, even if he didn't want to go with her. Every time he needed a sign that things might be okay, she had come through. Whether through something simple like reminding him of the stars or grabbing his face and forcing him to stare into her eyes; she did everything she could to keep him at ease. She spent several nights at his house, hushing him to sleep, stroking his hair as she would her little brother.

She even sang to him on occasion.

"I know my singing isn't the best," she'd tell him. *"But it might help."*

Amber had showed such strength from day one, even after Brayden's death. She believed, even when he didn't believe in himself. He made her a promise and he'd been doing his best to keep it. Sometimes he faltered, but he knew that each day in the fight was another day to change, another day to get better. If for no other reason, he knew he had been sticking around to be better to Amber.

His phone buzzed. It was her again. He just stared at his phone. Amber texted him throughout the day, but he'd ignored her. He'd began to run out of things to say back to her when she worried about him.

"I'm sorry you worry so much," he said to her even though she wasn't there.

He plucked a bottle out of the fridge and walked out to his back deck. Instead of swigging the bottle down, he climbed down the steps of his back deck and out into his backyard. He stared deep into the forest before taking a sip and winced. It was the first sip of alcohol he'd taken since the day he blew up on the baseball field and knocked David Grant unconscious.

"Damn near four months, right down the drain." He sighed.

He shook the bottle of pills inside his pocket and felt the banging of only a handful left. He popped the bottle open and dumped the circular white pill into his hand. Tossing it into his mouth and washing it down with another sip of beer, he treaded into the forest.

He looked around the dense forest, listening for cars whizzing through the streets nearby to make sure he didn't trek too far in. Even though everything looked the same, he knew where he was. About a quarter mile away, laid the same cabin he and Amber had discovered the day after Brayden's death.

He had used it as a place to get away from the world for a while. He followed a makeshift trail he had created that led him straight to the cabin. He ran his fingers across the rotted doorway and once inside, peered through a window with glass long shattered.

Part of the roof lay in what he imagined to be a living room, collapsed from decades of rain, snow, and other weather.

He tucked himself in a fireplace, the only part of the building untouched by time. The stone had held up far better over the years than the rest of the wood foundation. The moss underneath him squished under his weight. He rested his head back against the inside of the fireplace and polished off the rest of the bottle, letting his thoughts wander.

Don't you wish I'd just shut up? That voice returned.

"With everything I have."

There's only one way to make that happen. Are you brave enough to cross that line?

Everything within Logan's common sense told him not to listen, but he felt out of control. Within the confines of that house, Logan heard his next command, an idea he played around with since Brayden's death.

Bang. Get it over with. It's your fault he's gone.

A tear fell down his face. "You're right."

Maybe that was the only way to escape. Ever since the elbow injury, those thoughts burned. At night, he prayed maybe he would just take one too many painkillers and he'd slip away in the quiet of the night. Maybe he would just collapse down on the floor, only for his mom to find him just a little too late.

If he were to end it all, it'd be quick and painless. He pounded the back of his head on the stone, trying to shake those thoughts from his head, but couldn't.

"Get out of my head!" he yelled into the forest.

Make me.

The more he thought about it, the more vivid the idea became. He sat the bottle down in front of him and sat the rest of his pills next to it after peeling the labels off. He stumbled up to his feet, almost in a trance of sorts. He looked at his messages again from Amber and debated answering her with an apology for what he felt prepared to do. Suddenly, calm came over him, as if he finally came to grips with it all. He was ready to go. Picking up his phone again, he typed out a response to Amber, an apology.

I'm sorry I couldn't beat this, he began. *I'm sorry I let everybody down. Most importantly, I'm sorry I let Brayden die. I wish I could say I was strong enough, but the truth is, I'm not. People will look back on this and think I was selfish, and maybe I am. The fact is, I'm debating leaving the world. That's how I want it. Amber, I sincerely hope you find someone worth your love and kindness. You were the only beacon of light I had left, and I extinguished it. I'm sorry I ever dragged you into this, and I'm sorry for what I'm putting you through. I realize that the only person I'm being unfair to is and always has been you, but it's time for me to rejoin Brayden and be with him for good. I can't live another day with him there and me here, all alone. I just can't. I hope you never had a doubt about love in your heart, because I truly love you, and it's because I love you that I can't bear to see you again feeling like this. I'm sorry. I love you so much, Amber. Love, Logan.*

Before he sent it, he locked his phone. The draft sat there for Amber never to read. If he sent it, it would only sprout doubt and fear. He was weeping now.

"I'm so sorry."

He took a deep breath and stumbled from the cabin in the woods back towards his house.

Every step felt one step closer to an execution.

"This must be what it's like to be on Death Row."

A throbbing developed in his head.

Time's up. The voice returned.

He wavered as he walked back inside his house. He made his way upstairs to his room. He looked around, eyes red from failing to fight back tears. He picked up a trophy he won in little league baseball and tossed it aside. Before leaving, he found the binder of memories between him and Brayden. He ran his fingers across the cover.

"I'll see you soon," his voice echoed off the walls.

He rummaged through his drawers to find his Springvale T-shirt, with his last name and number on the back. He gazed at it for a moment before tossing it aside near the trophy. He debated on writing to his mother and father, apologizing in the same way he apologized to Amber, but decided against it.

A little more, the voice taunted.

He entered his mother's room. He rummaged through her drawers for the object he sought after. Finally, he checked under her bed, where he saw the unblinking eye staring back at him. He pulled his mother's pistol from under her bed. She kept it for protection, in case anyone ever tried to break into the house, a last resort of sorts. To Logan, it represented a twisted sense of salvation. He checked the chamber and found it empty. He dug further under her bed for ammunition. After all, he only needed one shot.

He found a high-end shoebox that housed several boxes of bullets. Ejecting the magazine, he loaded the bullet in and slid the magazine back up into the pistol, which shook in his nervous hands. He took another deep breath trying to recoup his emotions. He crept out of his mother's bedroom and looked back into his room one more time, almost in tears. He marched back downstairs and into the garage. From the garage, he flipped a small light switch to illuminate the basement underneath him. The basement stairs creaked with every step. It seemed too dark for him. He paced around the basement before finding a string dangling from the ceiling. He pulled on the chain and another bulb flickered above him.

Again, he took a few more deep breaths. He pulled the magazine back out and stared at the bullet inside. He rubbed his face.

"I can't do this! I can't do this." He sobbed.

You can. You will. The voice drew a final line in the sand, except this line would lead him right over a cliff to which there was no return.

He loaded the magazine back in and chambered the round. He felt paralyzed. He put the gun down and sat on a stack of crates, burying his head in his hands.

"I don't want to die yet."

But don't you want to get rid of the pain?

He felt his life flashing before him like a flurry of events. He could feel his heartbeat in his eardrums. The air felt heavier, and the silence was deafening. He stared at the pistol on the ground and bent over to pick it up once again. He tapped the barrel against his head a few times. He rose up off the canvas one final time, in hopes he could land a lucky punch and put depression away for good. He felt as if his body would split into two separate pieces. A war raged inside of him, and he wasn't sure which side was winning.

He felt the cold steel up against his forehead as his hand trembled. He threw up on the floor. Sweat dripped off his head and onto the pistol.

Without thinking, he put the gun up to his temple, closed his eyes, and pulled the trigger.

Nothing happened. The trigger remained in place when he tried to pull it. He reopened his eyes and exhaled.

"The fucking safety."

Gave yourself a second chance?

He still had a chance to change his mind and continue his fight.

"But I was willing to do it."

He felt his palms sweating and tears burning his eyes, much as they did the night of Brayden's death.

He disengaged the safety and felt the steel grinding off the side of his skull from his hand shaking so much. His finger slowly slid up towards the trigger. He closed his eyes once again, and took a deep breath in, hoping for the shot to be painless. Once his finger found the trigger, he moved in to pull it. His phone buzzed again in his pocket, and he put the gun down. Amber's name sat atop the screen, with her picture lingering in the background. He watched it ring repeatedly, and he looked into her eyes in the picture. His thumb hovered over the red decline button, but finally he picked up.

"..."

"Logan?"

"Hi."

He slid the gun out of his immediate grasp and sat cross-legged on the floor.

24

Moments Earlier

(Amber)

She hadn't heard from Logan all day. She tried calling him, but after a few rings, only got his voicemail.

"Logan, call me back, okay?" She left the message.

Rather than stay cooped up in her room, she knocked on Michael's door.

"Want to toss the ball around?" she asked him as he perched in front of the TV.

"Yes! Let me get my ball!" He popped up and grabbed a ball from the floor.

She made her way back to her room and slipped on a pair of flip-flops and a black, flowy shirt over a tank top that ran past her shorts. Before she could leave her room, her brother ran in, grabbed her hand and pulled her downstairs and out of the house into the front yard.

"Catch!" he shouted, tossing the baseball to her, which she almost dropped.

After every throw, she stopped to check her phone to see if Logan had responded to her yet, and he hadn't. Something was wrong. She put her phone in her pocket and kept tossing the ball with her brother. Michael had started developing affection for sports ever since Amber started dating Logan. She missed the days before Logan got hurt when he'd come over and show Michael how to throw different pitches. He liked watching professional games on TV now, and Amber always watched with him because he wanted her to.

"When is Logan going to be able to come over again play catch with me?" Michael asked.

She frowned. "I don't know. Logan hurt himself pretty badly. It won't be for a little while sweetie."

"Is Logan okay?"

She sighed. "He'll be okay eventually. He's just banged up right now."

His questions did her no good in trying to keep her mind off Logan's non-responses all day. She checked her phone again.

Mom should be home soon. Maybe I can go over and check on him then.

The ball came back to her and hit her in the stomach. She laughed while losing her breath.

"Michael! I wasn't paying attention!" She started to chase her brother around the yard for catching her off guard.

She caught up to him and wrapped her arms around him as he giggled in her grasp. She took him down onto the grass and kissed him on the head before he wrestled away from her. Still, looking at her interlocked hands at the bracelet brought her back to Logan once again. She corralled her brother and led him back inside while she tried calling Logan again. Once again, his phone rang, rang, and went to voicemail.

"Hey, it's me again. Um, I haven't heard from you and I'm getting a little worried. Call me when you get this, okay?" She paused. "Love you. Bye."

She frowned and put her phone back in her pocket.

Maybe he's just asleep or doing physical therapy.

She thought of every reason possible for Logan not answering her. She walked into the kitchen and made Michael a peanut butter and jelly sandwich in the meantime. He swung around behind her and tugged her shirt.

"Can I have a glass of milk please?"

She laughed. "Of course you can. Go and sit down on the couch. Lunch will be right out!"

She walked in a couple minutes later with his lunch.

"You make better sandwiches than mommy!" he exclaimed.

"I think so too!"

She sat on the couch beside her brother and looked over at the picture on the end table of her family. She almost never looked at it ever since her dad died. She looked over at Michael for a moment and thought about how differently she and her mother had raised him from how her father raised her. Her father had acted so cruelly to her, that it was hard to look at that picture and not think of anything but those memories. However, there were times when he seemed to be a loving father.

Every time she looked at Michael, she saw a little bit more of him. She just hoped she and her mother had influenced Michael enough to make him forget about his father. Though he never received the punishments, Amber did. He had witnessed their father hurt her a few times. Almost an hour passed, and still she had heard nothing from Logan. She tried calling him one more time. It rang several times. It felt like it was ringing for hours.

Finally, it clicked on. She looked down to make sure he didn't ignore the call. He didn't, he was there, but he wasn't answering.

"Logan?"

"Hi." His voice was shaky, even in saying hi.

"Is everything okay?"

"Yeah…uh…everything, everything is okay."

Her heartbeat started slowing. "So, what are you up to?"

He uttered a forced laugh. "Nothing really. To be honest, I just wanted to hear your voice, I guess. I miss you."

"Miss me? We talk all the time, except, you know, today! How come you didn't answer me earlier?"

"I…um…I was busy. I missed my therapy, so I was doing it on…my own."

"Do you want me to come over?" She felt nervous still. Something still didn't seem right.

"Umm…" She heard some rustling on the other end of the phone. "Yeah, yeah if you want. Don't you have to watch your brother?"

She looked at Michael. "I'll have my neighbor watch him for a few hours until my mom gets home. He loves the dogs. I'll see you soon."

"Okay." His voice sounded a little lighter and a little less crackly. "I love you."

"Love you too."

Her lips started to quiver, and she felt what color she had in her face leave her. She began to panic but didn't know why. He was reaching out, but there was something he wasn't telling her. It would take her awhile to walk to Logan's. She just wanted him to be okay.

She got up. "Michael, I'm going outside for a second. Stay right there."

She walked next door to her neighbor's house. She rang the doorbell far more than she needed to before an older gentleman answered the door with dogs barking in the background.

"Amber?" he asked. "What's wrong?"

"Could I ask you for a huge favor Mr. Torres? You let Michael play with your dogs all the time and he likes you and your wife. Can he come over for a few hours, or until my mom gets home? I have to go out for a little while."

Mr. Torres looked at her. "Is everything okay?"

"Yes. No. I don't know. That's why I have to go."

"Yes, okay sweetheart, anything you need. Bring him over. I'll look after him until you or your mom comes home."

"Thank you so much Mr. Torres!" she answered before rushing back to her house to get her brother.

"Mikey, I have to go see Logan, okay? Mr. Torres said you can stay with him until mom or I get home."

"Do I get to play with his dogs?"

She sighed. "Yes, of course. Now come on." She led him outside back next door.

"Thanks again Mr. Torres!" she said from the driveway.

She took a deep breath and began her walk to Logan's house. She called him again.

"Hey," he answered.

"I just wanted you to know, I'm on my way, okay?"

There was silence.

"Logan, okay?"

"What? Yeah. I'll see you in a bit."

She felt her stomach flipping in circles. She made her way down the block and into town, passing by the strip where Mr. Brooks' shop was located.

"Hi Amber!" Stephen Brooks waved her down.

"Hi, Stephen. Um, is your grandpa around?"

Stephen nodded and went to retrieve Mr. Brooks from inside the store.

"Amber, are you alright? Where's your mom? You walked all the way here?" the old man asked.

"Did you see Logan leave today or anything before you came to the shop?"

"No. I haven't seen him all day. Only his mom and she left this morning. Hadn't seen a soul move about that house. Is everything okay?"

She nodded her head. "Everything is fine. I just wanted to go check up on him is all…"

"Did you want me to take you?"

"No! No! You run the store. I'll be fine," she answered half-smiling.

"Well, okay. You take care."

Her heart kept beating faster as she made her way past *Dianne's* and onto the other side of Springvale. She stopped to collect her breath. The heat made her feel dizzy. Her heart felt like it would burst out of her chest soon if she didn't slow down, but her mind raced all over.

"Please, please let him be okay," she prayed.

She tried to keep her calm and focus, knowing she would be at Logan's soon. The Sun shined high over the tree line. She again took a few deep breaths after tiring out again. She rested in the shade for a second, feeling as if she were about to have a heat stroke. She found each breath more difficult. She made her way into Brayden's neighborhood and almost stopped at his house.

"I have to do this myself."

Finally, she saw the street sign for Church Street.

"I don't know how he does this every day."

She looked and noticed his mother's car wasn't in the driveway. She made her way up his red and grey-bricked walkway and pounded on the door.

"Logan! Logan! Are you there?" She got no answer.

She rang the doorbell a few times and got no answer again. She pulled on the door, but nobody unlocked it all day. She let the handle go and felt like crying. She made her way around the side of the house that Logan's room was on and tried to hit his window with a few rocks. Again, nothing happened. She bit her lip, running out of ideas.

She made her way to the backyard, scaled up on Logan's back deck, and pulled on the back door. The back door opened right up. She breathed in the cool air upon reaching Logan's dining room. Not a single light was on in the house.

"Logan? Logan are you here?"

Nobody answered her. She crept up the stairs, checked the bathroom and found nothing. She walked into Logan's room and flipped the light on. She found the binder Logan made for him and Brayden tossed down on the floor alongside one of Logan's baseball t-shirts. She scoured his room and looked at his messy bed, looking for any kind of clue as to where Logan might have gone. She checked the drawers she knew he kept his medication and only found one-half empty bottle of Vicodin. The other medication was missing.

"Logan!"

Leaving Logan's room, she walked into his mother's room and found various drawers left half-opened, but nothing seemed out of place. She tried to think of anywhere else to look. She trotted downstairs and opened the side door to get into Logan's garage. Again, she looked around and not a single soul was in sight.

She looked over to the right and saw the light switch to the basement flipped on, and she propped the basement door open and saw the lights were on downstairs. She snuck down the stairs and her heart beating faster with every step she took. She peeked down under the railing and Logan was sitting on the floor, cross-legged, as if he was in some sort of trance.

"H…hey," he said, nervously. "Sorry, I um, I didn't hear you outside."

"Are you okay?" she asked.

He closed his eyes. "Honestly? No…no I'm not. That's kind of why I wanted you to come over. Could you just come and sit here with me?" He sobbed. His eyes were already red.

"Of course," she answered. She took a few more steps down and sat down next to him. "I'll sit here all night if I have to."

His hand was shaking.

"Logan, what's going on?"

"I don't want to lie to you anymore. I don't even want to stretch the truth. I've been thinking about Brayden a lot."

"Of course. I think about him all the time."

"No, that's not what I mean. I've been thinking a lot lately about being WITH him."

"You mean…"

"Yeah, and it scares me to think like that. It's never gotten this bad before. You know, everything everyone says about me getting better? When I have thoughts like this, it makes me think I'm getting worse."

She put her hand on his thigh. "You know he wouldn't want that. You know what he'd say if he were here!" She was trembling.

"That's why at first, I didn't want to tip you off or talk to you. I…I was scared to." he moaned between cries. "But then I picked up the phone and I heard your voice…and it was like that all went away."

"Did you…did you try, did you think about it?"

He bit his lip. "Yeah, yeah I did. And I don't want to scare you. It was never a life-or-death thing, but yeah, before I answered the phone, I did. I'm sorry."

She took a deep breath, rushed into him, and grabbed a hold of him. "I'm just glad you're okay."

"I'm sorry for putting so much on you," he cried into her shoulder. "I just want you to be proud of me. I want you to see I'm trying."

Every part of her body shook, but she refused to let go of him. She felt him shaking too. She stood there, frozen.

"Logan, I know you're trying. I know. You don't have anything to apologize for."

"I have more to apologize for than you know."

She still held him. She heard him sobbing over the top of her. He fell back way from her to the floor as she fought back tears of her own. She wanted to cry for him, so that maybe everything he was feeling would just vanish from his face.

She kneeled in front of him and hugged him again. "Why did you think this was the way?"

"Sometimes…I don't know…sometimes I feel like I'm so lost, like there's no hope anymore."

"There's hope right here, looking you in the face. You always told me it made you happy when I smiled, right? But I've always just been as afraid as you."

"What?" He sniffled and looked her in the eyes.

"I've always had this nightmare…that…" She tried to collect herself. "That you'd try to leave me here all alone, and I can't…not after Brayden, I can't lose you too. I won't lose you, Logan. I won't." A torrent of tears started to fall again.

"I'm…" He choked. "I'm so sorry."

She slapped him. "Don't ever scare me like this again. I can't handle it. Do you know how freaked out I've been all day not hearing from you?"

"I…I didn't…" He continued to cry, "I'm…sorry!"

"Don't leave me. Not today. Not ever! You don't leave me Logan Anderson, promise me. Promise me and mean it!"

He paused for a moment, collecting himself. "I…I promise. I'm so sorry Amber."

"You're going to get through this, okay?" She grabbed his head just as she did the night she asked if he loved Melissa Davenport. "You, Logan Anderson, you are going to get through this. And you won't get through it because of me, or anyone else except yourself. It's okay to need help, but nobody can pull you from this completely."

"That's where it starts." He wiped his eyes. "I get it now."

She finally let him go. "I'm not letting you do this alone anymore."

"I'm so sorry for all of this."

"The only thing you should apologize for is making me walk all the way across town." She let out a nervous laugh, unsure if it was okay to laugh or smile.

"You walked all the way here?"

She nodded and wiped smudged make-up from her eyes. "Yeah. I did."

He reached out, hugged her, and kissed her. "I don't deserve you. You're truly an angel."

"I'm not an angel. I just love you too much to see you go. I'm not letting you."

"I'm not going anywhere. I know that now."

You get better and stay right here with me." She closed her eyes and buried her head in his chest. "You don't leave me."

"I'm so, so sorry Amber. I love you so much."

"I love you too, Logan." She leaned up and kissed him, feeling the faintest taste of beer in his breath, but it didn't even matter.

She stayed knelt in front of him and he ran his hands near her waist and wrapped his arms around her. Her phone buzzed, but she ignored it. The only thing that mattered was the person in front of her and keeping him alive. Her heart still refused to slow down, and her head started pounding. She reached her hand up to her head and started thinking about what Logan had said to her. Was he really going to commit suicide? Is that why he called? For some reason, the image of her father lying on the ground the night of his heart attack flashed in her mind.

It could have been Logan this time. She pounded on his chest. "I don't care what time it is, if you're doing something you know you shouldn't be doing, or thinking something you shouldn't be thinking, you call me first."

"I didn't…I didn't want to bother you."

"Bother me? Logan, I love you. You call me before anything else, and I'll answer every single time. I don't care if it's in the middle of the night, the middle of the afternoon, sunrise, sundown. I don't care."

"Okay. I promise."

She leaned away from him. "There is always a choice, Logan. It doesn't matter how low you feel. You always have the choice to keep going."

Her hands still shook wrapped around Logan's back as they held one another for several minutes.

She grabbed the sides of his head and put her forehead on his. "Promise me again," she repeated as sweat stuck their heads together.

"I promise," he answered. "I'm done breaking promises."

"Good, because you're all out of promises to break to me."

He removed his arms from her and stood her up alongside him. For the first time, she saw him standing and he looked horrible. It was as if the stress from the entire day was manifesting itself on his body. They walked into Logan's room together. Sweat dripped from his face and his shirt was soaked. She walked over and picked up the Springvale baseball t-shirt he threw on the floor earlier in the day.

"Put this on." She picked up the binder. "You dropped this too"

"He'd hate me right now," Logan said looking at the binder.

"No, he'd just be glad you made the right choice, to keep fighting." She sat next to him.

"No more. I can't be like this anymore," Logan admitted.

"You can beat this. It's going to be really hard, but just trust me and trust yourself that we'll get you through this, Logan." She put his hand over his. "But please, think about seeing someone."

"I will. Maybe it'll help. It's better than this…I don't know." He stopped and ran his hand down her cheek. "You're an angel."

"I would have gotten here sooner if I was. I could have flown."

"It does make me happy," he answered out of nowhere.

She tilted her head.

"Your smile. It makes me happier than anything in this world does, and I don't want you to smile to be afraid anymore. You're too beautiful for that."

"Then give me reasons to smile without being afraid."

"I'll try."

He kissed her as the two fell back onto Logan's bed.

"Amber. I'm so sorry, again"

She put her finger over his mouth. "Stop apologizing. Words can only mean so much. You have to prove to me that you mean every apology and every promise."

"I will."

"No more words. Actions. I'm not leaving you alone today. I hope you know that."

She never thought that he was in that bad a shape that he contemplated ending it all. It never came up. He never discussed it. That's what scared her the most. She started to cry again thinking about losing him. She felt his hand wiping away her tears. She looked over into his sleepless, red eyes and rubbed heads with him again before kicking her shoes off and snuggling up on his bed.

"Looking into your eyes now is the only reason I need to never think about that again," he said.

"Find a reason within yourself, not just in me. You need to be here for you too." she answered back.

"In time, but right now, you're the only reason I need." He kissed her on the cheek.

Her heart fluttered again. The doubt would never really go away. She knew he truly loved her. Could that love transcend even the darkest parts of his spirit? It wavered once. But something felt different. This was the moment she feared the most. She thought about the prayer she made to Brayden, asking him to give her the knowledge of what to do in this exact situation. Logan was there with her. Surely, that meant something.

Thank you, Bray.

She got up off his bed to wash the smeared make-up off her face and freshen up from the sweat.

"You should clean up too, to clear your head."

As she washed and looked into the mirror, she could see what the fear had done. She brushed her hair back out of her face and looked into her own eyes. She never saw what Logan or anyone else saw in them. They never seemed brilliant or special, just ordinary and hiding so many feelings and emotions.

Eyes are supposed to be windows to the soul.

She thought hers to be transparent, but Logan's eyes, those hazel eyes; she didn't know what she saw anymore. To her, his windows were shattered and nobody could see inside.

She fumbled around trying to rinse the rest of the make-up out of her eyes. Logan walked in behind her, and she watched him wrap his arms over her shoulders and rock her. She looked in the mirror again and saw something different in his eyes. It was faint, but she saw a glimmer of confidence. The bags spoke to her as much as the red tinge within them. He looked like he hadn't had a good night's sleep in weeks. His hair looked greasy, and his face had lost its glow long ago. She wondered how she missed it all this time, but now, staring at the two of them in the mirror, she saw it all. He was fighting. Somewhere in there was the old Logan Anderson. He just needed to reawaken it

The contrast between the two of them was incredible. She reached up and touched her own face before running her hand across his and feeling how coarse his skin felt compared to the smoothness in hers. Even her arms started to get more color than his did, as if he hadn't seen the Sun in weeks.

"Logan, I'm sorry."

"For what?"

"For not noticing how bad it's gotten."

She leaned back and he looked into her own eyes again, and she jolted forward, reminded of their tense moment downstairs.

"Are you okay?" He asked.

She led him back into his room. He sat back down on his bed with his arms stretched out for her and she obliged, falling into his arms. She turned her back to him and he caressed her arms.

"I am now. Because, now I know, we're both going to be okay in the end."

25

August 27th
Senior Year
(Logan)

His alarm beeped and screamed. He swung his hands, trying to find his phone to turn the alarm off for good. After shutting it down, he flopped flat on his back and stared at the ceiling. He reached up and pulled the silver pendant Amber had given him for his birthday around his neck to his chest. He twirled the star between his fingers still looking up at the ceiling. He reached over to his phone.

Good morning. I'm up.

She wouldn't be awake yet, but he felt better texting her. After finally rising out of his bed, he looked at the near empty bottle of painkillers sitting on his dresser. He scoffed at them and grabbed a pair of cargo shorts and a T-shirt from his dresser drawers. Even on days his elbow bothered him still, he stayed away from the pills.

"I made a promise."

He removed his shirt and looked at himself in the mirror. What remaining definition his abs possessed had vanished for good more than a month ago. A bruise permeated above his boxers near his hip from a nasty fall he had suffered going down the stairs one night a week ago.

He looked at the bottle again and his fingers twitched.

"No more. You're killing yourself. Keep fighting. You don't need it," he told his reflection.

That moment in his basement between him and Amber continued to shake him to the core whenever he thought about it. After a turbulent winter and summer, he hoped the new school year would finally aid the change he sought after. Once again, he'd be forced to wear a mask and put on an act, this time for a whole year. His arm served as the lone symbol of anything healing. His doctor allowed him to start throwing a ball, albeit not hard, but it was better than not at all.

He walked into the bathroom, flipped the light on, undressed and turned the water on for a quick morning shower before school. He took a few deep breaths and closed his eyes as the water poured over him. Calm came over him as well for a change. He ran the water so hot that his back felt like it began to burn, but he didn't care. Frigid air blasted him upon his exit from the shower as he dried off. He slipped his outfit on and wiped the fog off the bathroom mirror to fix his hair.

His book bag had seen better days. Rips and tears started to widen at the bottom and a sizable hole developed near the loop at the top over the past couple of years. He looked out the window to his backyard towards the woods, towards the wooden cabin hidden within. He hadn't gone back to that twisted sanctuary since the day he wanted to die.

Maybe it'll just fall down.

As he passed by Brayden's house around the halfway mark, he thought back to the first day of school last year, when Brayden had met him at the front door and Logan asked how he felt about finally graduating.

I was so anxious about you leaving, but I never thought it'd be forever.

He sighed, passing by the silent Lewis home and continued towards the school.

Finally, the tree line gave way to the wide-open site of the Springvale campus. He watched a couple busses motor past him to park and wait to let the students out. He took his usual position at the front door, waiting for the secretary to open the door, which she did upon noticing Logan at the front door. The door buzzed, clicked, and Logan walked inside.

"Good morning and welcome back Logan!" the cheerful secretary greeted.

"Good morning, Miss McCrery!" Logan answered with a smile.

Not long after he made it through the main hall, the other students soon followed him in like a stampede. He passed his locker, walked around the corner, and posted up at another. He checked his phone, glanced over his class schedule a few times, and tapped the side of the locker until she arrived.

"Forget where your locker was?" he joked.

"Shut up!" Amber pushed him aside after kissing him.

He noticed small streaks of brown starting to break back through the end of her long hair, which still ran near her waist, just as it had the last two years.

"Might be time for some more dye," he stated wading his hand through her hair.

"I don't know. I was thinking of maybe letting it be brown again. I've missed it in a way."

"Oh, really? I've always really loved it black, but, I mean, I liked it when it was brown too, if I can remember how I felt in third grade." He laughed.

195

"We'll see. I haven't made up my mind yet. My mom wants me to dye it black again too. Anyway, let me see your classes!" She snatched the paper out of his hand.

He watched her eyes run up and down the lines, and she smiled.

"Well, we don't have first period together, but we do have Pearsall's honors class at the end of the day! And lunch of course." She hugged him. "Are you alright?"

He looked down into her eyes. "Getting there."

"Good. Keep going, okay? Now get to your locker and put your things away so you aren't late to your first class! Senior year, time's up."

"Don't remind me. I'll see you in a bit. Love you." He kissed her again.

"Hey! You kids keep that stuff at home," a peering teacher snapped from inside his doorway.

Logan laughed and shrugged at Amber before heading to his first class. He turned back for a moment to watch her. He watched her unpack her things into her locker and chuckled as she fumbled her things onto the floor, hoping nobody noticed. She tossed a brand-new satchel-like bag across her shoulder and stopped. She turned and caught Logan staring, and she smiled, and pointed at him.

"Get to class!" she yelled.

He sighed, lifted the pendant between his fingers, and flashed it at her. In reply, she flicked her wrist in the air showing the amethyst bracelet he had given her for her birthday in February. He walked into his first class, an honors history class, with the faintest sense of confidence.

"How's the elbow?" one of his teammates asked.

He looked around the room and it was as if everyone's eyes were on him at that moment. It was the first moment when he could decide to keep everything hidden, or to open up a little more, even in this small moment in time. He pulled the neoprene brace he wore down near his wrist so they could see the remnants of the scar.

"I think I'll be ready to go for the first game, if Coach still wants me on the team."

"He definitely does. We all do. So many kids graduated, including John. That could open up room for a decent amount of freshmen this year," one of his teammates replied.

Logan thought for a moment and shook his head. He still remembers the excitement he felt when he saw his name on the list of players who made the cut. He tried to snap himself out of thinking about Brayden but lost himself.

"Hey, Logan, you okay man?"

"What? Yeah. Sorry, just spaced out for a second."

He ran his hand through his hair and sighed again, waiting for class to start.

* * *

As he reached his final class of the day, he slumped down in his seat. He was lucky to know that his favorite teacher taught his final class. It also didn't hurt that Amber was in the class too. Logan and Amber took up the same seats they sat in last year in Mr. Pearsall's class and waited for him to walk into the classroom. Suddenly, he whisked in as he always did, sleeves rolled up, except now sporting thick rimmed black glasses and his hair cut to a short buzz cut, instead of its usual brown curls.

"So, these are my seniors," he said. "Wonderful. Welcome to the first day of the last best days of your lives. I'm Mr. Anthony Pearsall. You can call me Mr. Pearsall, Mr. P, whatever fits your attitude. If you give respect, you'll get it in return. I promise you."

He looked into the room and spotted Logan, and he smiled as he picked his syllabuses up from his desk and began passing them out.

"Good to see you here, Mr. Anderson."

"I'd be lying if I said it was easy Mr. P," Logan answered looking away.

Mr. Pearsall looked at Amber and then went back to Logan. "We'll catch up in a bit after class, deal?"

Logan nodded. He read over the syllabus and figured the class would be challenging as much as Mr. Pearsall's other classes. In a way, it gave him something to look forward to day in and day out. He always learned something throughout Mr. P's classes; be it course material or just about life.

"The first book," Mr. Pearsall opened. "Is Erich Maria Remarque's All Quiet on The Western Front." He continued passing out the novel to the class. "About the struggle of not the allied forces in World War I, but the German soldiers. Not only will this book provide insight into you about 'the other side' as it were, but also the harshest reality of war in a way you've never quite been able to imagine just watching clips on the news. Not only that, but you'll also learn about loss and fear during war, and the effects that those things can have on a human psyche. After all, these men were just humans. We'll say, let's see, the first 50 pages by Wednesday?

We'll have a discussion then. Read up. You're in for a wild ride with this one."

Logan thumbed through the book.

Easy enough.

"Alright. You have your contracts. You have your assignments. Normally this is where I'd pass out cards and have you all write things about yourselves. However, since you're seniors, I think you know enough about each other by now." He laughed. "Take the class to get to know each other, get our class energy in place."

Mr. Pearsall always took it easy on the class on the first day. Just as in his other classes, many of the kids made their way over to Logan to ask him about his elbow. A lot of them were there in person when it happened. He showed off the scars again. The scars freaked some kids out; some kids thought the scars were somewhat cool.

When the bell rang, Mr. Pearsall called Logan over to his desk.

"Want to take a walk?" He asked.

"What? Where?" Logan laughed.

"Just come with me." Mr. Pearsall looked at Amber. "Well, say goodbye to the missus before we go."

Logan's face flamed as he turned to Amber.

"I'll call you in a little while." He kissed her on the lips.

"Call me? That's different!" she teased.

"Kind of like your hair."

She shook her head, hugged him and vanished out the door to catch the bus. He grabbed his back off the front desk and followed Mr. Pearsall out the door. Mr. Pearsall kept quiet the whole way.

"Why are you doing this?" Logan asked. "Where are we going?"

"We'll talk soon. Don't worry."

They walked almost all the way across the school before coming to the auditorium. It was so vast with just the two of them in there.

"I never realized how big this place is," Logan remarked.

Mr. Pearsall laughed. "How do you mean?"

"It's just, I've only ever really been in here for assemblies. You know? The whole school is in here. With just us in here, man, it makes me feel so small."

The stage was dark, except for one lone stage light shining down in the middle of the stage. An empty mic stand was just off to the side. Mr. Pearsall hopped up on the edge of the stage and waved Logan over.

Logan followed suit and hopped up. He looked out into the sea of empty chairs. In a weird way, it made him feel more nervous to be sitting in front of an empty auditorium than it did standing on a baseball mound. This wasn't a game. He didn't have any face to wear or any persona to try to emulate. He was himself. He was vulnerable.

"And I always thought the theater kids had it easy performing up here."

"Not as easy as it looks, is it? Here." Mr. Pearsall tossed him a water bottle. "Have a drink."

"Are you going to tell me why you brought me here now?" Logan asked.

"I just wanted to talk to you for once, not as a teacher and a student, but as a man and a budding young man who I know has been in rough shape over the last several months."

Logan sighed and looked away. "So, it's therapy."

"No. Not in the least bit. For one, I'm not charging you, and two, I just want a dialogue with you Logan, to know what's going inside in your head. This isn't like last year. I only had you for half a year after Brayden died. I just don't want you to vanish in and out of class, or worse. So, how have you been?"

Logan kept his eyes away from Mr. P. He wasn't sure whether to tell Mr. Pearsall the complete truth or just to keep things simple with him. How much did he really know?

"The summer was pretty rough, with my elbow and all, and you can pretty much guess how everything before then went."

"I know you weren't sleeping. I know you probably dove into those pain medications a little bit more than you should have been."

"How did you…"

"Did you forget I told you about my experiences in college? I know the signs when I see them, Logan. What else?"

"I…may have messed around with sleep medication early on because I couldn't sleep without getting terrible nightmares. I needed something to knock me out at night." He bit his lip. "And then…when I got hurt, the doctors, they, prescribed me some pretty heavy pain meds to manage the rehab. I might…" He started choking up. "I might have taken more than I needed to on some days."

"Logan, I'm so sorry you've endured that. Nobody should have to go through that at your age…"

"It wasn't a matter of having to go through it. I just didn't know what to do. My life still isn't in control. I don't know."

"Still taking that stuff?" Mr. P asked concerned.

"No. I've been trying to quit everything the past few months. It's super hard, harder than anything. I get these urges...you know? They're physically painful sometimes, but those aren't the bad ones. It's the ones up here." He pointed at his head. "Those urges are way worse."

"I understand, Logan. Believe me, I do."

"You're not going to...you know; tell other teachers or the principal, super intendant or anything, are you? About me? About my problem?"

"I already told you, Logan, right now, we're not teacher and student. Anything you tell me is safe with me. I promise you. Any other thoughts?" Mr. Pearsall asked.

"I mean...it was hard not to think about, you know, leaving." Logan paused. "But I never acted on those thoughts. It wouldn't be fair to the people I care about."

"Depression isn't any easy thing for anyone to deal with, Logan. But the thing about it is, you never should have to battle it alone. I know you have Miss Donovan there for you, but is there anyone else? Mom? Dad? Anyone?"

Logan laughed. "That's real funny. My parents got divorced last summer, not that my dad was that good to me anyway, and my mom, well, the divorce took its toll on her. I kind of understand what she was going through now since I'm kind of going through the same thing, but no, nobody besides Amber. I've been seeing a therapist every week though."

"She must be a strong influence."

"Stronger than you'll ever know."

Mr. Pearsall pulled out his wallet. He took out a tiny picture, of a man, a little bit older than himself. "This is my father," Mr. Pearsall said.

Logan plucked the photo out of his hands.

"That was one of the last pictures my dad ever took."

"What..." Logan collected himself. "What happened to him?"

"Not long after I graduated college, he went out to the bar one night. My father, he drank, sometimes too much. He decided to drive home from the bar without calling me or my mother, and they found his car wrapped around a tree, parts scattered everywhere throughout the woods."

"Jesus, Mr. P, that's rough."

"I didn't get why he did it. I still don't. Even in my darkest days, I never considered doing something so stupid. I was angry with him for robbing me of living the rest of my life with my father if I needed him. It killed my mother. I tutored at a community center for a while to stay close to home, to stay close to her. She swears up and down that my staying home for those couple of years got her through losing my father, but I knew that eventually, she'd have to move past it, because I wasn't going to stay home forever. I couldn't...Do you see what I'm trying to say?"

"That...I can't rely solely on other people to dig me out of the hole I'm in. I know that. I'm just not sure I'm ready..."

"Maybe not, but you also need to consider how Amber feels too, not just release all your problems onto her. She's only a human after all."

His words echoed what he said earlier describing the characters in the book they were to read for class. Even though they were soldiers, they were still human and could only endure so much horror before it consumed them.

"I can't remember the last time she talked about her life to me." Logan said.

Never once did he ask how Curt treated her or her mother, how far along her brother got with all the silly baseball things Logan taught him, or how she felt about Brayden. For all he knew, she was hurting just as badly as he was, but she put on a front to be strong for him. He never considered how much he put on her, and how much of a miracle it was that she stayed with him for as long as she had.

"Thanks for this, Mr. P. I needed this, I think." Logan peered over at his teacher.

"I figured you never talked much about it. You don't have to fight the battle alone, neither of you do. Logan, I never want you to feel like you have to put that burden on one person. I'm here for you all year. Okay?"

"I appreciate it Mr. P. Seriously. It means the world to me."

"Don't mention it." Mr. P extended his hand to Logan.

He thought for a minute and instead of shaking hands, Logan embraced his teacher. "I'm going to go see Amber and see how she's doing."

Mr. Pearsall smiled. "Good boy. You take care of that girl, and she'll take care of you. And you will be able to get through this. I promise. You make sure your arm heals, but more importantly, make sure your mind and your spirit heal as well."

201

"Thanks again. I don't honestly know where I'll end up, but I'll try to keep this all in mind."

"That's all I can ask of you. I'll see you tomorrow?"

"Count on it."

Logan hopped down off the stage and approached the doors. He looked back at Mr. P, still seated on the stage and smiled, not a full smile by any stretch but enough of one to show that what Mr. P said mattered to him. He jogged out the front door and made his way over to Amber's house. Once he got there, he saw Michael staring out the window and it didn't take long for the boy to run outside to greet him.

"Logan! Logan!" Michael ran over and hugged Logan, who he hadn't seen since the middle of the summer.

Logan rubbed Michael's head. "Hey, bud. Look, my arm is getting better, in a few weeks, we can start playing ball again, okay?"

Michael smiled and ran back inside. He pulled Amber outside to the surprise.

"Logan? What are you doing here?"

"I figured this was better than calling. It's nothing bad. Don't worry." He smiled.

"Then, what?"

"Let's go for a walk. I…" He froze. "I just want to see how you're doing."

"Can I come?" Michael asked.

Logan and Amber looked at each other, laughed, and nodded at the same time. Amber stood in the middle and grabbed each of their hands.

"You seem, happier, in a way. Are you sure you're feeling okay?" She looked up at him.

"Yeah. I'm fine. I'm fine because I know I'm not alone, not anymore."

26

October 20ᵗʰ

(Amber)

"I know, Logan, but…" She sighed as she pulled the phone from her ears. "I know it's not going to just disappear overnight, but I'm not sure I want it to." She laid a pair of tights out on her bed. "No. I'm not mad, just a little disappointed. I know. Love you too. See you in a little bit. Be safe."

Even though she and Curt were on somewhat okay footing, she wasn't sure when to let her guard down or start to accept him. It was nice, though, to be able to talk to Logan about things going on in her life. He seemed like he was getting better. He was more open and more willing to listen.

"Everything okay, sweetheart?" her mom asked from the doorway.

"I'm fine. It was Logan, just talking. Nothing crazy," she lied.

"I understand." Her mother sat at her bedside. "But you two are going to go out and have a nice dinner! I can't remember the last time you two went out like this."

"That's what I'm hoping. Thanks mom."

She ran her fingers through her hair, which sat around the middle of her back now rather down near her waist as it used to. She had finally decided to dye it black again, but she added bronze streaks to the end that popped right out of the darkness. From her closet, she pulled a familiar dress that she hadn't touched since Brayden's birthday dinner last year. The black dress with white pinstripes had hung too long tucked away in her closet. She'd never found another reason to wear it. She laid it out on her bedspread.

She spritzed herself with sweet, scented perfume before throwing the dress over her head. She turned in the mirror and the dress twirled around her near her waist. She laced up a pair of black boots and flipped her hair down over her shoulder, brushed through the newly dyed brown streaks, and flipped it back over her head. She took a deep breath and sat on her bed, waiting for Logan to show up. She looked down at her bracelet. Something caught her eye, and she moved over to her bedroom window. Pulling the blinds up, she found nothing but the night sky. She dimmed the lights for a moment to look out at the stars. She isolated the three brightest stars her eyes could see.

"Our fates. Our destinies," she echoed Brayden's words aloud after choosing them.

Suddenly, a knock on the door broke her concentration.

"Come in!" she shouted.

She turned in time to see Logan walk into her room, dressed more sharply than he had in quite some time. His reddish-brown hair stood completely crisp and still.

"You're going to have to start shaving soon!" she teased noticing a semblance of stubble under his lips. She saw a collared shirt peeking out from underneath his baseball sweatshirt. He moved over to kiss her.

"I hope you planned on bringing a jacket or something."

She nodded and took a black overcoat from behind her door. She swung by Michael's room.

"Don't stay up waiting for me! I'll be home later."

"Have fun!" He ran over and hugged them both before they left.

"Have fun kids!" Amber's mother shouted from the bathroom before they left.

As the two walked, Amber kept looking over at Logan. He seemed more nervous than usual, grabbing his right arm.

"Does your arm hurt?" she asked."

"What? No…no, I'm okay."

"Then what's wrong?" She pressed him.

"Nothing's wrong. I just, I don't know. I'm actually pretty hungry."

They opted to eat at Dianne's, as they had a year ago. Amber hoped that rekindling the most positive of memories the two shared with Brayden would alleviate both of their minds. Logan looked around the dining room in a trance of sorts. He hadn't been back there since last year either.

"Follow me this way!" the cheery waitress said. "I'll give you two a honeymoon booth."

They took their seats in a small booth, tucked away from the rest of the main dining room. For the first time in quite some time, she felt a little shy around Logan.

"We haven't ever really gone on a REAL date," she said, laughing nervously.

"Mhm."

She frowned. Something wasn't right with Logan at all.

Suddenly, Logan remarked, "It's been a while since you wore that dress, huh?"

She darted her eyes down at the table. "Almost a year."

"Oh," he replied. "You haven't worn it since…"

"I never had a reason to."

"It still looks as amazing on you as it did then, you know." He smiled.

"Thank you. Do you know what you want to eat yet?"

He shook his head and sifted through the menu. The waitress came around and delivered a glass of water to Amber and a soda to Logan.

"Still need a few minutes?" the waitress asked.

The kids nodded. As her eyes scanned the menu, she kept glancing up and catching Logan fixing his gaze on her. Every time she caught him, she flicked a pinch of water towards his face, prompting them both to laugh.

"Is your arm almost done healing?" She kept trying to get him to talk.

"I don't really know. The doctor said I could start throwing from the mound pretty soon. I want to get a few of the guys together and throw a bit sooner rather than later."

"I just don't want you to feel like you have to rush…"

"It's fine! Trust me. I'm not going to push it. I know how important this is." He pointed at his arm.

When the waitress returned, they ordered their meals and waited again.

"How's your mom?" She tried to open him up further.

"Finally starting to get her crap together, I think, I hope," he answered. "She doesn't talk about much, especially not, you know, dad or anything like that."

"Have you heard from your dad since the divorce happened?"

He ran his tongue inside his lip. "A phone call here and there. He called me after he heard I hurt my arm and asked how long I'd be out and stuff like that. He didn't call me at all when everything with Brayden happened. I don't really know much about what he even does anymore." He pounded the table. "It's like…it's like he forgot about us after he left. It feels like he stopped caring."

She frowned. "I don't think he stopped caring. I don't think parents are like that, even if they separate or divorce. He still must have love for you in his heart. He pushed you to play baseball in the first place, didn't he?"

"Yeah, but I don't know. He was always a hard ass about everything. Like, nothing I did was ever good enough, you know? When I reached a certain age, he stopped praising me entirely. He just wanted my best all the time and life just doesn't work like that. Our relationship really started to get messed up at the end right before he left. I mean, you understand, don't you? You and your dad never got along."

"Never got along is an understatement. You know that." She glared.

"I know. I'm sorry. I didn't mean to make light of it."

She nodded and whipped around as she heard the waitress approaching with their dinner. She set the plates down and Logan didn't wait before going right after his meal. He paused, looked across the table at her, and laughed. She giggled.

"It's fine! Eat your heart out."

She picked and prodded at her own meal, almost feeling a lost appetite of her own. Logan scarfed down his hamburger and salad as she just stopped to watch him, almost impressed with how fast he polished off his meal.

"What?" he spewed with a half-full mouth.

"Oh, nothing. You look hungry!" She pointed out. "And don't talk with your mouth full silly."

"Sorry, mom," he teased back.

"Everything okay?" The waitress appeared from out of nowhere.

"Yes. Thank you so much," Amber replied for the both of them.

"I'll just leave the check here. Have a great night you two."

"I don't remember who paid the last time we went out." He frowned.

She thought for a minute. "I think you did…"

"Well, then I'll take the tip then?"

She nodded her head. "And I'll take the bill. It's a fair trade. Just remember this for next time!"

Logan left a nice tip for the waitress as Amber picked the bill up to pay at the counter. She struggled to get her coat back on before the nighttime reintroduced to the cold upon exiting the restaurant. The black and gold sign illuminated their way towards the park, where she planned to take Logan next.

"Are you sure you want to go?" she asked.

He nodded. "I think we should."

They made their way through town in the direction of the park. Before approaching an adjacent neighborhood, Amber noticed a scruffy silver husky with icy blue eyes mirroring Amber's own, sitting next to a table set up near Mr. Brooks' shop. Amber made her way over to it without hesitation. She reached her hand out to try to call it over to her. She leaned down to the dog, which sniffed in her direction before a deep, booming voice stopped it.

"Apollo!" Amber jumped.

A middle-aged man came from Mr. Brooks' shop. Amber stood still in her tracks, losing her breath for a moment.

"I'm sorry," the man said, "I didn't mean to startle you."

He looked cold. He didn't have any sort of coat, instead wearing a dirty navy cut-off sweatshirt. His pants were tattered above the right knee and just under the left thigh. He wore battered, old sneakers, with soles grinded to the rubber. Her heart sank seeing both this man and his dog in this situation. His eyes looked red, as if he hadn't slept in weeks. She still hadn't moved towards or away from the man, who himself hadn't taken a step since calling the dog back to him.

"I was just inside talking to the man who owns the store here," he said.

"My neighbor, Mr. Brooks." Logan entered the conversation. "We should really get going," he whispered.

She nudged him in the gut. "What were you talking to him about? What's with the table?"

"We had a home once, him and I," the man said suddenly. "Lost it though. Been moving in and out of town ever since. The cops chase me out; we stay away for a while. We come back. The shop owner gave me this table here and is going to let me set up a little donation place here, in case anyone wants to help out." He pointed at the husky. "Going from place to place has taken its toll on him and the spot in the next town over doesn't allow pets so here I am."

"How long?" Amber asked.

"Amber, can we please go?" Logan reached out for her, and she snatched her arm away trying to listen to the man.

"Been over a year now." The man began to cough. She looked back down at the dog, whining behind his owner's legs.

"I thought of giving him away to a shelter, to find a better home for him you know, but it'd be like giving away my best friend."

Amber nodded her head fighting back tears. "I understand. I do." Without thinking much more, she took her coat off and moved towards the man.

"What are you doing?" Logan warned.

She glared back at him before moving towards the man some more and stretching her arms out with her coat in her hands. "Take this."

"Are you serious?" he asked. "What am I going to do with this?"

"I…I don't really know. I know it's too small for you to wear, but maybe a blanket for you to keep warm with or bedding for him. I want you to have it. It kept me warm!"

"Young lady…I, I don't know what to say." He rubbed his wild brown hair.

"Don't say anything. Just take it and do your best for both of you. Survive. Life will get better if you survive. Every day is a chance for life to turn around. Just keep believing. Don't ever quit, okay?"

"To be a child again," the man lamented. He smiled. "Okay, I'll keep believing. Thank you, young lady…"

"Amber." She stopped him. "My name is Amber."

"Derek and this is Apollo." He pointed at the dog that had already made his way to Amber and licked her face. "That young man over there, he's your boyfriend?"

She nodded.

"You hold onto Miss Amber and make sure she's safe!" he yelled over to Logan who didn't answer back but walked towards them.

Logan pulled his wallet out and handed Derek two twenty-dollar bills. "Take care of yourself and keep him safe too."

The man laughed. "Thank you both. I don't know how many kids your age would stop and talk to someone like me, nonetheless help. You are very solutions-oriented Miss Amber. Thank you, again, I can't repay you obviously…"

"You can. Like I said, live, survive, and try as hard as you can to get out of this. That's how you can repay me. Promise?" She extended her hand.

He chuckled. "Promise." He reciprocated her handshake.

She rubbed Apollo down one more time after he flopped down on his side, panting.

"You survive too, okay? Promise me." She whispered.

Apollo licked her face as she got back up. She waved goodbye to Derek and Apollo and heard the dog whine as she walked away with Logan. She looked back, saw Derek lay her coat down on the ground, and tried to get Apollo to lay on it.

Maybe I'll see you again someday.

"You're going to freeze now," Logan teased. "And probably get sick now."

"Maybe," she answered. "But if I get sick, I'll get better. If he gets sick, he might not be so lucky."

"Do you remember last summer, and I told you that something about you just lets you know just the right thing to do or say?" Logan asked.

She nodded.

"You told me then it was just body language, but it isn't. Nothing about what we just were a part of was body language. You literally gave the shirt off your back to a guy you didn't know. That's not body language. That's a heart unlike anything I've ever seen."

"Logan it's…"

"You need to learn to give yourself credit for the good you do for people."

She laughed. "It's not my credit to take."

"Can we just go back to my house? I'm getting kind of tired."

She shivered on the way back to Logan's.

"You want my sweater?" he asked.

"No. I'm fine."

She texted her mom and said she'd be home in the morning as they made their way back to Logan's. It wasn't the worst thing in the world. Maybe she was better off not being home tonight. She got worried about Logan whenever he was over-complimentary towards her. It usually meant he was on the verge on some sort of breakdown. Logan didn't look at her or say a word when they got back to his house. They went in through the side door. She breathed a sigh of relief after hitting the heat inside his house. They made their way upstairs to his room and she unlaced her boots, kicked them off to the corner, and walked into his bathroom to freshen up. She washed the dirt off her hands and arms from petting Apollo and washed her face as well. She picked up one of the brushes on the counter and picked through her hair to unknot it. When she returned to Logan's room, he tossed a pair of his old sweats and a T-shirt to her to put on.

She tossed the shirt back. "I'll just sleep in my tank top. It's fine."

"Well here." He tossed her an old pair of sweats. "I haven't worn these since I was thirteen probably, but they'll probably fit you."

She made her way back to the bathroom to change. When she returned, she found him just sitting on his bed cross-legged, fidgeting with his hands.

"Are you…okay?" She asked leaning in.

"Yeah. I think. No. I don't know." His answers were all over the place.

209

She slowly closed his bedroom door. "Want to talk about it?"

"I...um...I want to ask you something."

She was puzzled, walked over to him and sat next to him on the bed. "What's wrong?"

"Nothing's wrong, but." He bit his lip. "Have you ever thought that we might be..." He froze. "Ready?"

Her eyes widened. "Ready? Ready for what?"

"You know...I'm sorry, I'm making this super awkward. I had this worked out much better in my head..."

"Sex, you mean?" she smiled.

He sighed. "Yes. Do you think we're ready?"

Her face grew hot. "I mean...God, Logan, I don't know. I'd be lying if it never crossed my mind, but..." Her hands went behind her back. "I don't know. Now? Like, tonight?"

"I think I might want to try."

She felt a pit in her stomach. "Are you...I mean...do you have protection?"

"Yeah! I mean, I mean, yes. I do." He moved over to one of his dresser drawers and pulled a box out.

She tried to relax. "I mean...if you want to try. I suppose... I suppose it's okay with me."

He slid over to the far side of his bed and waited for her. Her heart started beating faster and faster as she approached the bed. She lay down and they snuggled up close for a few minutes before he rolled over and messed around with the box of condoms out of her eyesight. In a way, she found it surprising that he was still a virgin after knowing about all of his flings throughout high school. She laid down flat on her back, not really paying attention to what he was doing, but rather her thoughts started to scatter all over the place.

"Ready?" His question jolted her back to the moment.

"Mhm."

As he pulled himself nearly on top of her, she felt his hands move down by her waist and he started to pull the waistband of the sweatpants down her thighs. He started to kiss her neck, and she closed her eyes. Thoughts battled back and forth, over whether she wanted this or not. His lips made their way to hers and they shared another passionate moment. He panted, and she felt a drop of sweat tap her chest. He slid her pants further down and she kicked them the rest of the way off.

"Logan, wait!" She broke out from underneath him. "I don't…I'm not ready for this."

"What? What's wrong? Did I do something?" He sat up.

"No…no it's nothing you did. I just…I don't think I'm ready for this."

"I don't understand."

"It's just not time yet. I'm sorry."

He stood up with his back to her messing around with his shorts. "I'd be lying if I said that doesn't really suck to hear," he admitted. "But, if you're not ready, that's fine."

"I'm sorry." She looked down, feeling nearly naked with just her tank top and underwear.

"No, no. Don't apologize. It's okay. I'm glad you said something. To be honest, I don't think I'm ready either. I just, I don't know, wanted to experience it finally. I got a little ahead of myself. I'm the one who should be sorry. I feel like I forced you into it."

"No, don't you apologize either. We just made a decision, but it's not time, not yet." She smiled at him.

He picked the sweats she wore up from the base of the bed and tossed them back to her, and she put them back on as she noticed her hands shaking. He went into the bathroom to wash up, leaving her alone with her thoughts for a minute. She was afraid to say no at first. Logan had never given her reason to be afraid of him but part of her worried how he might have reacted if she said no to him. She knew what a commitment that was at such a young age. She wasn't sure when it would ever come up again.

Just then, Logan came back, and he hugged her. "Amber, I'm sorry if you felt pressured."

She looked up at him in his arms. "Not pressured, just a little nervous. Thank you for listening."

"I wouldn't make you do anything you don't want to do, not now, not ever."

"Good to know."

He kissed her forehead and pulled her back down onto the bed. She stretched her arms out over her head and turned her back away from him. He turned over himself and put his arm over her shoulder. She felt his thighs up against hers and it made her breathe a bit more rapidly. It wasn't the feeling, they'd slept in the same bed a few times, but coming down from that kind of passion and emotion put her on edge. She stayed awake for what seemed like hours thinking about everything that happened tonight. She thought of anything other than what just happened. She sighed over his snoring as he fell asleep. She wiggled free from his arms, separated herself from him, and turned back over careful not to wake him. She pulled the blanket further up near her shoulders and rolled back over to her side.

I can say no. It's okay to say no.

It was reassuring that Logan wasn't the type of guy who made her feel guilty about saying no or worse yet, forced her into something she didn't want to do. It confirmed a lot about him that she already felt, but never really knew.

One day, she thought. *But not yet.*

She finally felt her eyes start to sag and she felt herself dozing off, timing her breaths with Logan's, creating a sweet symmetry between them. Once Logan straightened his life out, the two of them would not only be inseparable, but together, they'd be unstoppable.

27

December 24th

(Logan)

Amber had invited him out for a Christmas Day celebration of some sorts, but she wasn't telling him what kind. He felt bad if she had gotten him anything spectacular because he hadn't gotten her anything at all. He feared all day that she was planning some kind of grand adventure for the two of them that he couldn't reciprocate to her. His mother wasn't home because of "last minute Christmas shopping," or so she said. He was pacing around his living room, anticipating Amber knocking on his door any second. Instead, there was a furious ringing of his doorbell.

"What the…" he peeked out the front window towards the door and didn't see Amber, but a shorter figure standing. It was her brother.

He opened the door and Michael rushed in and hugged him. "Merry Christmas, Logan!"

He chuckled. "Hey, buddy! Merry Christmas to you too. Where, um, where's your sister?"

"She's in the car with mom and Curt, come on!"

Michael took his hand and led him outside into the snow and sure enough, he saw Amber alone in the backseat waving. He got in and sat between the two Donovan siblings.

"Merry Christmas," Amber said as she kissed him on the cheek.

"Ditto." He laughed. "And Merry Christmas Curt and Mrs. Donovan. But what's going on?"

"Amber put together a little Christmas get together with us and a few other people. She kind of wanted to surprise you with it, but that's where we're headed."

"Close your eyes!" Amber said.

"Seriously?"

"Yes! No peeking."

Logan rolled his eyes before he shut them tight. He felt Amber close to him, examining him to make sure he wasn't cheating. The car pulled out of his driveway, and he wasn't sure which direction it was heading in. The car ride wasn't long, or maybe it just seemed that way because his eyes were shut. He felt the car turn, slow and eventually come to a stop.

"Does this mean I can open my eyes now?"

"Yup!" Amber answered.

He opened his eyes, and they were in another driveway. The route was a familiar one and he should have known. He looked up and they were at Brayden's house. He looked out the window near Michael and saw his mother's car in the driveway.

"What is this?" Logan asked.

Amber opened her door and waited for him to exit. "A family dinner." She smiled.

Logan exited the car and made his way up the driveway. When he opened the door, he saw Brayden's living room transformed for Christmas Day. They had moved the couch towards the kitchen and in its place was a Christmas tree that stood nearly to the ceiling, fully decorated. He walked towards the kitchen where he saw his mother and Mrs. Lewis setting an extended version of their dining room table.

"Merry Christmas, sweetheart," his mother said when she saw him. She kissed him on the forehead.

"M…Merry Christmas, mom." He almost forgot to say it back because he was so shocked.

He hugged Mrs. Lewis and heard footsteps pattering down the hallway. He saw Julian and Angela come around the corner and put him in a dual embrace.

"Hey, guys," Logan said with a smile.

He walked down the hall past them and into Brayden's room. "Merry Christmas, Bray," he said into the air.

"It looks like he could come and move back in tomorrow," Amber's voice came from behind him.

"What's with the get together?" Logan asked.

"It's kind of like a Christmas present from everyone to everyone. It was my mom's idea. Don't let her give me credit for it. She called Mrs. Lewis and asked her if it would be okay for us to all come to her house and have dinner and just be together."

"Your family continues to amaze me, you know that?" He hugged her and they walked back towards the kitchen.

Logan went outside with Amber, Julian, Angela and Michael and the two teens stood in front of the door watching the kids play in the snow. This was the reason that Mrs. Donovan brought everybody together. The kids trudged through snow in the front yard deep up to their shins. An errant snowball hit Logan in the chest. He wiped the snow off his chest and smiled. He reached down and balled up snow tight.

"Logan," Amber warned.

"It's a snowball. I think my arm can handle it." He tossed the snowball up in the air and caught it behind his back.

"Always a showoff." Amber rolled her eyes.

Logan walked out into the yard where the kids were all playing. When he stepped on, they stopped and looked at him. He narrowed his eyes to identify his assailant.

"Now, which one of you hit me with that?" He said in a playful tone.

The kids remained silent.

"You've all seen me play. You all know how hard I can throw a ball. Don't make me pick one of you at random!"

Angela covered her mouth with her glove-covered hands and giggled. "Julian! Julian threw it!"

Julian pushed his younger sister towards the snow. "Did not! She's a liar!"

Logan walked slowly towards Julian and showed him the snowball. "Was it you? Did you hit me with a snowball?"

Julian's eyes lowered and he laughed. "It was a pretty good throw, wasn't it?"

Logan chuckled and walked backwards. "It was. The problem is that you didn't take me out with it. Now I get to give you payback."

Logan leaned in as if he was standing on a baseball mound and packed the snowball even more tightly. He shook his arm out and wound up. Before he could throw, Julian took off and ran away. Logan came back set and pursued him. He slipped and trudged through the snow trying to keep up with the boy. He looked back at Amber.

"A little help?"

She giggled. "This is your crusade. You can't catch a kid?"

Two more snowballs flew in and hit Amber in the shoulder and in the leg. She stood with her mouth open looking at Angela and her own little brother.

"Betrayed by my own little brother," she said in a mock-stern voice. "Michael, how could you?"

Michael shrugged, looked at Angela, and the two of them took off across the front yard also. Logan stopped running and handed a second snowball to Amber.

"Trying to join my crusade now, my dear?"

She looked up at him and kissed him before taking the snowball. "Let's show them not to mess with us."

Logan and Amber ran out towards the kids and Logan hopped forward, fired a snowball and hit Julian square in the back. The child giggled and fell into the snow. Amber tossed her snowball at her brother, and he dodged it, and quickly created a ball of his own and returned fire at his sister. Logan pushed Amber aside, took the brunt of the snowball and fell into the snow.

"Ah, I'm hit. I...I don't think I'm going to make it," Logan groaned.

He lay in the snow for minutes, feeling the cold on his neck and cheeks. He closed his eyes and just stayed there. Suddenly, the laughter of Amber and the kids started to disappear, and it was just him alone with his thoughts and himself. For the first time, there weren't a million things going on inside, but he felt like he was at peace. He heard footsteps approaching and his eyes snapped open. It was Amber peering over him.

"Oh, oh dear. This isn't good at all," Amber said standing over him.

She knelt and ran her hand over where the snowball hit him. "I don't know if you can ever bounce back from this."

Logan coughed and smiled. "I always bounce back." He reached up, grabbed her arm and pulled her down into the snow with him.

"It's so COLD," Amber yelled.

Logan laughed. "I'm sorry, but you didn't think you were going to emerge from this battle unscathed, did you?"

She lay down on top of him and stared down at him. Her hair was hanging down in front of her face, and he pushed it back for a second to look into her eyes, which fit right into the wintery environment.

"You are so beautiful," he said to her.

She smiled and kissed him.

"Gross!" Michael yelled from behind them.

Logan sat up with Amber still sitting across his legs. "It's the power of love. It brought me back from the void. Nothing is stronger than that. Never forget it."

"Kids! Dinner!" Brayden's mother yelled from the front door.

Logan slapped the sticking snow off Amber's back and helped clean the kids up as well, and they all headed inside. When he got inside, he looked at the table set for everyone. Brayden's father and Curt were already sitting, waiting for all the kids. They all sat one at a time. Logan and Amber sat across from each other while the kids all sat at the opposite end of the table from Brayden's father. After Mrs. Lewis and Logan's mother took their seats, Mr. Lewis said grace. Logan thought to himself for a minute, about how he had lost his faith so long ago, but listening to Mr. Lewis say grace to a God that, if he believed in, took so much from him over the past year. It must take an incredible amount of resolve and faith to continue to believe that God had their best interest at heart.

"I want to just thank you all for being here today," Mrs. Lewis said to the table. "This is our first Christmas without Brayden, and we weren't sure how it was going to go."

"But having all of you here," Mr. Lewis interrupted, "Has reminded all of us that Brayden always had a family outside of us and that we have the same as well. If our son was here today, I know he'd be happy to see all of us together."

He was right. Sometimes in loss, people fall apart from one another. It isn't because they want to, or that they resent each other, but grief has its own way of creating a boundary between people. Logan had walled himself off for so long from almost everyone in his life, but as he looked around the table. He saw everyone how were before Brayden died, before even his father left. He looked at his mother and saw in her everything that he admired and loved before the divorce took its toll on her and before she seemingly stopped caring. That wasn't it. She never stopped caring. Logan just never gave her a chance to care.

He looked at Julian and Angela, who'd be growing up the rest of their lives without their big brother guiding them. Julian had become so much more like Brayden in the year he'd been gone that it was scary. He took all the things he looked at in Brayden and applied them to himself. He'd be okay. He watched Julian packing Angela's plate full of food. It was that little act that let him know that Julian would always watch out for her and protect her like Brayden would have.

Logan picked his glass up. "For Brayden." He watched all the others, even the kids raise their glasses as well. "This is his family. This is our family."

"And we always will look out for one another," Amber said afterwards.

* * *

Amber had her mom and Curt drive Michael home as Amber and Logan decided to walk back to his house on their own. When they got back to his house, they stopped on the front stoop.

"You know," Amber said. "There's one thing we have to do, that I know neither of us have done."

Logan swallowed hard. "What's that?"

"We have to go see him."

Logan didn't answer. He thought about all the times he walked to the cemetery but never walked in to visit Brayden. Even a year out, with all the strides he'd made lately with himself, he wasn't sure he was ready.

"I don't...I don't know if I can."

"Well, I'll be there. I'm not going to force you, but on the anniversary of his death, I'll be there." She looked down. "Besides, there's one another thing I have to take care of."

"Your dad?"

She didn't answer but she didn't have to. Amber needed her own closure.

"Okay," Logan said. "I'll be there."

She smiled. "Deal."

He opened his front door for her and led her inside. He stood outside and looked up at the sky and the snow falling.

I guess I'll see you soon.

28

January 19th

(Amber)

"I'll take you if you want," her mom offered.

"No. It's fine. I can go myself."

She didn't know how long she would take, maybe minutes, maybe hours. She'd never visited, never once, in the year that Brayden was gone. Rain drizzled down on the hood of her jacket, and her pant legs were soaked from the puddles she stepped through on the side of the road. A year ago, she had lost two of her best friends. One left the world, and the other became detached from it. At least Logan had returned.

Brayden wouldn't be the only person she'd visit. She'd never said goodbye to her father either. She wanted to keep the spirit of Brayden alive, while burying the demons of her father and her past. She didn't know how it would feel, standing over his grave. Would she be mad? Would she cry? Or had she coped enough to confront the last remaining idea of a man who, despite acting like he was protecting her, had ravaged her childhood? At least he got part of it right. The things he had put her through made her stronger, but at a price. The scars were souvenirs she'd never lose.

When she reached the cemetery gates just as dusk set in, she froze. Finally, she walked amongst the tombstones, wondering about the stories and lives of every person buried there. She caught dates of people who had lived long and prosperous lives, some nearly century. Dates of lives taken far too soon had also filled the plot of the land. Some graves housed toddlers, some prepubescent kids, and more kids her age.

"How many other parents had to bury children?" she asked. "How many kids had to watch their parents be buried here?"

She made her way across the graveyard, weaved in and out of rows before coming across an unassuming headstone which prompted her to stop.

WILLIAM MICHAEL MATTHEW DONOVAN
APRIL 7TH 1970 – FEBRUARY 2ND 2017
A HUSBAND LIKE NO OTHER
AN IRREPLACABLE FATHER

She could think of many better fathers that could have replaced hers. Her reaction to those lines still hadn't changed. The flowers at the base of the tombstone had seen better days as well as the grave itself. Her mom hadn't visited the grave as often. She imagined him under the dirt, his body decaying in a casket. She remembered his wake and funeral as if it had just happened. Memories came back to her in a rush.

This was a mistake.

She felt something stir in her chest. She was angry about the things he had put her through in her life, and something else too.

"I...I never got to say goodbye to you," she muttered to herself as she dropped to her knees. "Dad, as much as I hate the things you did...I didn't want you to go without saying goodbye. I prayed, believe me, I prayed all the time that you would go away and stop hurting me, but I didn't mean like this...nothing so permanent." Her eyes welled up with tears. "Now I feel stupid for ever wishing it. I'd like to think, as I got older, we would be able to fix things...that maybe you'd be proud of me eventually. I always held on to hope that.... you'd change. In the back of my mind, I always thought you'd fix yourself, and I like to think that you wanted to. What I mean is..."

She paused for a second. She contemplated apologizing for wishing him ill or hating him for so many years. It would only justify certain things her father instilled in her.

"If I do, you'd be right again. I'd be wrong again. Just like you always thought."

Everything she had done had always displeased him. She stood at his grave, running her fingers through her hair, the same hair that had made her father furious when he had seen that she dyed it.

"This was my fifteen-year-old statement."

She had her own mind, no matter how many times he tried to alter her thinking. She had developed her own set of values far different from his and he hated it deep down.

"I'm sorry that I harbored so much resentment all these years, but I'm not sorry for the bitterness I held when you were alive. That's the conclusion I came to. I can't allow myself to feel guilty anymore for what happened between us. You had every chance to fix it, and every chance to try to repair our relationship, but I don't know why you never did. That hurts more than anything does, don't you understand that? You never gave me answers!" she screamed into the pouring rain.

"I always dreamed of a fantasy where, I would grow up and move away, and we'd never speak. Years would go by and after time passed, we would sit down together and reconcile for the things you did and the things we said to each other. And you…" She shut her eyes. "You robbed me of that moment of penance the night you died." Her lips quivered. "I'll never get closure with you, and that hurts me more than anything. I'm sorry dad."

She reached across her body into her bag and pulled a small pink ribbon from it. She had worn that ribbon in her hair almost every day when she was a child.

"And this is my statement now."

She gazed at it for a number of minutes before leaning down and placing it on the grave. She mouthed the words, "I'm so sorry" before turning and walking away before she started to cry. She looked back one more time, shook her head, and left the guilt of her father's death to rest along with him.

She felt her arms shaking as she walked through the graveyard in search of one more plot. She moved about more rows before coming to a hill with more graves. Her foot slipped in the mud on the way up, but she caught herself before falling. She noticed a bright colored bouquet pop from the sunset preparing to transition to nightfall. She kneeled and ran her hand across the engraved granite.

BRAYDEN OWEN LEWIS
DECEMBER 19TH 1999 – JANUARY 19TH 2018
DEARLY LOVED SON AND BROTHER
A STAR BURNED OUT FAR TOO SOON

She couldn't stop herself from tearing up just reading Brayden's gravestone. The day of the funeral, they didn't have a gravestone yet because Brayden died so suddenly. Brayden's family was there to support her. She was there to support everyone else. Now, as the wind began to howl across her face, she stood alone. She looked down at her muddy sneakers, thinking about Brayden's body underneath her. She kneeled into the damp ground and put her arms around the grave.

"The days seem so much longer without you. Every day I spent with you seemed like an adventure. I miss you so much. I miss your hugs the most, as silly as that sounds. I miss how you'd pick me up off the ground and leave me breathless. You had this…annoyingly booming laugh that I grew to love because it could make you stand out in any room that you were in." She sniffed and leaned back. "It's weird because we didn't even know one another that long, but it feels like I've known you all my life. I didn't even know you a year before you were gone, but you had this…magnetic personality. Your spirit always brightened my day. I always felt safe and secure around you even when I had nothing to be afraid of at all. You never said much at all, but when you spoke, you said everything. Some of the things I learned from you…Brayden, I'll never forget them as long as I live. You showed me so much about life in such a short time. Here! I brought you something that you'd probably like."

Once again, she reached into her bag and pulled a thick, black double-sided picture frame. Sitting in the front of the frame was Brayden's makeshift stick figure picture of him, Amber, and Logan. On the backside of the frame, Amber had placed her enhanced drawing of the three of them.

"I got better at drawing, I think. You'd be proud of me. Who knows? Maybe one day I'll be better than you were!" She tried to laugh but felt breathless. "I came here to know once and for all that you're never coming back. Like Logan, I always held this hope that I'd wake up, it'd be summertime and you, and Logan would come knocking on my door to take my brother and me somewhere. I imagined opening the door and you'd storm in, swoop me up in the air like a doll, and laugh at Logan and me all the time. I kept holding on to this idea that you dying was just a terrifying nightmare I couldn't wake up from, no matter how hard I tried. But…"

She felt tears roll down her cheek. "But you're not coming back. Reading your name on this stone is sobering. It tells me that you've been gone for a year now, and I haven't gotten over it. I'm trying to take care of him and he's trying to take care of me."

She ran her hands across the letters. "You always knew what to say to calm him down and bring him back to Earth. You made it look so easy, always knowing what to say and do. Why'd you have to go, Brayden? God must have needed the strongest soul he could get his hands on. I just wish he kept you around longer before he called on you."

She rested the frame against Brayden's headstone and kept kneeling in the mud. She came from her kneeling position and sat cross-legged in the intensifying rain, allowing her tears to mix with the raindrops peppering her face that snuck under her hood. She looked up at the sky and watched the moon rising behind the rain clouds.

"I know you're in a better place, but no place here feels better without you Bray, and this is always going to hurt, no matter what. I…I still have a hard time believing everything that happened that night. How did everything unfold the way it did? Logan never talks about it. He can't bring himself to…I only told him once and he got mad at me for saying it, but…I wish I was there with you." She started to break down again. "I…I always keep it in the back of my mind that if I was there, nothing bad would have happened. I should have gone with you guys that night, and I didn't, and it hurts that the last time I saw you alive, we were saying goodbye, not knowing it would be goodbye forever…"

"I thought I told you to stop blaming yourself." She heard a voice from behind her.

She whipped around to find Logan standing behind her.

"What happened to him wasn't your fault, Amber, not in the least." He put his hand on her shoulder.

"But I…"

"No 'buts,' this isn't the time for guilt," he replied as he knelt on one knee beside her. He looked down at the picture, picked it up, and flipped it to reveal her drawing. "You drew this?"

She nodded.

"It's really good, better than anything I could have ever done. I like to think of him like that…with wings…"

"…And watching us from up there," she said pointing towards the sky.

"Must be nice to be able to fly anywhere at any time."

"I wish he was here to fly with us instead."

Another strong gust of wind blew just as she finished her sentence.

I know you miss us too.

"The body disappears, but the soul survives," she said aloud.

She looked on as Logan said words of his own to Brayden. She held his hand as he spoke.

"If you could see the mess I put myself in, you'd be so pissed." He laughed breathlessly. "I messed my arm up. I missed the whole season. I got myself into a fight with alcohol and different kinds of medication, so that's good. I need your strength more than ever."

She felt him shaking from underneath her.

"I have a hard time believing that some God is looking out for me. That's her department. But you, I feel like, in a weird way Bray, I feel like you're right there with us still. I feel like you got us through, even though you're gone."

"I want to believe too, Logan," she said.

"I love you. You're my brother. Forever and always. I'll do my best to get through all of this and make you proud, make Amber proud. She's the strongest person I know. You'd be proud of her."

Logan stood up suddenly. "I can't be here anymore."

"I understand," she said as she wrapped her arms around him.

"Can we go to the park?"

She nodded. "I'll catch up in a minute."

She blew a kiss into her hand and placed her hand over Brayden's grave one more time. "This won't be the last time I see you. I promise. I love you Bray, and I always will." She choked up again. "I...know you're here with us, and you're here with me," she said putting her hand over her heart. "And I know that whenever my strength wavers, I only need to look up to the sky and find our stars...no matter how cloudy it gets, and even if I never see them, I know they're there. I know that I'll never see you again in this life, but I know you're always there, and that comforts me the most. Take care love. Rest in peace and harmony Brayden." She winced as she rose to her feet. "I'll be sure to tell you all about all the good things that come next time. Your light will never burn out as long as I'm here. I'll make sure of it. Until next time, goodbye."

She sighed and struggled to pull herself away from the gravesite. She felt drained of energy. She knew it'd be hard to come to grips with two deaths in one night, but she wanted it that way. She felt lightheaded. She saw Logan standing up against the cemetery gates with his arms crossed waiting for her. He started walking before she reached him and walked ahead of her with his head down for quite some time.

"Are you alright?" she asked.

He didn't answer.

She wondered what he must feel now. He seemed just so sealed off at times. She worked most of the time to try to figure out what he was thinking at any given time.

He felt some sort of responsibility to be a jovial, self-assured beacon of positivity for everybody at school because that's how everyone had grown up knowing him. Sometimes she wished he existed in more obscure ways. The popularity felt like such unnecessary pressure. She quickened her pace to keep up with him on the side of the road as two cars whizzed by them at an unsafe speed.

He looked back after catching the two cars fly down the street and waited for her before tucking her towards the lawns of the houses they passed by and positioned himself closer to the street. She smiled even though he didn't say a word. They walked in silence for what seemed like hours before coming to park, looking worse for wear. The nets on the basketball hoops were tattered and falling, the backside of the building in front of the park became tagged in graffiti, and a few of the swings on the swing set sat next to a dumpster close by.

"When did it turn to this?" she asked.

Logan again, didn't answer her. He seemed entranced by it all. He moseyed over towards the baseball field and looked up at the sky as he stood atop the tiny mound. With her arms crossed inside her jacket, she made her way over to him as his face became drenched from the rain.

Suddenly, Logan started to laugh at the sky as thunder boomed above him and the lightning lit up the sky as he smiled. His drastic change in demeanor surprised her. He started laughing loud and it became infectious as she began a nervous laugh of her own.

"Come here." He turned to her and motioned.

She obliged. He pulled her close and took her hood off her head.

"Logan!" she shrieked. "I'm going to get soaked!"

He didn't answer with anything except laughter.

She gritted her teeth and growled as she felt her hair begin to dampen from the intensifying rain, which started to evolve into a freezing drizzle.

"You always thought I took myself too seriously," he said out of nowhere. "Now I want to let loose and laugh a little, and you want to be mad at me? You're a confusing girl." He chuckled.

She didn't know what to make of what was happening. Maybe he cracked. Maybe he came to an epiphany.

"What…happened at the cemetery Logan?" she asked.

He wiped rain from his eyes and replied, "A moment of…clarity. You know? Despite how messed up I am upstairs, I just need to keep smiling. We sat up there." He pointed to the dugout. "And Brayden opened up about this craziness about stars, destiny, and fate and I didn't really get it then, but I get it now."

He walked over to the dugout and gripped the roof of it before swinging himself atop it. He sat with his legs swinging over the edge and extended his hand out to her. She looked at the shine of the water resting on the roof and became quite nervous.

"I…I can't! What if I fall?" she stuttered.

"When have I ever let you fall?" he answered.

She thought about it for a moment. "Never once."

"Never once."

She smiled and tried to walk over to him. She reached her hand out towards his and he gripped it tight. He extended his other arm up near her shoulder and told her to jump. She closed her eyes and squeaked as her feet left the ground, and he swept her up ono his lap. Her eyes remained clenched as she felt her feet still hanging over the edge.

"You can open your eyes now and crawl up," he teased.

She re-opened her eyes staring at Logan's chest before looking up and meeting his smile. She scrambled off him and struggled to sit comfortable next to him.

"You just said you 'got' what Brayden was talking about with the stars and stuff, what do you get?" she asked him.

"What he meant," he responded. "They're always there, just like he's always here. No matter how dark it gets, like it is now, and there are no stars, they're still there. They never go away. They're tiny bits of light that are always shining. The funny thing is, some of those same stars might have died in their galaxy, but their light still shines in ours. It's incredible really."

She wanted to reply but found herself speechless.

"…And…even if that star is gone, you still see it, you know?" She knew he alluded to Brayden as she heard his voice crack. "And you can't ever forget that star because…without it, you don't have anything else to believe in. I'm starting to not make sense." He pounded his head with his open palm.

She shushed him. "It's okay. I know exactly what you're trying to say, calm down sweetheart," she answered as she rubbed his back.

"No. You can tell me when I'm starting to sound crazy because I'm just saying words, hoping they link together right now, trying to compensate for the fact that even though I made fun of him for his little speech, it made way more sense than anything I'm trying to say…" He started to tear up."

She didn't know what to say to him.

"We have these vivid memories of him, and I think that's really important to hold on to." He sat up a bit straighter. "When he got his scholarship, the first thing he thought of was us going to college together when I graduated, and he held onto this fantasy that we'd both go pro together and get drafted by the same team." He paused and wiped rain or a tear from his eye. "It was that kind of endless optimism that made us so close. I always teased him for being too much of a dreamer, but it was that attitude…the attitude that prompted him to be such a great friend. I see that now. Brayden brought everyone so much, and people need to see how many people he affected. Life is measured by how you live and what you do, and Brayden did so much for so many people. God, I miss him so much!" He screamed out to the sky as another crack of thunder boomed across the night sky.

"I know you do. I miss him too." She bit her lip. "But what you said was right. Even though he's gone, he's still here, in our hearts, and in our minds, and the impact he left on us won't ever go away. In that sense, he's never really gone, you know?"

He sighed. "I want to believe in all that afterlife and heaven stuff that you believe in, but it's hard to think that he's just here, floating around watching us from wherever he is. It's hard to imagine him in any 'up there,' and even if he was, why would he waste our time watching us in this place?"

"Because he loves us and misses us just as much as we miss him!"

"I wish I could believe like you do, but it just never added up to me…" He bowed his head.

"You don't have to believe like I do, Logan," she reassured him. "Believe what you want so that it makes sense in your head. You don't have to convince me or anybody else. If you want to believe that he's watching over you, and he's always with you, then believe it with all your heart and that's as real as it needs to be."

He leaned over and kissed her on the cheek. "You always know what to say, all the time." He smiled.

She reciprocated his smile with one of her own. "The silence kills me."

She ensnared his left arm with both of hers and put her head down on his shoulder staring out over the baseball field with him amidst the freezing rain. He lifted her head off after, hopped down, and once again extended his arms out to her.

"This again?" She frowned.

"Ah, what did I say about trusting me?" he answered back.

She nodded and closed her eyes tight and leapt down into a strong embrace. She heard him grunt a bit from the little pressure she put on his bad arm, and it made her panic. The panic soon lifted when she felt her feet leave the ground once more and he swung her around to put her back to the pitcher's mound.

227

"I know we still have a few months until prom," he said. "But, may I have a dance?" He extended his arm out to her.

She watched the frozen raindrops break across his sweatshirt sleeve before taking his hand. He drew her in close to her and she leaned her head back, touching his chin. As soon as he drew her in, he spun her back out towards the mound and their hands separated, but their fingers remained touching at the tips. When she came to a stop, she separated from him and skipped around him several times, watching his head try to keep up with her as she laughed and flipped her hair up over her head, splashing Logan with droplets in the process. He reached out and grabbed her arm and she giggled when he drew her back towards her and started rocking her as she rested her head against his chest. She closed her eyes and listened to his heart beating faster, then slowing, and then picking back up again.

"I'm going to make it. I'm going to be okay," he reassured her. "I promise."

"I know. I'm going to help you. We get through this together. We never leave the other's side, no matter how dark things get, and no matter how much we don't think we can. We have to know that we can get through this," she echoed a promise they made after Brayden's death.

"I remember. I haven't forgotten." He rubbed her back and squeezed. "And I never will leave your side. We're in this 'life' thing together now, and nothing from the Heavens above or the Earth we stand on now will ever get us apart."

They departed from the field not long after that moment, walking hand in hand back towards Amber's house. After the emotional evening, it warmed her heart to be here with him, in this moment, feeling like they both had turned a corner. It took a year, but it finally seemed as if they started had started healing.

I hope you can keep this up.

She promised herself that she'd never let him slip away. She looked over at him and thought about how hard the coming months would be for them both. Despite the promises and despite the sweet words, reality once again loomed. She didn't know if he'd ever thought about it, but right now, it didn't matter. She wanted them to have this. She looked up again at the sky as rain peppered her cheeks, looking for something to ease her pacing mind. She found nothing but silence, rain, and wind. She looked over at Logan once more before seeing the light post in front of her house illuminating her front yard.

She stopped at her front door and turned to him. "Never apart you said, right?"

"I meant every word. Never apart, never again."

She grabbed his cheeks, kissed him on the lips. "Goodnight, Logan."

She cracked her front door open and turned to watch him fade into the darkness. She worried about him as he fell into the shadows. She eased her way through a pitch-black living room and searched for her stair railing. She found the doorway into her bathroom and flipped the light on. She stretched her arms out, looking at her soaking wet face and hair. She grabbed a towel and dried herself off before making her way into her room to change. She slipped into a long-sleeve tee shirt and a pair of Logan's sweatpants that he left at her house one night.

Throwing her hair back into a ponytail on the way, she opened her brother's bedroom door and found him fast asleep. As always, she leaned in, kissed him on the forehead, and stroked his cheek with her finger, causing him to stir. She backed out and walked back into the bathroom to wash up. She looked at herself in the mirror.

Upon returning to her room, she saw her phone illuminated on her bed, a text from Logan reading, *Home. Safe and sound. Love you angel. Thank you for the wonderful evening.*

She smiled and responded. She collapsed onto her bed. She tossed her comforter around in a messy fashion and buried her face in the pillows underneath. Before turning the lamp off on her end table, she looked at the photo of her and Michael and smiled. She grabbed her phone and scrolled through her messages down near the bottom to her last text from Brayden, a picture of the night sky with a fully illuminated moon.

"Thank you, for everything. I love you Brayden," she whispered to herself clutching her phone to her chest.

He left an everlasting impact on many people he touched. She wasn't sure where her path would take her, but she knew whom she wanted along for the ride. She wanted Logan beside her, her family behind her, and Brayden above her. She had feared the future, but now she felt ready.

Her life was somewhat of a beautiful disaster. A small tear trickled down her cheek. He had taught her so much in the short time they spent together. She knew his soul survived somewhere out there in the world and it survived through everybody he loved. She hoped Logan believed that too. She hoped he could grow and become even stronger than he once seemed. She pulled out her yearbook.

The school had published a two-page feature on Brayden after his death.

Inside the yearbook on Brayden's photo, she scribbled something. She closed the book and clutched it to her chest.

I can't wait until Logan sees this.

29

March 28th

(Logan)

It wasn't too long ago where he had shared the school gym with Brayden, tossing the ball back and forth, lamenting the idea that Brayden was going into his final season. Brayden had remarked about the scouts and with eyes no longer on him due to his college commitments, their eyes would solely be on Logan. The only eyes Logan wanted on him last season were Brayden's, but they weren't. What the scouts saw in the past season was a mental implosion and after a hiatus from the field, a catastrophic injury that prematurely ended his junior year. His arm had healed, and he was ready to pitch for the first time since the injury. He missed his entire junior year. His future, his senior year, rested on this very first game. He opened his locker, but the game ball wasn't there.

"What the Hell?" he asked aloud to an empty locker room.

There were footsteps within earshot, and he turned around to see Coach Stevenson walking into the locker room.

"Missing something?" Coach asked.

"Am I…am I not starting?" Logan asked, feeling a pit in his stomach. "I mean… I get it. I haven't pitched in almost a year. I got suspended. I wrecked my arm…"

"Logan!" Coach interrupted. "Take a breath son. I'm not benching my best arm. I just thought, maybe it was time we started a new tradition." He turned. "I thought maybe, it was time for some change."

Coach Stevenson opened the door and Julian walked in with Angela and Brayden's parents. Julian held the game ball in his hand and Logan leaned down to meet his eyes.

"This for me?" Logan joked.

Julian nodded and reached his hand out. Logan rubbed his head, hugged Angela tight and walked over to Brayden's parents.

"You know, last time we had this talk, it didn't go so well," Logan lamented to Mr. Lewis.

"Last time we had this talk, I don't think you believed you were ready," Mr. Lewis answered with a smile.

Logan didn't answer. Instead, he nodded and gave Brayden's father a hug. It didn't really strike him until that very moment; he hadn't received a hug from his own father in more than two years. He closed his eyes and let his head rest on Mr. Lewis's chest.

"You all always believed, even when I didn't."

"And we always will," Brayden's mother said.

Logan turned and moved to his locker where his new jersey was hanging. He had asked Coach for a new number, 36, a combination of his #24 and Brayden's #12. He slid it on and buttoned it up. Soon after, he closed his eyes for what seemed to be an eternity and felt a rush of air enter through his nostrils. There was silence and a slow exhale before he yelled to release all the nervous energy within him. His brows furrowed and he walked towards the locker room doors and out to the gym. He stopped before exiting the gym that led directly to the baseball field. He lifted the star pendant that Amber gave him for his birthday and kissed it.

"My star, my destiny," he said to himself.

Before long, he emerged with his cap in one hand, and a glove in the other. He turned back towards the door, kneeled, and bowed his head. He looked over at a crowd full of supporters and opposing fans alike. The entire team had already been in the midst of their warm-ups. He started to jog over towards them until he spotted Amber standing at the fence by the first baseline. The two shared a kiss much to the soundtrack of hooting and hollering from Logan's teammates. Amber's face flushed red, and Logan uttered a chuckle.

"How are you feeling?" she asked him.

"I guess we'll find out when I started throwing," Logan answered back.

Amber turned and looked behind her, as if she felt something creeping up behind her.

"What is it?" Logan asked looking over her shoulder.

"Nothing, just a feeling." She smiled. "Good luck. Take care, okay? I love you. Be safe." She reached over the fence and hugged him.

"I love you too, Amber. I'll be okay," he replied. "Broken wings mend in time..." He shook his arm out.

"And you're ready to fly again!" She finished his statement.

Logan nodded and ran out to the mound to warm up. He threw a few warmup pitches with a tick lower velocity than he was used to. He didn't throw a single slider in warm-ups. He looked the letters "BL" scribbled inside the palm of his glove and the letters "AD" on the outside of the wrist strap. Logan threw a final pitch, and the catcher threw the ball down to second.

232

"Play ball!" the umpire yelled.

As the first batter stepped into the box, Logan leered in to get the first sign of the game. For a moment, the catcher behind the plate vanished and Logan saw only Brayden behind the plate. He saw a single index finger laid down for a first pitch fastball. Logan wound up and fired a blistering fastball down on the inside corner of the plate, backing the batter up.

"Strike one!"

Logan smiled as he took the ball back from the catcher. He took his eyes off the game and looked over at Amber, who was still standing at the fence. She was looking up to the sky. The sun reflected off her eyes before she closed them and her face seemed to glow in the sunlight. The wind picked up a bit, lifted her hair off her back and she stretched her arms out.

Thank you for always taking care of me and believing in me, in us. I love you. I know you miss Brayden more than I'll ever know. But always know he's here for you. He's never going to be gone for good. Remember that

Logan turned his attention back to the game and quickly finished off the next two batters to end a perfect first inning. Rather than yell, he casually pumped his fist to the cheers of the home crowd and before returning to the dugout, he walked over to Amber.

"Hey," he said.

"Hey yourself," she echoed.

"I just wanted to say something before I really lock in for the rest of this game," he stopped.

"And?"

"He's the ground beneath us. He's the air all around you. He's everything. We'll see him again. We only say goodbye for now. If we ever need him, he's not hard to find. All we need to do is look up in the sky and know he's never far. He loved us, Amber, and he always will."

"You felt it too?" Amber asked, as if she was out there on the mound with him when he saw Brayden behind the plate.

"Yeah," Logan looked up. "Yeah, I felt it too."

Logan kissed her on the forehead and jogged back towards the dugout to go watch his team hit at the bottom of the inning.

* * *

It wasn't a perfect game. It wasn't a no hitter. It wasn't even a shutout. But Logan fought tooth and nail to both start and finish this game. He needed to prove he was capable physically and mentally. The team was up 5-2, so it was a comfortable enough lead. He could afford a few slip-ups and still walk away with a win. He had retired the first two hitters in the inning. The next batter approached the plate and laced a ball into center field for a single. Logan glanced at the runner and then to home plate. As he wound up for his next pitch, the runner took off and the throw wasn't in time. The next batter walked on five pitches. Coach Stevenson jogged out to the mound.

"I have arms ready, Logan. Just say the word."

"You've been coaching me the last three years. Do you really think I'd give you the word?" Logan exhaled a laugh.

Coach Stevenson smirked. "No, I reckon not. But I know you can get one of these guys. So, I'm gonna sit those guys and let you ride this out until the end."

Logan nodded. "Thanks."

As Coach Stevenson walked away, he bellowed, "Besides, if you do blow it, we still have a bottom!"

Logan rolled his eyes and zeroed back in on the next hitter. His catcher dropped two fingers for a first pitch curveball. Logan obliged and the umpire called strike one. The next two pitches were a ball and a strike. Logan peered in to get what was finally the final pitch of the game. The catcher flashed a few signs before settling on a fastball. Logan nodded, but then he stepped off the mound to collect himself. He exhaled his breath and took his hat off.

He looked down at his glove and saw the initials of the two people he cared about more than anyone else and the two people who had been his closest friends for as long as he's been alive. He shook his head and returned to the mound. It didn't take him long to nod and come set. He fired a fastball with as much behind it as any he'd thrown all game, and the batter put a good swing on it but popped it straight up. Logan looked up and lost the ball in the Sun.

"I got it!" he heard a familiar voice yell.

He looked forward and saw the catcher's mask on the ground and much like at the start of the game, when he looked at his catcher, he didn't see anyone but Brayden. The ball fell into the catcher's glove, and the game was over. Logan jumped in the air as if they had won a championship rather than the first game. He ran over and hugged the catcher.

I've got your back, always, he heard Brayden's voice in his head in the midst of the embrace.

"You alright?" his catcher asked.

Logan took a step back, the image of Brayden faded, and he saw the catcher again. "Yeah, yeah, I'm fine. You called a great game today."

"Well, if I'm going to stand out. I have to develop a good relationship with our best player!" His catcher, a sophomore, answered.

Logan smirked and got in line with the rest of his team to shake hands with his opponents. Coach Stevenson gave him a firm slap on the back and congratulated him.

"Good game, 36," the opposing coach said at the end of the line.

"Thank you, sir," Logan answered.

He shook away from the rest of his team and met Brayden's family in the stands. He got a big hug from the kids and Brayden's parents welcomed him with big smiles.

"You played outstanding, Logan," Mr. Lewis said.

"Couldn't have made it back here without everyone's support."

"I disagree," Brayden's mother said. "You made it back here because you never quit on yourself. The most important part in recovering is knowing the part YOU played in your recovery too. Everyone else's effort means nothing if you don't want it. You wanted to be back out here." She hugged him tight.

"I did, more than anything."

"Your biggest fan is still waiting for you." Mr. Lewis pointed behind Logan.

He looked at the bleachers to see Amber clutching a book in her arms. He ran down and embraced her.

"You played so well. I'm so proud of you!"

"Thanks, what's uh, what's with the yearbook?"

She stretched the book out. It was last year's. "I wanted to show you this sooner, but I'd hoped you'd win today so I could show it to you now."

She opened the book up to a two-page spread that the school yearbook staff ran on Brayden after his death. He smiled looking at the pictures and thinking about everything he saw on the field today, what he heard in his head. It really was like Brayden never left in the first place. He ran his hands across marker writing scribbled across the pages.

"You?"

She giggled. "Who else?"

"I love you," he said kissing her.

"Broken wings mend in time..." she repeated his words from earlier.

"And we're ready to fly again." He smiled.

She turned it towards him and he ran his eyes across the page:

Sometimes the road isn't always clear. Sometimes life will do unexpected things that you won't always understand, and you might think fate is changing. Sometimes, you won't see your star in the sky because it's too cloudy or the stars are hidden or you lose it in the sea of space, but you still know it's there. Your star is your destiny. It's yours for the rest of your life.

Your star will always burn bright in the sky, in my heart, in my spirit, and in my soul. Until next time my friend, farewell, goodnight, and goodbye

End

Acknowledgements

To my friends and family, who have always supported my passion for writing and my dream of one day publishing this story to share with the world.

To my college mentor, Cecelia, without your guidance, encouragement, and support, this story would not be shaped into what it is today.

To Brittany, my brilliant cover designer, thank you for bringing my vision to life through your incredible art.

And finally, to you, the reader, for welcoming these characters into your life. I hope you enjoyed their journey as much as I enjoyed creating it.

About The Author

Robert Peck lives in the Pocono Mountains of Pennsylvania. *In Pursuit of Starlight* is his debut novel, born from a lifelong passion for storytelling and the belief that even one story can make a difference.

A Note from the Author

Thank you so much for reading *In Pursuit of Starlight.* This story has been years in the making, and it means the world to me that you chose to spend time with Logan, Amber & Brayden.

If the book resonated with you, I'd be truly grateful if you could take a moment to share your thoughts in a review on Amazon or Goodreads. Reviews help other readers discover new stories, and your words can make all the difference for an author.

Thank you again for being part of this journey. Your support means more than you'll ever know!

—Robert Peck

www.ingramcontent.com/pod-product-compliance
Lightning Source LLC
Chambersburg PA
CBHW032040240626
47154CB00003B/1009